WARMTH

Sam Wolfson

For my beautiful wife and son.

May the future be more forgiving.

Whether long-range weapon or suicide bomb

A wicked mind is a weapon of mass destruction

Whether you're soar away Sun or BBC 1

Disinformation is a weapon of mass destruction

You could a Caucasian or a poor Asian

Racism is a weapon of mass destruction

Whether inflation or globalization

Fear is a weapon of mass destruction

Whether Halliburton or Enron or anyone

Greed is a weapon of mass destruction

We need to find courage, overcome

Inaction is a weapon of mass destruction

Inaction is a weapon of mass destruction

Inaction is a weapon of mass destruction

Excerpt from "Mass Destruction"
Maxwell Fraser (Faithless)

JOHN STARED AT the massive structure in the middle of the blue green expanse of water. The grand white tiled arches jutted out with resilience as the occasional foaming wave brushed up against them. Its glass windows extended into the water's depths, now thickened with algae and salt. Barnacles claimed its lower limits. It gave the structure age, and yet it still retained some elegance of a time now lost.

"We'll go through our safety briefing now," said the dive master. "Today we're diving the front restaurant and kitchen of the Sydney Opera House. This used to be a popular place to eat in the city before going to a show, but it is now, as you all know, one of the top dive sites in Sydney. The water today will be warm, about twenty eight degrees, but it will be fairly murky as we've had a fair bit of rain. The vis' will be about five to ten metres, so be sure to stick close to your buddies..."

John stared into the water. It had been a year since his last diving trip, so he was itching to get back into the water. It was his weekend away, and after a heavy week at work and more than a three hour drive from Canberra, he thought he would do a SCUBA dive on the 'House' as a chance to relax.

Upon boarding the boat, John had been assigned a dive buddy who, even though he was roughly the same age as John, he was really starting to show signs of age with his weather worn skin and occasional scar that marked his face. The dive buddy was pleasant enough, but what annoyed John was the necklace that hung around his neck. What hung there was a gold pendant, a cross embossed over a drop of water rolling into waves – the emblem of the *Delugionists*.

John looked back towards the dive instructor who continued, "Just remember the emergency exits are, well... pretty much anywhere off the side of the boat. Now gear up and get ready to jump in. Just a reminder, as the Opera House is an Australian national treasure, you are not allowed to remove anything from the site and you must stay in my sight at all times. See you in the water!!"

"Pity they couldn't have saved it," said John quietly.

"Can't save everything," replied a young female passenger next to him as she began to don her gear. She was quite attractive with a fair complexion, dark brown hair and blue eyes. She reminded John of his ex-wife.

"Yeah, but it's *the House*," John responded. "A place of theatre, music and fun. You know it was designed back in the 1950's to emulate yachts on the water – a sort of tribute to the magnificence of Sydney Harbour."

"And now it's truly fulfilling its design," she replied with a wry smile.

They both laughed. John smiled at the thought and turned back to his assigned dive buddy who was deep in contemplation. He slapped the *Delugionist* on the shoulder as he reached across to grab his gear. "Come on mate. Let's get going."

The *Delugonist* glared at John briefly. He signed the cross and then started to get ready for the dive. He hardly spoke as he readied himself, but mostly wore a constant serene smile on his face that irked John. John sighed and started to put on his own gear.

By the time they had donned their SCUBA gear, most of the other divers were waiting in the still water. John and the *Delugionist* strode into the water and swam over to the group who were waiting for their final instructions.

"Remember, follow me close, stay off the ground and if you actually want to see stuff, don't kick up the silt!!" yelled the dive master. "When you're ready!"

John signalled to his buddy to descend. The *Delugionist* signalled in reply and said, "Praise be to God for today's dive. For without him, this dive would not be here." He signed the crucifix and rain from above, and then placed the breathing regulator in his mouth. John bit his tongue stopping himself from rising up in annoyance. He placed his own regulator in his mouth, took a deep breath and sank into the water's murky depths.

It was the year 2027 and the world was a changed place. Oceans had risen, nations had changed, and new religions had formed. The *Church of Delugion* was now the world's leading religion with over three billion followers.

Even though it had its early roots in Christianity, *Delugion* rose up in the late 2010's prior to the Great Global Flood, when a man from Nanaimo, Canada, only known by the name Clive, rose to fame. Clive made many predictions, but the ones of flooding and widespread devastation brought him the greatest recognition as they were disturbingly accurate.

His amazing claims stated that the Great Global Flood or as the *Delugionists* liked to call it, '*The Great Deluge*', would start in the early 2020's and this would not be due to man or nature, but would be caused by almighty God. He preached that *"This Great Deluge would cleanse the world of great sinners, being God's second great flood"*. People would then *"See the true light"* and follow the teachings of almighty God, Jesus and Clive himself.

The majority of Muslims, Jews, Christians and other religions initially rejected his preachings, saying that he was *"a madman, a schizophrenic most likely, and that his teachings were deluded"*. Still many people followed him, mostly on twitter.

Scientists from around the world including those of the International Panel on Climate Change, the IPCC, said that such a flood would not occur, that such predictions were flawed and ridiculous. They said that *"Yes, the sea levels will rise due to the impact of humans, but it would occur slowly over the next century, not nearly as high or as fast as Clive claimed"*. Clive ignored the scientific and public condemnation.

It was not gradual, as most thought it would be. It was a chain of relatively quick events.

Over the next few years, the Antarctic sheets continued to melt and dissipate. Greenland was greening, and the Arctic region was shrinking just as the IPCC predicted, but then the real changes started to happen.

Clive made several accurate claims in the weeks leading to what later was known by the religious circles as *The Start of the Second Coming*. He claimed that *"God's breath would flare and the Earth would warm causing seven years of God's wrath over humans abandoning him. And after the seven years, there would be a time of great peace and serenity for God's son was soon coming back."*

It occurred with the belching of methane from the Arctic tundra in 2021. Plumes of methane, the greenhouse gas, rose into the atmosphere acting like a gaseous blanket over the earth. Global temperatures rose, oceans warmed and large areas of ice and snow started to rapidly melt. Mountains were stripped of their white peaks, glaciers faded away, and ice packs disappeared. With heavy humid rains, rivers flooded, lands slipped and many towns were simply washed off the map.

The IPCC claimed that they always predicted this, but admitted their models did not nearly predict this level of change. They told the public that they should not be alarmed as methane would only last in the atmosphere for a maximum of ten years, and then it would not be as harmful. They told people it was a natural event and not God's wrath.

People became nervous. They were confused over what and whom to believe.

Clive then gave his second prediction in May of 2023. This became known amongst his followers as *Clive's Second Great Prophecy.* He claimed that sometime starting in the next two months, *"God's fist would come down causing the ground to tear worldwide and the seas would rise washing away the vain, the corrupt, and those following the wrong light."* He advised his followers to abandon their evil ways and to follow in the light of true almighty God to ensure that their souls would be saved.

Clive's predictions were fulfilled. On June 7, 2023, it happened. *The Great Quakes* as they later became known, superseded the massive quakes of the past modern records. The rising sea levels, by then only a metre, had unknowingly to the scientific establishment severely destabilised the Pacific Rim due to the extra weight of the increased amount of oceanic water.

The first quake was massive. The deep ocean subsidence sent a tirade of water up to thirty metres high across the pacific into many Asian countries wiping out large areas of Indonesia, Thailand, Sri Lanka, and India. The tsunami obliterated many island nations including the Maldives, Seychelles and Madagascar. Heavy aftershocks occurred throughout the region causing further deaths and destruction.

As the grounds gradually settled, the regions slowly recovered. Then only a mere two months later, the second great quake hit. The US San Andreas Fault shook devastating the American east coast. The US fell into a great panic as California fell into ruins and their western markets collapsed.

After '*The Great Quakes*', several volcanoes burst into life including many of Iceland's largest Volcanoes, most dangerously, Mount Katla and Mount Hekla. Together, they melted large glaciers and ice sheets sending great tirades of water through villages and towns washing them mercilessly into the ocean.

Off the east coast of Greenland, the warming ocean currents melted the seabed ice causing a massive sub-marine landslide. This great movement of an enormous region of under-water land sent a large tsunami towards the west coast of Ireland and the United Kingdom which destroyed many coastal towns and cities. This landslide released even greater amounts of methane that had been trapped there by earth and ice for thousands of years.

But there was still more, the global geologic instability had not ended. The volcanoes of Hawaii were next, bursting into action spewing vast amounts of lava and ash causing further volatility in the region. The Hawaiian flares and concurrent tremors caused an unprecedented disaster. A large section of the western edge of the islands received a massive undersea landslip that created a gargantuan tsunami. This made the pacific tsunami and the Greenland tsunami seem like a ripple in the ocean. A wave one hundred metres high spread across the Hawaiian island chain drowning and wiping out many of the Hawaiian cities and instantly killing hundreds of thousands of people, and injuring many more. The devastation was immense, but sadly not over.

The impact of the continual melt, warming waters and rising oceans caused great pressure on the ice sheets of the Antarctic. Ice packs were ripped off shrinking the size of the frozen continent. The release of pressure destabilised the Antarctic land causing small earthquakes and several dormant volcanoes in the region to erupt. There was now even more melt.

Sadly, to the world's amazement, within only a five year period, the oceans had risen an enormous eight metres.

Clive's predictions had come true. *The Second Great* Flood had come. Many people of Christian, Muslim, Buddhist, Hindu, Jewish, Sikh and other religious beliefs were stunned. Many atheists, agnostics and non-believers were stunned. Many saw Clive as knowing God's word. Many non-religious people reverted their beliefs back to God, to Clive.

Various religions then tried to claim that Clive spoke for them and them only. Fights and violence sparked. Militias formed. Clive quickly put a stop to this. He replied that he '*spoke for no one religion, but for God and God only. The Deluge that God has bestowed upon mankind was God's message that religions need to unite and follow his new teachings.*' He spoke of the Old and the New Testament. He spoke of the teachings of all religions as being of one. The Catholic and other Christian churches deemed that the third book – *The Modern Testament*–was now to be started as a new era of God had begun.

Religious leaders from the key faiths came together and met with Clive. Many of the leaders came out saying that Clive did truly speak from God and that they needed to follow the new teachings as they came, and the people who follow the teachings will be known as *Delugionists* – named after The Great Deluge that God had bestowed the Earth.

That was how the church of *Delugion* arose.

As the Earth settled, *Delugion* grew in popularity. Many people converted their faiths from Christianity, Islam and Judaism to hear and learn from their new teacher. However, many still resisted. Scientists tried to discredit Clive, but even they could not deny how precise his teachings were.

Clive continued to claim that *"God had punished all non-believers for their wasteful ways and for ignoring him."* Clive was often seen on television and heard on radio preaching the new church of *Delugion*. He had changed many of the old edicts modernising religious ways. However he said that *"God frowned upon the excesses of mankind"*, giving examples that *"The Great Double Global Financial Crisis and wars over oil was the fault of mankind"*.

Now, in 2027, the Earth's oceans had slowed in their rising and the Earth's crust had settled. Some governments had changed considerably, but many carried on in the same vein. Sadly, many tens of millions of people had died during the great global change causing immense grief and misery to many nations.

Despite all the turmoil and tragedy, the world was now at peace. Even the various religious tensions that had existed in Africa, Europe, Asia and the Middle East had settled... to some extent. Many had credited this to the strength of *Delugion*.

But life moves on. *Delugion* was now well entrenched in society, and nations had to deal with the reality of the global changes. So, with the higher oceans, various new enterprises had spawned to take advantage of the new coastlines. Several such enterprises had made it possible to SCUBA dive on twentieth and early twenty-first Century relics, which had become the new international craze. Diving on the Opera House was now a great tourist attraction in Sydney, and had only opened in the months prior.

The dive was over and the group had returned back on board the vessel. Everyone was buzzing about the *"amazing"* dive they had just done. John and the *Delugionist* started to remove their dive gear as the boat's engines fired up. John found it hard to talk freely to the *Delugionist*. Even though *Delugionists* were mostly harmless, John disliked them as a whole. He felt that they had prayed upon people's fears ever since the Great Global Flood.

The *Delugionist* smiled making his wrinkles fold up upon each other like a venetian blind. "Great Dive!!" he said.

"Yeah," said John curtly.

"God has done great work."

"Uh yeah, okay," said John, trying to avoid furthering the conversation. He looked away trying to hold back, but finally could not stop himself. "How can you guys say that 'God' is so great when so many people died from the Great Flood?"

"Only sinners died."

"So you think it's good that all those millions died?"

"It's God's will. I do not try to make harsh judgement on what God has done. But as Clive says, *We are blessed with what God has now provided.* Today's dive is a beautiful example of God's great work."

John shook his head. He knew that there was no use in arguing and let the issue settle. "Thanks mate. It was a great dive," he replied, and locked his tank safely in its bracket.

John towelled himself off. The *Delugionist*, in the meantime, had moved over to the other side of the boat and began talking with others. John didn't care being left alone. He had enjoyed the dive and this relaxed him after the hard week he'd had in Canberra. John sat back gripping the gunnels of the boat as it set off back to its berth. The Sydney harbour *was* stunning even with its new coastline. It amazed him that to allow nature to firm up the water's edge, many buildings had to be demolished prior to their land being submerged.

Obviously God likes people who live on hills, thought John. It just seemed ridiculous to him.

The wind whipped through John's sandy brown hair as the boat splashed along the harbour. No matter what, it truly was a beautiful Autumn's day, a little bit warmer than usual for this time of year, but still magical.

PART 1
DELUGE

THE DRIVE BACK to Canberra early Monday morning was longer than usual due to a trifecta of heavy rain, weekend traffic and an unfortunate accident along the freeway. John was a little frustrated as the delay meant he would be running late for work.

John was a political advisor for his good friend and colleague, Frank Tsoukalos. Australian politics since the Great Global Flood, and much to John's relief, had changed very little. There was still the usual array of political group, lobbyists and fanatical protestors that they had to deal with. According to his diary, Frank's morning was not very busy, so he felt that Frank should cope.

As the bleary sun tried to lift itself above the clouds, John called up Frank to let him know of his delay.

"No worries, mate. Just as long as you're back here by half ten," said Frank in his low drawl. "I should be right. I've got our meeting with the Greens all wrapped up. Hey, after the meetings, let's have a beer at lunch and you can tell me what this new tourist venture on *The House* is like."

"Sounds good," replied John. "I'll catch you soon." He hung up the phone and placed it down on the passenger seat as he continued driving his blue Ford along the concrete expanses of the Hume Highway.

The modern climate had changed Australia's Southern Highlands quite dramatically with the increased rain and humidity. Rivers flowed stronger, and the rainforest sections along the highway had started to expand and blossom. The gorges and valleys were now quite a sight to see.

John flicked on the radio. ABC radio, Australia's national broadcaster, was piping some 1970's song for the "golden oldies". John vaguely remembered his mother listening to this song and dancing around to it when he was a kid. The female presenter had all morning been promising a radio interview with a mystery international figure of whom she was very excited about. It was bordering on annoying, but as it was only coming up next, John persisted on listening. The song finally ended and a familiar voice came over the radio. John recognised Clive's strong Canadian accent.

Welcome Clive, thank you for joining us. I'm so excited having you here on the eve of your world tour, chimed the radio presenter.

Thank you for having me, replied Clive, *I'm looking forward to coming down under.*

And when will that be?

In three weeks. First I'm heading to sermons in Europe and the UK. And I know we'll have an even greater turn out in Oz.

We're so looking forward to seeing you, said the radio presenter with a slightly flirtatious admiring tone. *So it has been an interesting few years. We have been following you closely since your first grand prophecy, and it is amazing what God has been telling you.*

Absolutely, replied Clive. *I have been so blessed to be able to pass on what God has been showing me. It is a great time that we live in, in that we will be able to meet his son soon once again. With the events of the past decade, God has shown sinners the wrong that they have done and the true light that we must follow. God has cast down his wrath upon those who doubted him and followed the wrong pathway of greed...*

John quickly tuned the radio channel onto something different. John didn't care what, as long as it wasn't Clive. ABC radio had certainly changed. In fact, the whole world had changed. People had found religion again which troubled John as science and sense had taken a back seat.

The traffic started to dwindle and the road cleared as he drove on towards Canberra. He still had over two hundred kilometres to go and the rain was not easing. It was going to be a long day.

The storms cleared as John arrived at Australia's Parliament House, affectionately known to many of its inhabitants as 'The Hill'. The green grassed slopes of the grand sloped edifice glistened in the morning sun after the rain brought it to a full lush life. It was a lot later in the morning than John had hoped to have arrived, but, to his relief, he was still in time for the minister's main meetings.

John made his way through the grand marble lined foyer, and had his bags scanned at parliamentary security. Even though John knew the security personnel well, security checks were compulsory and always took a bit of time, especially now with the greater risks of terrorist activities.

"Do we always have to do this?" asked John, fully knowing what the answer would be.

"Yeah, come on John. You know the drill. Only last week, there was that attack on South African parliament by those green freaks. And one of them had hidden something in the parliamentary secretary's bag. You can never be too careful."

"I know," said John. "It's just such an arse going through all this."

"That it is, that it is…"

There was always the fear of rogue environmental groups. They were now seen as a great global threat, with several coordinated attacks around the world happening over the previous decade. No one took risks with them anymore.

Once security were satisfied that John was not a danger, they opened up the elevator doors for him to take him to his floor. The ride up was fairly slow and John was in a rush. Everything seemed to take forever which frustrated John further, especially with him running late.

The silver metal doors of the elevator slid open as he arrived onto his floor. John quickly made his way through the maze of corridors that permeated the building. Every room and passageway looked identical and he often wondered if he should lay down string and carry a sword in case he encountered a Minotaur.

John finally arrived at the minister's suite and grabbed a coffee from the percolator on the way past. He sipped the hot dark beverage allowing the caffeine to fill his veins and give him a sense of clarity and awareness.

"Morning John!" chirped Scarlet.

"Morning Scarlet!" replied John, waking from his momentary trance.

Scarlet was one of John's favourite parliamentary co-workers. She had been with Frank for the past ten years as his personal assistant and was hard working and diligent, which Frank valued strongly in his team.

John always had a slight fancy for Scarlet, with her shoulder length brown hair and penetrating blue eyes. She had a stunning figure and a keen fashion sense, but John knew she was too young for him, so he never pursued anything.

Still Scarlet often flirted with John and he returned the favour.

"Big weekend?" asked John.

"Yeah! Me and the girls went to a few of the bars in town, ended up at Mooseheads."

"Really?" said John. Mooseheads was one of Canberra's more seedy nightclubs. "I thought there would be too many uni students there this time of year."

"Yeah! There were a few. I might of went home with one... a bit of fun... but you know, young men and their hormones. A lot going on down there, but not much happening up top." They both laughed. "John, when are you going to come join us?"

"When you remember to invite me!" replied John with a smile.

"Oh come on! You're always invited," said Scarlet with a wry smile.

Even though John was in his mid-forties, John was considered quite a find amongst the office's female staff. His appeal was not unnoticed by those within the party. With his looks, charm and charisma, he had often been asked if he would run for politics by those further up in the party's ranks, but John preferred to work in the back rooms working out deals and formulating policies.

"More influence, less scrutiny," he would say, "especially on your personal life."

And on that note, his personal life, everyone left him alone. John had been married in his mid-twenties, but sadly it was relatively short lived, lasting just ten years. The marriage was a strong and happy one, the envy of all others, but tragically his wife had passed away after a dreadful motor vehicle accident. He found out later that she was six weeks pregnant at the time and was on her way to meet him to tell him the big news. They had been trying for many years, and to find this out on top of her tragic death only compounded his grief.

The tragedy devastated John, and he used his work to focus himself away from his misery. Ten years later, his marriage now seemed like a separate life that he sorely missed.

John tried to stay fit to help keep his mind clear and sharp for the political arena, often running around the foreshores of Canberra's Lake Burley Griffin. Every morning he would run on a twenty kilometre track often passing the prime minister who similarly would run on the water's edge flanked by his six security officers.

"Morning John!"

"Morning PM!!" John would reply as part of the morning routine.

"If you ever want to move up the ranks..." the prime minister would often yell out.

"No thanks. I'm happy where I am. Who else is going to keep Frank in line?" John would yell back with a smile.

John didn't begrudge the work of a parliamentary aide. Actually he loved it!

It all started in the early days of Frank's rise into politics. John had met Frank whilst studying at Sydney University, where they both joined the Young Labor group in the summer months of 2004. They became young active grass root party members. The environment was a strong passion of John and Frank, so they fought hard to get real action on climate change within the party.

Over the years, they both worked strongly within the local chapter, yet only Frank was seen by party seniors as an outstanding member. He was seen as one who could win people over to his point of view, but at the same time would take the time to care and listen. They pulled Frank up further, but Frank made sure John was there. John was his wingman, backing up Frank when needed, coming out with all the facts and statistics, being Frank's own personal database. It was only later that John's attributes were recognised.

When pre-selections for the 2007 Australian Federal Elections occurred, Frank got pushed into being a Labor candidate as there was great promise seen in him. The Labor Party won the elections that year and Frank became an official member of the Australian parliament.

Frank was quite daunted with the job, so immediately asked John to be his political advisor and confidant. John was over the moon. He was excited to enter the real world of politics, and most of all to be there with Frank in Canberra.

Frank started off in the government's back benches due to his relative youth and inexperience. He was only twenty-two at the time. He kept his head down, followed party doctrines and used his and John's knowledge on certain affairs when necessary. The combined pair was seen as a real asset to the party, and many people thought that Frank had the real qualities to be a future leader.

At the time, the Labor Government was confident and strong. To John and Frank's amazement, the government quickly signed the Kyoto Protocol, an agreement for cutting carbon emissions, early in its term of government.

This move was popular amongst the Australian public, as this treaty had already been ratified by most developed countries worldwide, and Australia seemed to be lagging behind. However Australia only joined it in the latter half of its lifespan, and there was nothing to succeed it when it ended. The world needed a successor to this agreement.

The hope was that it was going to be negotiated in Copenhagen two years later amongst the various world governments at the United Nations Framework Convention on Climate Change. Australia was now going to be one of the key members. So the Labor party, in light of the Australian public's approval, organised certain members of parliament to get ready for these negotiations to help drive a successful plan.

As the meetings approached, flatteringly and to Frank and John's amazement, Frank was asked to help prepare and join the government at these meetings. According to senior party figures, it was due to *"Frank's hard work in climate change policy in the Young Labor movement"*.

This meant a lot of hard work. Frank and John worked tirelessly collating material, learning about various countries' viewpoints and setting up strategies. On Frank's request, John accompanied Frank and the Australian entourage to Denmark in the winter of 2009.

Many meetings occurred during the convention; several lasting many hours, some that lasted all night, but nothing came through that resulted in a global agreement on climate action. What resulted became known as *The Copenhagen Accord* which was seen by many climate commentators as a dismal failure. Both John and Frank were deflated with the result, but they were both determined to persist to get some change.

Over the next few years, the Labor Government tried to introduce their own climate carbon schemes within Australia, but none were very successful or popular. The party's popularity started to falter and flounder, leaders changed, the party fell into turmoil, and eventually the Labor Party failed dismally at the polls. Frank barely retained his seat.

John was there for Frank when the party lost and Frank was there for John. When John's wife died shortly after, Frank took a leave of absence from politics to help John deal with the tragedy. John appreciated the friendship and the help he got from Frank.

For the next decade the opposing party, the Liberal-National coalition, ruled very much to Frank and John's dismay. Environmental and Climate Change projects they had instigated had halted. Similar things happened worldwide. Governments got distracted by social upheavals. It almost seemed as if the world just did not care about the environment. Then the Great Global Flood occurred.

With all the public confusion and anger over the climate changes, Frank's party won back the next election with a landslide victory as though they had been vindicated. It was a bitter-sweet win.

With their government return, Frank was seen as more senior in the party, and was made the Minister for the Environment, Agriculture and Climate Change. This was considered a very big portfolio, especially with the environmental challenges that had occurred. It was Frank's job to prepare the country to deal with the new climate reality, and Frank relied keenly on John for his steady head and knowledge. John provided this and through their teamwork, great strength was brought to the government.

"So how's Frank this morning?" asked John.

"Oh you know!! Beating his head against the wall because he's got another meeting with the Greens," replied Scarlet.

"Aw... Jim's not that bad," said John with a quiet laugh. "He's just a little bit too keen."

"Too keen? That's putting it mildly. I think *insane* is a better word. Frank's a bit dirty with you for running late and leaving him to deal with Jim," said Scarlet, "but I think he'll forgive you. Anyway, there's a pile of papers on Frank's desk for the next set of meetings. He wants you to have a look at them before his 10.45. So you better get your cute arse cracking if you want to get through them all."

John smiled at Scarlet's comment. He dreaded the thought of the pile of papers that awaited him. He knew it wouldn't be easy reading, and to get Frank up to speed was going to be a nightmare to say the least.

John thanked Scarlet. He wandered through the office suite, passing various lit up meeting rooms with pristine white tables containing the mandatory jug of water and minted sweets, and then passing by the dingy parliamentary offices containing staff members glued to their phones and sucking on coffees. John often felt a sense of claustrophobia in the parliamentary suite, as if the ceiling and walls was closing in on him. He was very glad to get out whenever possible.

Frank had only one early meeting that morning and that was with the Greens. John knew that Frank dreaded meeting with James Eastlake. James was the leader of the Greens Party of Australia, and Jim, as he was known by his friends, was a bit excitable with politics. Once again in Australian politics, the Greens had grabbed the balance of power, and so the Labor Party had to often negotiate with them.

Still, John had to get ready for the rest of the day. John walked into Frank's office which stood above the parliamentary court. The view was stunning overlooking the surrounds of the round Canberran streets with the blue hued mountains forming a vast scenic backdrop. Often John and Frank would have a whisky in the office late in the evening whilst looking over what Frank termed as *"The Commons"*.

John sighed and looked for the material he needed. Frank insisted on using paper as he kept on losing his tablet computers. The government security agencies were not impressed.

Frank's desk was covered in various folders and folios, and had the occasional photo frame scattered around as a fond reminder of times gone by. One photo which John often looked at with fondness was from a fishing trip they did together in the Northern Territory. John was holding a large Barramundi in his arms, whilst Frank was giving it a big kiss. He smiled as he glimpsed at the photo.

John found the folders and reached out to grab them. As he leant over, his elbow knocked the computer's mouse causing the computer screen to flash on with life. Frank, much to John's amusement, still persisted in using a mouse even though they had well and truly been superseded with touchscreens and motion sensors. John was about to walk off when something on the screen caught his attention. It was an email with the word *Delugionist.*

What the hell is Frank doing with those nutters? thought John.

Curiosity got the better of him, and he sat down and started to read through the message.

Dear Frank,

This email is of the utmost importance; hence we sent it through the usual security.
    Operation Warmth will continue and more funding is needed for the Delugionist Foundation. It is absolutely vital that the funding is to continue as we have so much still at stake. Them and the others have so far agreed. Stage 4 will start soon.
    Please reply using the correct procedures.

From TG!

John looked at the address bar. There was no "from" address, no electronic signature, just the message. John stared at the screen.

What's Frank doing?

John clicked on the forward tab and typed in his home email and pressed send. The message moved to the out box, and then to the sent items. John decided that he would look at the email in more detail later on in the day.

If Frank is going to get involved with the DF, then he better bloody well tell me, thought John.

He clicked in the sent folder, deleted the sent email, and then emptied it from trash.

Done! There should be no trace of it being forwarded on the system. John made sure the screen looked identical as to when he arrived and made sure the mouse was roughly in the same place.

John picked up his folders and started to walk out of the room. Just as he left the office, he crashed into Frank who was rushing in. The folders in John's arms were sent flying into the air spreading the papers all over the floor.

"Bloody Hell!!" said John.

"Sorry!" apologised Frank as he helped John pick up the fallen documents. "I swear I didn't see you coming."

"Yeah, no worries mate! Mind you, as collisions go, it wasn't bad," replied John.

"I guess if you're going to do things right, then do it with gusto."

They both laughed.

"Why in such a rush?" asked John.

"Oh, you know, with you being late and all, I wanted to make sure we had everything sorted for our 10.45," said Frank. "The meeting with Jim went much later than I expected. I should've known it would've taken a while. Jim just bloody kept yabbering on and on. I was lucky that I didn't develop tinnitus from the constant whine of his voice."

Frank chuckled at his own joke, then paused as he studied John's face. "What's wrong? You look all serious, like you've seen a ghost."

John lied. "Oh nothing, really! I was just looking out the window before and saw someone who looked like Rebecca. I still miss her."

"Yeah John. I know you do! But really, you've got to move on. It's been, what? Ten years? I worry about you sometimes." Frank sighed, and wandered over to his desk. The screen was still on. Frank's face flushed white and he quickly clicked the mouse several times in rapid succession and then wandered back.

John glimpsed over. The message had been removed from the screen.

With a slight jilt in his voice, Frank continued, "Did you hear that damned *Delugionist* Clive on ABC radio this morning?"

"Yeah, just a bit," John replied. John was now wary. He wasn't too sure if Frank was trying to find out if he had seen the message, or whether he was just being conversational. He thought it better to hide the fact, at least for the time being. "Is he really coming to Australia?"

"Yeah. As part of the world tour. Apparently I've been told I've got to attend."

"Really?"

"Really!!"

"I couldn't be bothered listening. I can't stand that prick."

"Me too. I might take some ear plugs," laughed Frank. "Just because we've now got a few *Delugionist* nutters in the party, doesn't mean we have to be bombarded by *Delugion* bloody everywhere. I know that we have to be seen to be seen to be supportive of *Delugion*, but thankfully everyone's staying with party policy and not bringing their religion into political decisions. Still, I'm very uneasy with Clive doing a tour of the country."

"Too close to home?

"Yeah, too close. At least he's only here for just a few days. It's too long as far as I'm concerned. His influence will do enough damage."

John picked up the final sheet off the floor and dusted off the folders. "Okay. You ready for this meeting. We need to get moving if we are to get there on time."

"No worries," drawled Frank in his trademark approach. "Let's knock 'em dead."

They headed out of the office through the parliamentary suite, and went back through security. The government car was waiting for them at the front entrance. They both got into the back sitting on the leather lined seats. The black sedan took off.

The car ventured through the spiral streets of Canberra, passing several anonymous large glassed buildings and various garish business centres. John and Frank continued to peruse the day's material.

"You on top of all of this?" asked John.

"Not really. Thought we would wing it," replied Frank.

John looked slightly shocked and was about to panic.

"Of course I'm on top of it, you idiot," said Frank with a grin.

The driver turned the corner sharply and pulled up in a small side street.

"Where are we?" asked John. They were supposed to be going to the CSIRO to discuss the latest scientific developments and research results on GM fisheries.

John turned to Frank. He looked as white as a sheet. "I'm sorry John," said Frank. Tears started to form in his eyes. "I think I know what's about to happen. I hoped, for dear God, that you hadn't seen it."

The driver turned around with a gun in hand and aimed it at John's head. The driver had a cold hard expression on his lacklustre face. "The email you sent," he angrily stated. "Why did you send it to yourself? Who do you work for?"

"Umm... I just sent it to myself... I... I... I just wa... wanted to see what it was all about!!" stammered John.

"Not good enough," replied the driver. "You!" The driver turned to Frank. "You are no longer needed." The driver aimed the gun onto Frank.

"That's not the way it's supposed to happen. I am one of the original..." yelled Frank as he struggled for the door handle. The driver shot him. The bullet tore through the flesh of the side of his neck taking out his jugular and part of his throat. Frank clutched at the wound. Frank's breathing started to rasp as blood poured out incessantly over his shirt and chest. Panic set in. Frank looked to John for help. John just sat there frozen, mortified, waiting inevitably for the gun to turn onto himself.

Suddenly, the door next to John burst open. An arm wrenched around his throat and before he knew it, his seatbelt was released. John was dragged out of the car struggling. He felt a sharp pain slam into his leg followed by an aching burn that travelled up his thigh. Things suddenly felt heavy and his vision started to blur and waver. Someone picked up his legs and carried him away. He was unable to struggle. He saw the browning leaves of the Canberran trees slowly moving in the breeze. He turned his head and saw another man carrying a slumped body over to the car.

"Put the replacement in the driver's seat and make it look good," yelled a detached voice inside John's head. He couldn't tell where it came from or for that matter if it was real. John could hardly keep his eyes open as everything started to fade away.

What the hell's happening?

CHAPTER 2

JOHN FELT HEAVY and uncomfortable. His head ached with a dull throb that faded in and out. There was a constant whirring noise that echoed inside his head. Now it was outside of his head. John tried to focus. *Footsteps!* Somebody was coming towards him. Sudden acid burning sensation in his leg. *Pain!* John fell back asleep.

John slowly woke again. His leg was throbbing and there was a small dried patch of blood on his trouser leg. He was strapped in a firm chair and could not move. Someone was yelling in the background. He looked around to see where the voice was coming from.

"You idiot! What do you mean you need to fuel up again!?! We are supposed to meet Egyptian services in three fucking hours. We'll be lucky if we make it there in time. They're not likely to sit around and have a cup of tea whilst chatting to their mums, are they!?!? And besides I only have one jab left and we'll need it to transport him once on the ground!!! What do you intend to do instead, bore him to sleep?"

There were some words John couldn't make out.

"Well I thought I had enough! I'm not a bloody pharmacist, am I?!? We haven't had to use this before from Australia. Who knew that this damn flight would take so fucking long. I don't even know if a person is supposed to have this much. For all we know, he may be a fucking walking vegetable."

There was some other indistinguishable yelling.

"Okay, okay! So I could have looked it up on the internet. Sorry Mr Computer nerd. And besides, why couldn't we have fucking flown directly to Egypt?"

Some more yelling in background.

"Damn fucking aviation rules! Anyway I make the rules around here. Get this fucking thing fuelled up and in the air! Unless you've got a time machine concealed up your arsehole, we need to leave now!!"

Suddenly two shots fired and the blurry figure by the aircraft doorway fell. There was more yelling in the background which John could not distinguish, but the voices were different. Two blurry figures appeared and rushed towards him from the door with some device in hand. They cut through John's straps and carried him out. John tried once again focusing but eventually gave up. He gazed around and realised he was now in a wide open area. He tried to move, but failed.

"Stay calm. We're here to help," said an English accented voice on his left that he thought was female. John looked to see where it came from and saw that it was someone with long hair. He knew he was right. It was a female! John was happy that he was right.

"Oh!" replied John in the best way he could in his drugged out state. He giggled. *What's so funny?* he thought. He giggled again.

"Get him to the car," said the right hand voice. This one was male. *Ahhh the perfect couple,* thought John. *Both of them enjoy taking people from planes... They match!!!* John smiled as they threw him onto the back seat of a waiting car.

"Will those guys be all right?" said the male voice.

"The seda-taser should wear off soon," replied the female voice, as the car started. "Besides, I doped it up with an added hallucinogen that I got off *Silk Road*. It will lay them out easily at least for the next two hours. They won't even know what's real."

John liked the voices. They were funny. He slowly drifted off back to sleep as the car whirred... *like a condor purring*, thought John.

John woke later wondering, '*How can condors purr?*' It just didn't make sense. Actually, not a lot made sense. John sat up and rubbed his head. He was sitting on an old cracked red leather lined sofa in a small low lit dingy room. The scent of stale beer emanated from the floor making him feel nauseated. He tried to make sense of what had happened. It gradually started to come back... strapped in a seat... car... gun shots...

Oh god! Frank.... .....did he? He must of!!! thought John. On the far wall, an old fashioned wooden door with ornate twentieth century handles opened and a woman with long red hair entered the room. She walked slowly towards John. He rested his head in his hands as his thoughts continued to swirl in his head. *No way he could have survived that. Where am I? I think I was on a plane. I must have flown here. Where am I?*

"Where am I?" asked John. The long haired woman grabbed an old wooden chair and took a seat in front of him.

"Where do you think you are?" she replied, arms folded. Her cool green eyes stared back at him.

"I don't know. One minute I was in Canberra, then Frank... ohhh Frank... poor bastard."

"Where were you being taken?"

"I don't know!!" growled John. His head was throbbing. "Where am I? Just tell me where the fuck I am!!!"

"You're in Barnstaple, Devon."

"Where?"

"The United Kingdom. You know, Devon, Devonshire tea – scones, clotted cream and jam country??"

"What the hell? How did I get here? Why am I here?" asked John rubbing his eyes as an ache pounded behind his left eyeball. His nausea waxed and waned.

"You got here by plane."

"But why?"

"That's what we want to know," replied the woman. "John, why are you here?"

"Well that's a dumb question," laughed John. "I just asked you that and you ask the same question back. What sort of moron are you? Hang on, how do you know my name?" John felt his pockets. They had been emptied. *She must have my phone and wallet.*

"Flattery's going to get you everywhere," retorted the woman sarcastically. "And yes, we've got your wallet." She threw it on the chair. John put it back in his pocket. "Well obviously they thought that you were important enough to take a private jet from Oz with a transit in the UK. So, I ask you again, can you think of a reason why you are here?" The red headed woman got up and started to pace.

"Errr...The email... wait a minute... who are you!?!"

"Jenny Fitzgerald. And we know exactly who you are. You are John Frankston, the political advisor to Frank Tsoukalos, the Australian minister for the Environment and Agriculture."

"Okay...."

"Yes. We know you. You are John Frankston, who grew up in West Ryde and rose up in the political ranks of the Labor party. *The* John Frankston who's wife passed away from a tragic car accident ten years ago. "

"Okay, enough!!! Anyone can Google that shit."

"Yes. We know you are *the* John Frankston, the political advisor who murdered the politician Frank Tsoukalos and his driver two days ago." Jenny threw a copy of *The Australian* newspaper onto John's lap. John's face was plastered all over the cover alongside Frank – 'Nation Mourns: Australia's First Political Assassination' rang the headline.

"Wait... what!?!"

"Yes. We know you are *the* John Frankston who is now on the run from authorities after it was declared that he shot Minister Tsoukalos apparently in the name of the eco-terrorist group, The Earth's Representatives for Revegetation, Order and Restoration, also known as tERROR."

"Wait... Stop it!" John stared in disbelief at the front page of the newspaper.

"Yes. We know you are *the* John Frankston, who is now wanted worldwide by authorities due to this political murder and his affiliations!!"

"Oh, God!!"

"So we know that you're important to them, but why?"

John's mind was reeling with all that he was hearing. It was all too much. There was something that troubled him. The name... *Jenny Fitzgerald.... Jenny Fitzgerald...* It suddenly dawned on him. John realised where he had heard the name before. Jenny Fitzgerald was one of the leaders of tERROR. This was a group of eco-terrorists that had done terrible acts in the name of the environment. tERROR were responsible for assassinations of various political figures, for bombing of fossil fuel organisations, and for disruptions of intergovernmental gatherings. Fear started rising in him. He now realised who he was dealing with. According to many reports, Jenny was brutal and ruthless in her eco-terrorist activities.

"You're that woman. You killed all those people in France."

"Yeah? And you killed that innocent politician and his driver!" retorted Jenny.

"No... No... I didn't...."

"Well, guess what Einstein?! Neither did I. Our group did *not* do any of these things. Yet, here we are, two of the world's most wanted. And now, apparently, according to the news, you are part of our group. So, I'll ask you again, why are you here?"

"Let me think..." John was confused. He looked back at Jenny trying to grasp the entirety of the situation. Jenny sat back on her antique wooden chair. Her long red hair was tied up in a tight pony tail which rested on her shoulder. She was quite attractive in real life, very much different to the images shown in the media of the angry volatile activist. John looked around at his surroundings. He was in a moderate sized room with wooden panelled walls covered in garish posters. The ceiling hung low with dim dingy lighting. A strong smell of musty stale beer and burnt logs wafted through the room and reminded him of English pubs, similar to the ones he visited after his university years.

John leant forwards on the tattered red leather couch and rested his head on his palms. The only other sign of life was a small television screen lit up in the back corner of the room. A laptop was perched up on a table and around it were several empty pint glasses with dried beer and lipstick on the edges. John looked back at Jenny's green eyes. She stared back with a sense of determination. John leant back. He thought back to when it all started.

"The email... I can't quite understand why..." John hesitated. "Hang on... what's all this to you anyway? Why am I telling you this? And am I in a pub?"

"Yes." Jenny smiled at the last comment. She got up and started pacing the room. "Yes, you are in a pub. We're in the back room of *The Reform* if you really want to know. You can let the authorities know that, but somehow I don't think they'll be all that sympathetic to you."

John still wasn't quite convinced he should trust Jenny. He kept silent, unsure of what to say or do.

Jenny sunk her shoulders in mild defeat. "You're confused, I know. You've probably been through a lot. I suppose I better explain a few things to clear things up, make you understand why we need to know why you are here."

John looked up, intrigued.

"You're very lucky, you know? You're very lucky that we were able to save you. As far as we understand, you were on rendition to Egypt. We believe you were going to be interrogated there and probably would have never left. We managed to intercept the flight during your plane's refuelling after a certain tip-off. It wasn't easy to get to you. If it wasn't for us, you would be in an Egyptian prison by now, most likely being water-boarded or worse."

John was shocked. It all had happened so fast, Frank being shot, then him being shoved heavily sedated onto a plane. But to be sent to a foreign prison and tortured, John shuddered at the thought. "I thought they stopped all that," he said.

"Yeah! And you continue believing that!!" replied Jenny astounded at his naivety. She paused briefly in a mixture of constraint and annoyance.

"As you probably know," she continued to explain, "I am the supposed current figurehead of tERROR. The group has been around for over twenty years, but the reality is that there is no direct leader, just different cells in various areas with their own causes. Anyway, enough about us. What do you know about Frank, and his involvement with *Them*?"

"Who?"

"*Them*!"

"I'm sorry, but are you quite right in the head? *Them*? What do you mean *Them*?" said John.

"*Them*, as they've called themselves, are a group that have been trying to control worldwide climate debate for the past twenty... thirty years." Jenny sighed in exasperation. "*Them* as we understand called themselves '*Them*' to make it easier to talk about themselves without revealing too much information. Also, whenever someone mentions *Them* in Blogs or internet chatter, it seems to the public more like paranoia and insanity than an organised group."

"*The paranoia is starting to appear quite true here too...*" muttered John under his breath.

"No!" Jenny protested. "You don't understand the severity of the whole situation. *Them* has influenced governments all around the world. *Them* is more interested in financial gains and maintaining control, than protecting the environment, than protecting the planet."

John looked at her incredulously.

"You don't believe me. Look, it was *Them* who kidnapped you and brought you here."

John wasn't convinced.

"Them have been monitoring your government for years... no... decades."

John had had enough.

"Fuck you and your mentally insane conspiracy shit!!" he said. "I've got to get out of here and try and sort this fucked up situation out." John stood up and started to walk towards the door.

"*Them* killed your wife!"

John stopped and turned. She had his attention. "That's not funny. Don't you dare fuck me around and try to bring my dead wife into all this bullshit."

"Frank had a secretary for the past fifteen years, long brown hair, blue eyes, about five foot four, flirtatious, named Scarlet? Ring any bells?"

John started trembling in fury. It was a low blow bringing Rebecca into this, but if there was any hint of truth, he needed to know. John calmed himself and sat back down. "Okay. I'm listening," he said.

"Before I start, I just want to let you know, I'm sooo sorry!" Jenny's eyes had welled up with sheer desperation. "We're all sooo sorry about this! The information you might have, we hope, is what we need, what we've all been looking for."

"Okay. Tell me what happened," said John holding back his anger through gritted teeth.

"Alright!! Back in 2009, we had high hopes for the various Governments from around the world in getting a successor to the Kyoto Protocol in Copenhagen. To bring about real global change."

"What's this got to do with Rebecca?" asked John in annoyance.

"Everything," replied Jenny. "I'll get there soon. I promise. Australia was seen as the latest nation to change its mind on Climate reform after they had signed the Kyoto Protocol. They were seen by a number of countries as a nation that had, as such, 'changed its mind'. In Copenhagen, it was hoped that Australia could convince other countries that weren't part of 'Kyoto' as to why they changed their view.

"Our organisation had several insiders to monitor the two week event. We knew that Australia's government was stymied by a number of internal elements, but Australia's team in Copenhagen seemed initially to be real reformers."

"Get to the point!" said John.

"I will," replied Jenny. "You were there with Frank Tsoukalos. Frank, as you know, was one of the big 'behind-the-scenes' negotiators on the reforms. We had big hopes with him. He seemed like he could change things, but after the Friday of the first week, his views altered – not radically, but nonetheless they were different.

"He no longer was as passionate as he was before. He even seemed to hold back on a number of fronts. Something was wrong. In fact, he started to advocate a number of ideas that many knew were going to be ineffective. We were concerned that someone somehow had got to him."

John sat back. He knew of the meetings she referred to, and he remembered how pissed off he had got at Frank for going for weaker options. Frank had just said that he had *'been shown the science and that these other so-called milder schemes had great merit'*, and that *'we were not going to be able to get a binding international CPRS through'*. John was flabbergasted. He asked Frank for the supposed information he talked about, but all Frank said was, "In time..."

It never happened.

"So, what's this all got to do with my wife?" asked John.

Jenny replied, "We believed that someone had got to Frank in Copenhagen, and we wanted to know who. There was no chance of finding out at the Convention, and we knew that whoever did, would stay in contact with Frank. We could no longer watch your government from afar. We needed someone on the inside. We needed a mole, someone we could trust.

"A few years later the opportunity arose. One of our organisation's newer UK members at the time was a young Australian – Scarlet Jones – a young environmental law student dropout who had a keen passion for politics and the environment. She had come to the UK for a gap year after dropping out of university and, through her friends, got to know our organisation quite well. She volunteered a lot and helped out. She always said that if we ever needed any help back in Oz..."

John leant back. The picture was starting to clear. "Go on," he said.

Jenny continued, "So when the time was right, we took her up on her offer. We told her that the job could be dangerous and might take some years 'til we got results. Scarlet thought it definitely would be worthwhile as she felt this was the best chance for her to make a change.

"She really was ideal for the job. Scarlet had a clean record, no history of protests or arrests, and at the same time was sensible, very keen and clever. She was willing to do whatever it would take.

"Her role was to infiltrate Frank's office and find out what happened those years back in Copenhagen and potentially more. As you know, Scarlet initially volunteered in your electoral offices and was very quick in getting close to you and Frank."

John felt uncomfortable. He remembered how Scarlet came to work for them in the party, how she impressed John and Frank with her zeal and enthusiasm towards politics and environmental affairs. It was what won them over for her to be their political aide, and ultimately Frank's personal assistant. Her background in law, no matter how short it was, was seen as a great plus.

"As we all hoped, Scarlet managed to get a job in your government office very quickly. And as Frank moved up in politics, she followed along as his loyal dog's body.

"Scarlet was great for us in tERROR. She passed on information that she thought was important and we would go through it and let her know what else to look out for. Scarlet was very careful in the way she passed it on. She made sure she wasn't detected. The information that came through initially seemed to show that Frank had just changed his stance on his own, which was, needless to say, disappointing. But, as time went on, Scarlet found some more information that changed this view.

"She overheard a conversation where Frank kept on saying that he's done a lot for them, but wouldn't be controlled by them. We asked her who he was referring to. She said he didn't say, but apparently he was arguing with someone who she thought he was afraid of, as he was pale and sweating profusely when he came out of his room. He apparently was swearing and muttering to himself about *them* and *since Copenhagen.*

"It was what we were after... confirmation, but it wasn't enough. We still didn't have any details or concrete evidence that Frank was being manipulated or part of some conspiracy.

"Then Scarlet found some more information in Frank's office. It made us realise that there was a larger group that was coordinating all of this, the group that we now know as *Them*. It was a major breakthrough for us. We tried to post some stuff up on the internet, but we now realise that was a mistake.

"*Them* had started to suspect that there was a leak and traced it back to your office. We believe they had your office under surveillance for several months. Scarlet said there were strange phone calls coming in. She said that one time she found her files in slight disarray and her computer was slightly altered. Scarlet from then on lay low."

Jenny took a deep breath somewhat nervous about the information she was imparting to John.

"But even so, she still managed to send us more information. Unfortunately for your wife, Rebecca, *Them* found one lead that took them to the wrong person."

Tears started to roll down her cheek.

"Someone must have come to believe that your wife was the leak. So, late one rainy night, they ran her off the road and made sure it looked like an accident."

John dug his fingers into his legs. He kept quiet whilst Jenny continued. "We know it was *Them* because of a conversation that Scarlet overheard between Frank and some person. Frank was furious and adamant that 'the leak' couldn't be Rebecca, but *Them* apparently convinced him that he was wrong. According to Scarlet, Frank was truly devastated by the loss of Rebecca and the supposed betrayal of someone so close."

John was beyond words. For Scarlet to betray Rebecca and allow her to fall on the sword was beyond comprehension. Scarlet wasn't just a work colleague. In fact, Scarlet and Rebecca had been very good friends. Whenever Rebecca came into the office, Scarlet and Bec would go off and have a good girl's chat and gossip about the various ministers and their mistresses or, for that matter, their toy-boys. They both used to come out of the staff kitchen red faced and laughing their heads off. John would shake his head in amusement whenever he overheard their conversations.

So, the fact that when Rebecca was killed in the crash, Frank and Scarlet appeared to be particularly crushed, it now seemed to be an outright lie. John originally had put it down to their close friendships to him and Rebecca, but now he knew they both had other reasons... guilt!!

Jenny found it hard to look at John. She stared dejectedly away. "Scarlet was a nervous wreck after that. A close friend, the wife of a colleague had been murdered, and she didn't ever want it to ever happen again. We barely managed to convince her to stay on. We had to remind her that it was for the greater good, and so much more was at stake. She took a lot of convincing, but reluctantly agreed.

"For a safe measure, and to let her settle back in, we told her to stop sending us information for at least a year to ensure that they didn't search for any more leaks or for that matter kill anyone else. With your wife's death, *Them*, we believe, had assumed that the leak had been sealed."

John stared at Jenny in silence and in anger. Tears started to form in his eyes. He wiped them away.

Jenny rested her head in her hands racked with guilt. She was now a little more demure. "Eventually, Scarlet started sending us information again. Over the years Scarlet got us more and more material, this time being far more careful. We tried to make sure that there wouldn't be any linkage back to your office, and nothing came up, until now.

"*Them* must have had their suspicions again. So, whatever you did must have made them think that you were the mole. Whatever you picked up or saw must have been vital for them to want to interrogate you, rather than kill you. This is why we need you to remember what it is that they were upset about. They have killed at least two people over this, including one of their own. They will have no qualms in killing more."

John couldn't take any more. His mind was in freefall. He had to get some air. He stood up and stormed for the door.

"Wait!!" yelled Jenny, but John didn't care. Tears rolled down his face as he burst through the door into the next room. The room was larger and brighter, but still had the same booths and wood-lined walls. Plastered over the walls was a range of old fashioned advertisements telling people to drink their favourite brews from the nineteen forties and fifties. A dozen people were sitting around the bar having ales, lagers and various beverages. One pale leggy blonde haired man from the group quickly stood up and started to walk over. John headed for the main door and burst through into the night.

A wave of cold air hit him. Outside in the street, it was dark and freezing cold. He looked around and saw that he was in a narrow alleyway at the base of a hill. The smell of Indian food emanated from a small brightly lit takeaway store next door to the pub. John moved from the alleyway into the main street and started to walk quickly up the steep hill. He didn't care where he was going. He just needed to get away.

John stormed past many old stone buildings that abutted one another like books on a shelf. They were grand and tall, some several storeys high. It made the bitumen road appear narrow and cramped. Cars were parked close together like a game of dominoes. Many rooms had various coloured curtains blocking their lit windows, stopping people from being able to peer in. He passed several small shops that were closed for the night with their wares displayed in darkened windows.

After walking for only a few minutes, John came by another pub – *The Chichester Arms*. He looked around for some form of familiarity, but he was lost. He felt for his phone, it was gone. He didn't know what to do. Dejectedly, he went into the pub. The pub had a cosy feel with a roaring wood fire warming the slate floors and felt lined booths. A barman stood wiping down the wooden bar, whilst several people sat in their booths eating their dinner peacefully. Similar to *The Reform*, the ceiling was low, and the room had a musty smell, but it was warm. John went over to the bar and sat down.

The stubbled barman picked up the phone and dialled.

"He's here," said the barman and put the phone back down.

John sighed. He went to get money out for a beer and realised he only had Australian dollars. There was no point running. He had very little money in his wallet, he was wanted by the Australian Government, and *Them*, whoever they were, were apparently after him. John realised his new rescuers-abductors were now his main hope of coming out of this alive and somewhat free.

The door of the bar opened and Jenny came walking in followed by the leggy blonde man. The blonde man took a seat near the door guarding the entranceway. She walked over to the bar and sat next to John.

"There was nothing we could have done for her," said Jenny, nodding to the Barkeep for two beers. "We had no idea that they suspected Rebecca, otherwise we wouldn't have dreamed of putting her in that danger."

"Yet you still kept going!!" replied John staring at the wall straight ahead. "After Rebecca died, you still kept going. You still kept stealing information and for what!?! To infiltrate an organisation that might have some influence on a small nation like mine? We're not big players! We're a tiny fucking country compared to the rest of the world. And because of your spying, my wife is dead, now Frank is dead, his driver is dead and I am fucking framed for their murders. Are you guys actually capable of learning?"

"Yes... We learnt that they have their fingers controlling policies of many nations including Australia, the US and the UK. *Them* is influencing global policy, yet we still don't know who they exactly are," replied Jenny.

John took a sip from his beer. "Okay. You want to find out who they are? I know who we can find that out from. I will need a proper sleep, a shower and a change of clothes. But, as soon as you have your information and I am a free man, I'm out!!"

"Okay," agreed Jenny.

"Do you by chance know the way to the Cotswolds?"

CHAPTER 3

*J*ohn was driving *down the Hume Highway. His phone rang. He smiled. It was Rebecca. He reached to grab the phone. He was now sitting next to her in her car. She was still talking to him on the phone, laughing at one of his bad jokes. He reached over to stroke her face as he often did but could not reach her. He called out to her, but she could not hear or see him. Rebecca continued to talk on the phone to him. "I must be driving in another car," thought John. John looked out the window. They were at the end of a T-Junction on a darkened country road. Rebecca was waiting for a clear run of traffic to cross the highway. A large truck was coming down the road. Rebecca looked absolutely stunning, all dressed up to meet him for dinner. She was gently caressing her belly. Suddenly there was an engine roar from behind and a massive jolt. Rebecca screamed in a panic as her car flew forwards veering under the oncoming truck.*

John woke bolt upright sweating.

By the time they were organised, it was late morning. John had been told that he needed to change his dress style so as to make him blend more into the local scene. The suit that he had been wearing was not the usual dress of *The Reform*. He was told that he stood out like "tits on a bull". The bartender beamed, proud in having used the Australian vernacular. The barman gave John some of his spare clothes, ones that he had come back wearing from the latest music festival. John appreciated the thoughts, but felt that the outfit did not hide him very well. It instead made him look more like a confused middle-aged man in a mid-life crisis trying to find his youth again. Still his so-called new friends insisted.

When the time came, Jenny grabbed some bags stacked up in the front room and took John out to the front of *The Reform*. The street looked a lot friendlier in the light of day and consisted of townhouses from a different bygone era. John wondered which century they were from.

"They're back from the time of *The Doomsday Book*," said Jenny seeing him study the area. "It's the reason the council saved the buildings."

"What's *The Doomsday Book*?" asked John.

Jenny smiled shaking her head.

Soon, an immaculate white van pulled up out the front and two men and one woman jumped out. A ginger tom cat came running up the street obviously happy to see one of the van's occupants. It started rubbing up against the woman's legs in sheer delight. The young woman was glad to see the cat and picked him up whilst giving it a scratch under its powder white chin. The cat's engine started purring.

"You still have them!!" smiled John with some admiration. "I thought the old British white van had died out over a decade back."

"They're a classic, always loved them," said the driver in a welsh accent. He was a tall young man with a dark olive complexion, and short cropped hair. The driver walked onto the footpath and put his arm around the young female passenger whom John assumed was his companion. "So who's your boyfriend?" the driver asked.

Jenny held up the front page of the Australian newspaper, and slapped it against the driver's chest. "Work it out yourself. You're late!!" she said. Jenny started to pack the back of the van as the driver looked at the paper. His eyes widened.

"Oh fuck! This guy's all over the news. The Aussies are hunting for him. They think he's still in Australia. Why do we have him? What's he doing here? Have you checked him over? Have you made sure he's safe? More importantly, have you got rid of his phone?"

"Yes, I've checked him over, and no, I haven't got rid of his mobile. I thought we better keep it as it might have some important details that we might need," replied Jenny, now holding up John's phone. John looked intently at the mobile. It was his lifeline. It had all his contacts, addresses, numbers, emails... It had the email!! Jenny continued, "John was kidnapped by *Them*. They thought he was one of us. We managed to free him and get him away just in time. They obviously want him as they didn't kill him, so we wanted to know why. John must have found out something important. Hopefully he is of more use to us than them."

John felt a little uneasy.

"But they'll be able to find us! They can use the phone's signal to pinpoint us!"

"That's all you focus on!?! You idiot!! I turned it off and pulled out the battery as a safety measure. They can't find us while it's off. You don't think I'm that daft, do you?"

"Well I just wanted to be sure."

"To be sure of what?" said the second man. "That she turned it off, or that she's daft?" He had a big grin on his face. John recognised him as the same leggy blonde guy from the night before. In the daylight, he was able to survey his most recent set of abductors a little better. The second man, John felt, would have had many a woman fall under his gaze with his strong physique, pale blue eyes and short blonde hair. Even the small scar on his cheek hid in his dimples whenever he smiled.

"Oi, you guys!!" piped the short young dark haired woman under the driver's arms. "That's enough! Let's get on the road. And come on, where's your manners? Hello. I'm Karen. This idiot is James. And that lanky bastard is Ahmed."

Ahmed came over to shake John's hand. His fair complexion did not seem to suit his name whatsoever. "Yes. I met you yesterday," said Ahmed. "From what I remember, you were quite rude."

John looked puzzled.

"Well, I picked you up from the airport, drove you four hundred miles, gave you free accommodation and when I joined you up the road at the pub... and you didn't even shout me a beer."

"Next time, mate," laughed John. "Definitely, next time. Nice to meet you all."

"Okay!! Come on! Everyone in!" yelled Jenny.

The group started to pile into the van. Karen suddenly looked up concerned and grabbed James on the arm.

"Hon', can you put Fred inside?" she said. "I don't want him getting hit by some idiot driver."

James mumbled something incoherently under his breath and jumped out of the van. He grabbed the cat and threw it inside *The Reform.*

"Sometimes I swear she cares more for that cat than James," whispered Ahmed. "Though, to be honest, I wouldn't dare argue with her."

"Why not?" asked John.

"Let's just say she is very well trained. Mind you, she's trained him too."

James returned back to the van and jumped into the driver's seat. He started the van, "Where're we off to?" he asked.

"The Cotswolds," replied Jenny. "John said his so called pal, our climate minister, Phillip Cudsworth should know why John was kidnapped and probably quite a bit more."

"Really? Him?" asked James. "But he's old!"

"He's not that old!" said John. "He was there when I reckon it all started in Copenhagen. He must know."

"Yeah, James. It's not that surprising," replied James. "I guess we always suspected the Environment minister was somehow involved."

"Really?" asked John somewhat incredulously. "So if you guys thought he was dodgy, then why haven't you chased him before? Let's face it, I know you guys aren't afraid of confrontation and for that matter getting your way with violence."

Jenny scowled at the inference. "John, parliamentary security are not going to let people like ourselves get close to a Secretary of State without good reason. And even if we did get to him, do you think the minister is going to chat to an activist about stuff that's happened in secret meetings?" Jenny gritted he teeth and took a deep breath. "And regarding violence, we don't like using it and as I said before, Paris was not us!"

Obviously a sore point, thought John.

The Paris bombing was still one of the world's most notorious eco-terrorist activities that had ever happened. It had occurred twelve years earlier when environmental groups and many in the general public were getting annoyed with the general inaction on changing climate.

Many blamed the oil and mining companies for causing delays and misconceptions. Soon targeted protests and clashes occurred at various mining and intergovernmental congregations, often requiring riot police to intervene.

The Paris bombing happened at *Le Palais des Congrès de Paris* during an international mining convention and killed approximately three hundred people. There was mass confusion and panic after the event. It was thought that eco-terrorists were to blame. More specifically, governments came to believe that tERROR was involved. tERROR vehemently denied any responsibility.

John remembered being briefed by the Australian intelligence service, ASIO. ASIO believed that tERROR's leader, Jenny Fitzgerald, was the one behind it all. They deemed her to be extremely dangerous and a high risk to national security. Her whereabouts at the time was unknown, but there were often reported sightings in the UK, US, Africa and even Indonesia. None of them were ever confirmed.

After the Paris bombing, many governments increased their security measures as they believed that governments which supported mining and exploration would be targeted next. Everyone feared tERROR and especially Jenny Fitzgerald.

After himself having been set-up, John was no longer sure that what he was told was true. He no longer knew what to believe.

Jenny took a deep breath. "Look John, the minister is more likely to talk to you. You were there at Copenhagen. You know him better than any of us."

"Fair point," John conceded.

Jenny was right. John had grown to know Phillip quite well over the many years in politics. Whenever Frank and John were in the UK, they would often meet and catch up with Phillip to discuss the latest policy developments in both countries. There was a strong bond between their departments. Eventually a robust friendship sprung up between them all which John valued quite fervently. In fact, the friendship was so strong that both Frank and John had gone to Phillip's daughter's wedding two years back, which was a raucous affair.

The van pulled out from the front of *The Reform* and headed down the narrow alleyway to the main street. As they rounded the corner, they drove past a three metre high sea wall. John now understood Jenny's earlier comments. *The Reform must be below the flood level,* thought John. *Amazing structure.* The wall was a high set steel structure, with large mesh drains at the base. A large pump was visible every ten metres along its vast length.

Soon, they drove out of Barnstaple onto the freeway. Everyone was silent as they contemplated the day ahead. The van rolled its way through the green Devon country-side. The fields were stunning with the grassy hills of the moors rising and falling like giant landlocked waves. Rivers slivered their way through the open valleys as their waters rushed along the banks on their way to the open sea. The grass seemed thicker and greener than John could remember. *A product of the increased carbon in the air,* someone once told him at an environment conference. John smiled as he thought about it. *The problem is we need more fertilizer now,* the person had explained, *because the nutrients are used up faster.* The van continued its way southwards.

John sat up and leaned forwards. "I need to get the address off my phone," he said.

"Sorry?" replied Ahmed.

"I need to get the address off my phone," repeated John.

"Hang on. No!" Ahmed was slightly taken aback. "Mate, we won't put up with any of your shit. You are not going to get your phone.

You heard what James said. They'll pinpoint us as soon as you turn it on and use it to work out where we're heading. No! We can't risk it."

"Look, I need it for Philip's address. I'll turn it on, get the info and turn it off. It's not that hard. I'll be quick about it."

"Don't you understand? No! They'll identify the car on satellite through your phone signal and follow us. It's like watching a cockroach from above, and then squashing it before it scuttles off. We can't risk it!"

"Besides," James butted in, "you said you knew where he lives. How do we know you aren't making this all up, like, to send a message or make a call or something?"

"Look, I know where he lives in London. What I don't know is where he lives in the Cotswolds," explained John. "He has a house there that he uses on weekends and parliamentary breaks and that's where I reckon he'll probably be. UK parliament isn't sitting in at the moment. I know that because we had a departmental email from them tellingus that they would have minimal contacts over the two weeks of break. So, I assume he'll be there in the Cotswolds.

"Now, his phone and address are not on any public database. I've got his address on my phone as he's invited me there once before. The other option is we get his phone number by other means, but if I call him, somehow I think he will know it's me, who is now wanted by police, so I don't think he'll want to stay around to catch up and have a cuppa. And he won't give his address freely out to strangers. So once again, we'll need to get his address off my phone."

"Hey you two, stop it!" said Jenny trying to break up the argument. "I trust John. *Them* were attempting to take John to Egypt for extraordinary rendition! So, I really don't think John wants to risk getting caught again. Besides, Scarlet always said that she trusted John, and for that matter given the circumstances, so do I."

John could not help but imply a subtle warning in Jenny's comments. He certainly didn't trust Jenny at the moment.

"Jenny's right! We should trust him!" Karen piped up trying to bring herself into the conversation.

"Okay, okay!!" said Ahmed, still not looking convinced. "How are we then going to safely turn on the phone without *Them* identifying which one is our van?"

"Can't you take out the Sim Card and then turn it on?" asked James.

"Keep up with the times, you idiot!" replied Ahmed. "They got rid of sim cards ten years ago. Phones don't have them anymore."

"We can do what we used to do in the IDF if we wanted to hide the signal source," said Karen, now satisfied that she could make some valid contribution.

"The IDF?" asked John.

"Israeli Defence Force," replied Ahmed.

"What? Were you in the army?" asked John.

"Yes," replied Karen miffed at the inference. "I was a Segen Mishneh... Second Lieutenant in the IDF, and I am a bloody good shot. And yes, I will be the one saving your arse if necessary, so show some respect!!"

"Sorry," said John, suitably chided.

Ahmed whispered under his breath, "They say that a man wears the pants in a relationship, but the woman tells him which pair to put on. Karen... she has organised the whole wardrobe."

John curbed a smile.

Karen looked at them suspiciously. "Okay! So, here's the plan."

Karen explained in great detail what John would do to get the phone activated without identifying himself. It seemed straight forward and not too complex.

"Unless they are in the same building," she continued, "which is unlikely, we have probably a maximum of fifteen minutes from the time you turn it on till they could possibly get to you."

John looked up nervously. "What? They'll be that close!"

"Not necessarily, but if they are, that's how quick they could be. They're probably counting on the fact that we wouldn't have moved too far away from the region, and they would be right. Who knows how many people they have looking for you spread out over the country."

John's fears were not eased.

"The other option is that you can give us your password and we can do it for you instead. It'll save you any worry," she added.

"No," stated John emphatically. He felt it was important to keep his cards close to his chest. He wasn't completely sure that they would not just abandon him, or potentially worse.

The van turned off the freeway and made a detour into the large town of Taunton. They drove through various streets, finally pulling up at an open car park of a large shopping centre.

"This centre's safe. We've used it before for meetings," said Karen. "It only has four CCTV cameras in the vicinity and more importantly they're not linked to the internet. Pretty old fashioned!! In any case, they're on record only. So, no-one from the outside can access it. It's a clear day, so our biggest issue will be satellite imaging and tracking if they work out where we are.

"Okay, now remember, wait fifteen minutes before you turn your phone on. That way it'll be hard for them to know which one was you going into the centre and which car you came from if they try tracking you straight back. It's a big centre, so there will be lots of people coming in and out over that time. It will make it confusing for them to work out which one is you. Now we can't have anyone go in with you because they will be expecting you to have company. Having more than one person coming back to the car might identify us irrespectively."

Jenny gave some further instructions on how to remain inconspicuous and what to do if identified. She handed John his phone and battery. He grabbed them and placed the battery back in.

"Just don't cock anything up!" said Jenny. "Remember, it's you they want!"

CHAPTER 4

JOHN TOOK A deep breath. He was slightly surprised at the level of group's paranoia, but thought better than to question matters. John exited the side of the white van and walked confidently into the shopping centre. The building was moderate in size and reminded him of similar large centres in Australia. There were various clothing retailers displaying their garish wares, electronic stores spouting the latest technical fashion and food stalls filling the air with their sumptuous smells. John wound his way through the centre and found a small dumpy cafe slightly tucked away in the corner of the centre. He took a seat.

A young gruff male waiter looked up slightly annoyed that someone had disturbed him in the middle of a game on his phone. He idled across carrying a small tattered notepad. On his face was a slight look of disdain due to the fact that he might need to finally do some work. The waiter's eyes had darkened rings around them which John suspected came from too many wild nights with little sleep. *Those were the days*, thought John with a smile. The waiter flipped a page and readied his pen.

"What can I get you, mate?" said the waiter with a strong Australian accent. His voice sent a shiver down John's spine.

Shit, I hope he doesn't recognise me, thought John. *Hopefully he hasn't heard or seen the news from back home. Mind you, he's probably too hung over to have noticed anything.*

"Ah, a latte please," replied John. He took out the ten pounds that Jenny had given him to '*help kill fifteen minutes with*', and gave it to the waiter. The waiter wandered off with the money, totally uninterested in anything to do with his patron, and started to make the coffee.

John reached into his pocket and took out his phone. He looked at it with new meaning in all that it held. This small rectangular object now represented his past, his present and his future.

John looked around the centre. The building was full of people going about their daily tasks. John was impressed. Karen had chosen well in finding a place where John could merge into the crowd. There were suited people from local offices getting their lunches of curries, fried food and pasties. One mother was dragging her young child around by his arm, the kid kicking and screaming in a tantrum. A young couple was arguing at the checkout of a nearby sandwich bar, whilst a tall man in overalls walked past with a bucket of water and a squidgy ready to clean the window of some mundane insipid display. It all seemed surreal compared to the new reality of what was now happening in John's life.

John started to breath quickly. He wanted to go back to his old life of meetings, dinners and the peace of his apartment. A sense of panic entered John's heart. He looked at the exits. *What if I run? I could make it out of here. It's crowded. No one would know that I am gone.* He looked around. *No... No... I can't! I have virtually no money and what would happen???* The coffee arrived, saving him from his thoughts. He thanked the waiter, cracked open a sugar, and poured it in. He started to stir. John came to the conclusion that there was no use in trying to escape. He sipped his coffee. *Too hot.* He put the coffee back down and waited for it to cool.

John looked at his watch, it was 12.35pm. Only three minutes until he had to turn the phone on. John tried to relax and took another sip of his coffee, hoping enough time had passed for it to cool a little. There was a loud bang. John spilt some of his cup. He turned to see where the noise came from. It was the emergency exit door slamming. *Everything's okay. Just stay calm.* John took another deep breath.

12.38pm. John looked at the phone. *Time to turn it on.* He pressed the power button and it flashed to life. *Jenny must have charged the battery.* John waited for it to properly start. *Come on, come on!!* The phone finally loaded up and asked for the unlock code. John typed in the four digit number, and flicked through the settings to flight mode. The screen glared back at him showing the symbol of an orange aeroplane and the sliding button on/off. John poised with his finger over the button. The phone suddenly buzzed. John hit the home button. The display flew back through its screens to its front page and the phone mail box flashed up – seven missed calls, four voice messages left.

John stared at the phone. People had tried to contact him. *Of course!* He did not dare to touch the phone and change the screen in case he lost the fact that he had four voice messages in his phone. John took a deep breath. He needed to know. He needed to find out who called. *What if they could help me get out of this damn situation?* thought John.

John made up his mind and pressed the voicemail button. As he put it up to his ear, the ring of the phone emanated from the speaker, then a voice appeared.

"You have called voicemail. You have four missed calls. Message received March 15 at 12.15pm," said the androgynous voice.

A stern male voice wafted from the head of the phone, *"G'day Mister Frankston. This is Senior Constable Corey Jones from the Canberra Police. We would like to ask you a few questions about some serious events that occurred earlier today. If you could come down to the station at London*

Circuit, or call me on…" John grabbed a napkin and found a pen left on another table. He wrote down the number.

Could come in handy, thought John.

"Message received March 15 at 5.02pm."

A female voice resonated out of the earpiece. John recognised it. It was his sister, Sarah. Her voice was concerned and panicky. *"John. What the fuck's happening? What the fuck have you gotten yourself into? You're all over the news! For the sake of you and the family's reputation, hand yourself into the police."* She paused stifling some tears. She calmed her voice and took a deep breath. *"We will help in whatever way we can. Just don't be stupid. And remember, no matter what, we do love you."*

John wiped a tear away. In all that had happened in the past few days, he had forgotten about Sarah and her family, and what the news of the murders and his disappearance would have done to her. He adored them dearly. Hopefully everyone would leave them alone. John was comforted in the fact that she was a lawyer, and was resourceful and strong in character. She could handle herself and the police well enough. It was *Them* and what they might do that he was worried about most.

"Message received March 16 at 10.20am."

Another familiar voice emanated from the phone, one he had spoken to just a few days earlier, but this time there was sense of terrified panic. *"John, this is Scarlet. I'm scared!"* She paused and breathed deeply. *"I left Canberra as soon as I heard of Frank's assassination. Everybody's saying that you did it, but I don't believe them for one minute. A good friend of mine works at the airport. I checked and she told me that a private medical jet has left Canberra airport with three people in it en route to England. One was supposedly ill and had to be carried on a stretcher. They said the person needed urgent overseas medical treatment. Don't ask me why, but I'm worried that it might've been you. I've let some important friends in England know and hopefully a person called Jenny will try and intercept the plane. She still thinks that you might have done the assassination, so be careful. Explain everything to her! I know you didn't do it, but trust her.*" A window smashed in the background. Scarlet continued in a sobbing terrified whisper, "*Fuck!! It's Them! They're here. I've got to run. And despite what I know you may soon think, I never meant for that terrible accident to happen to Rebecca. I promised myself I would never let anything like that ever happen again, especially to you. Be strong! Be safe!*"

John repeated the message on the phone. A tear rolled down his face. Despite his anger towards Scarlet for her inadvertent role in Rebecca's death, he still cared for Scarlet's safety. It now made sense how Jenny and her group knew where and when to intercept his plane.

"*Message received March 16 at 7.58pm*"

An older female voice came on the phone. "*John. This is Director General Jan Cover from ASIO. We have reason to believe that there may be several possible illicit organisations that might be behind the assassination of Minister Frank Tsoukalos and we are unsure in which way you are involved or even if you are involved. In any case, it is imperative that we talk to you. We believe you may be in immediate danger. You can reach me on a secure number by dialling...*"

Hopefully, someone who can help, thought John. He wrote down the number below the first and placed the napkin in his pocket. *Only four messages though, thought there would be more. Mind you my number is silent.* John was about to hang up, when his phone buzzed again in his hand. He looked at the phone's screen – it showed another new mailbox item. Nervously, John held the phone back up to his ear.

"*You have one new message. Message received March 18 at 12.47pm*"

Oh Fuck, that's just now. John looked around in disbelief. Someone had just called him just a minute before. *Fuck, fuck, fuck!!!*

The phone's earpiece blared into action. "*Johnny, my son. Nice to know you are using your phone. You got off our plane a bit early, didn't finish your trip. Very rude!! Must have been the shite in-house entertainment. Never any good. Anyway, I hope you are enjoying your coffee. Just do us a favour, be calm, stay where you are, and you won't get hurt. We are watching."*

John spun around on his chair trying to see where they could be. *They're bluffing, they've got to be fucking bluffing,* thought John. *Karen said fifteen minutes. It's only... oh fuck... thirteen minutes.* He had stayed on the phone too long. John hung up and went to the phone's flight mode and quickly switched it on to sever the connection. The reception signal disappeared replaced with the symbol of a plane. According to Karen, the phone was supposedly safe. John ran. *They can't see me inside with satellite. But how did they know I was having coffee. Extra CCTV cameras?!! No, they got rid of most of them in the UK – privacy freaks – God bless them. Oh fuck! Oh God! I hope they can't.... Maybe the phone towers? Triangulation... shit!! Gotta get going.*

John quickly deleted the recently dialled numbers. *Don't need the tERROR guys knowing that I've fucked up!* John finally reached the main car park exit. A large set of metal and glass sliding doors guarded the exit to the car park. People were still bustling in and out desperate to grab their lunch. *Okay, can't run now, don't want to be obvious. Karen said I need to wait at least two more minutes after turning off the phone before leaving, then walk slowly to the van.* John looked at his watch. *12.51pm.* It was cutting things fine. Various people walked in and out of the centre as John waited.

When he was ready, John stepped out into the car park and started to walk directly back to the van. He looked around to see if anyone was following. No one. People continued to walk in and out of the centre, heading off in various directions. *That's good. As Karen hoped, enough of a cover.*

John continued walking through the busy open car park and found the van. He went to grab the same side door he had come out of when Karen yelled out the window. "Not the side door! They'll pick that out as an anomaly. Go to the driver's seat. You should be the one driving off."

John opened the side door and threw in his jacket so as to not look too unusual that he went to the side. He shut it and then walked around as instructed and got into the driver's seat. As he sat down, he breathed a sigh of relief that what should have been such a simple task of turning on his phone was now over. He laughed at the thought. Suddenly he felt a jolt of pain in his back.

Karen had pulled out a pistol and held it up pointing through the worn seat. John felt another jolt of pain as it butted against his spine. Jenny said to John, "We have a gun pointing at your back. We don't know you. And we don't entirely trust you at this moment either. So tell us, what the fuck took you so long?!"

John started stuttering in reply. "I... w... w... was..."

Ahmed leant forward and whispered in Jenny's ear. Jenny continued, "Hold on! Don't bother answering yet. Give us your phone, NOW!! Is it unlocked?"

"Yes," replied John. He handed the phone over.

"Ahmed!" Jenny continued. "Check the phone. Is it on flight mode? Did he call anyone?"

Ahmed searched through the phone. "Yeah, it's on flight. There's no reception signal. Last call was... err ....three days ago. He's fine."

"Okay. John, start the car and drive out of the car park. Karen, put the gun away. Ahmed, give John back his phone."

"Yes, Mum!" replied Ahmed sarcastically under his breath.

"Fuck off with the jokes, Ahmed! Don't play me. It's not the time. Okay John! What took you so long? You should have been here ten minutes ago."

"I thought the waiter at the cafe recognised me. The bastard called over a police officer. So I pissed off and had to lie low for a while..." John lied.

"What? Why would he recognise you?" asked James somewhat dubious. "The minister's murder has only been covered in the Australian media, not much here. Most people still think you're back in Oz. There's no photo of you in the British press. Unless he got an Aussie paper or looked it up on the net, no one in the UK would even know your photo."

"The waiter *was* Australian. You know, a lot of Aussie backpackers take on these jobs," said John sarcastically, but slightly nervously. He hoped his bluff would work. He didn't want them to find out that he used his phone. "You can go and check it out if you like – it's the cafe next to the curry house."

"Okay, okay! Everyone enough!" said Jenny. "We've got the phone on. We can now get the address. Everybody's fine! That's all that's important. I guess John just had to powder his nose." John was about to arc up again, but Jenny butted in with a smile. "John, just drive."

John drove slowly out of the car park. As he reached the exit, he indicated to turn onto the street. Suddenly a large dark green four wheel drive came racing up the road and flew past them. It skidded to a halt by the shopping centre's front doors. Two people in dark blue suits jumped out and ran in a panic barging people aside as they raced inside. John took a deep breath. Jenny stared at the four wheel drive, barely able to speak as they left the car park.

"It's *Them*," whispered Jenny to herself. "It's got to be *Them*. So lucky.... so very, very lucky..."

John sighed deeply. *Them were bluffing. Thank God Them were bluffing!! They hadn't seen him.* John decided he would be far more careful in the future.

CHAPTER 5

T HE PALE WHITE van left the confines of the windy streets of Taunton, and made its way back to the safe anonymity of the freeway. James was back in control of the driver's seat after swapping with John at a set of traffic lights. Conversation was sparse. Everyone was a little shocked as to how close John came to being caught. Karen was visibly upset as she felt she had miscalculated the risks of the situation.

James flicked the van's digital radio on hoping to lift everyone's spirits with a little bit of distraction.

The Radio Presenter chimed through the speaker: *You're listening to BBC4. Today, we have a fascinating interview with a modern marvel, a living legend, someone who has brought millions of people's faith in God flooding back. Some of you believe he is the new prophet, a soothsayer as such; others believe he is the second son of God, Jesus reincarnate if you prefer to call him. In any case, he is now one of, if not, the most important and influential persons of our modern times. Yes, you've guessed it. We are very lucky to speak today with this remarkable man, ahead of his upcoming European tour, that most of you know as 'Clive'. My name is Charles Sekinger and this is 'THE LONG TALK BACK'.*

The show's music intro started.

John groaned, rubbing his temples from a building tension headache. "I can't stand that annoying arsehole. Can we change the station?"

"Charles Sekinger is a brilliant interviewer," said Karen, somewhat miffed that an Australian was passing judgement on one of her favourite interviewers.

"No, I meant it's Clive I can't stand," explained John.

"Ah..." said Karen slightly embarrassed at her gaff. James leant over to change the channel.

"Leave it on!" said Ahmed, still annoyed and not wanting to give in to John. "I always say, know what your enemy is doing."

John couldn't follow his logic. "Enemy? He's just a delusional idiot with some crazy ideas who got lucky..."

"...who is now the most powerful and important figure in the modern world," said Ahmed. "What he says changes public opinion and government policy. He is far more influential than you are led to believe. His claims that it was God and not man that has destroyed the environment has set green technologies back more than twenty years, not to mention the impact of his social and religious power on people."

John was about to argue back, but realised that Ahmed was right. Clive had great influence amongst his billions of followers. The Church of Delugion was now the strongest religion in the world reaching into every dominion and dominating every continent.

The gaudy introductory music stopped.

Charles Sekinger, the now identified presenter continued: So, who is this man, that some of you call THE GRAND DELUGION. Clive, born in 1976 as Clive Jutras, was the son of a primary school teacher and a fisher. He grew up in the great city of Nanaimo, Canada, famously known as the Bathtub racing capital of the world. Amazingly, both parents were agnostic, shunning religious certitude, and often attending sceptical functions in the local area, which is quite a contrast to the religious figure we have today. His early life was fairly conventional. Clive's schooling was non-denominational. He never attended church. He never was officially schooled in any religious directives. So how did this seemingly non-religious man rise up to be one of the world's greatest religious figures? He is here in London for the Delugion Dictate, and we are privileged to have Clive join us here today in our New London studios. Your Religious Excellency, Welcome.

Clive: *Please I preferred to be called Clive. I by no means want to be referred by ridiculous titles or covenants.*

Charles: *Sorry... umm.... So, Clive, from a person who seems to have been brought up with no religious convictions, how did you become the centre of this phenomenon, this modern religion of Delugion?*

Clive: *Well, my father as a teacher was very much a man of learning and he felt that it was important that I was educated in as much as possible about all that influences the world, what makes it go round. So as part of my education, he taught me about all religious beliefs, their readings and how they influenced the way people are and the way they act. It was then, when I was a teenager that I read the Bible for the first time and I suddenly realised that there was something I was missing. I felt a holy connection, one that I never could imagine. It was as if my eyes were opened.*

"Oh please! Come on!!" said John. "This is just tripe. There's nothing new here. It's just propaganda."

"Don't underestimate Charles," Jenny replied. "He actually digs quite deep. It should be interesting. Besides I want to know what ridiculous things Clive's now telling people."

Charles: *So when your metaphorical eyes were opened, is that when your now famous prophecies started, should I say, coming through?*

Clive: *No! I thought nothing of it at the time, my eyes being opened. All I thought I had was a religious awakening. This is something that happens to many people. The prophecies you mention were a different matter altogether. That happened some years later.*

Charles: *Really? Do go on.*

Clive: *Most people don't know much about these ones. I can remember the first set of prophecies as clear as day. It happened on February 1st, 2010...*

Charles: *"The Incoming Calling"?*

Clive: *Yes. You know these?? Clive chuckled. The Catholic Church gave it that name... don't know why they chose that, but I digress. On February 1, I woke in a sweat. You see, I had a dream. It was a powerful dream. I dreamt that I spoke to God and he told me of what he was planning for humanity. He said that I had to pass on his message. In this dream, he told me of six events... six events that would happen – some great, some small–and on the fifth, I and others would know his message was true and from then I would have six followers who would help spread the word throughout the lands. The sixth event would start the spread of the message to the masses. I thought I was going insane, and didn't tell anyone initially of these events. I thought that if I had any more of these dreams I would get myself a psych evaluation...*

"Probably should have," said James under his breath. Karen gave James a look of disdain.

Clive: *So I went to seek comfort from my pastor, Jean-Pierre, a great man, someone who I still have a deep respect for. I told him everything that had happened in my dream. I told him every detail. He just said that many people have dreams about God, and that these dreams are just dreams, and are nothing more. He said that I should feel blessed to have such great dreams, but they were unlikely to be real. His words were soothing and logical, and I did not argue. I thought nothing more about the dream, that is, until the first prophesy occurred.*

Charles: *And what was that?*

Clive: *The severe earthquake in Chile in February 2010. I had been told by God that this earthquake would happen before the next full moon.*

Charles: *So, by the end of February?*

Clive: *Yeah. That earthquake happened to be the eighth largest earthquake in history at that time. The Pastor thought I was lucky, or I guess, unlucky for the many who died. It wasn't until the second prophesy came true that the pastor started to pay closer attention. The prophesy was of the tragic Crash of the Polish airplane a month later, the one that killed the President Kaczyński of Poland.*

Charles: *You predicted that awful crash back then too? How do we know that you just didn't predict a general plane crash, and cherry picked the one that occurred conveniently, nonetheless significantly at that time?*

Clive: *Because I was specific enough that Pastor Jean-Pierre called me within five minutes of it happening and asked me to have a council with him and some of his colleagues. I was scared and initially refused. He assured me that it would be alright. He said that it was important for others to know. I thought about it and then agreed to it, but asked if I could have my friend come along too, as I didn't want to be ganged up upon. You see, I didn't quite understand the messages I received myself, and I was afraid. I wanted an independent witness, someone I knew and could trust.*

Charles: *So how did that council proceed? Who came along to this meeting?*

Clive: *They are now very well known... the ones who came to that meeting... that is the six. As for the council, we met at the church on a Tuesday evening in March. Pastor Jean-Pierre was there, and his assistant Claude. There was also Rabbi Peters from the nearby synagogue, and the Muslim Cleric Yusuf Yasin. I brought along my co-worker from school, Crystal Lewis. And by chance, but unintentionally, there was also a cleaner in the church, Maria Rodriguez.*

Charles: *Interesting! So Maria was never invited to the meeting as such?*

"Maria is a piece of work," muttered Ahmed.

Karen glared at Ahmed. Ahmed poked his tongue out at her.

Clive: *No. She had only started there a few days before, but importantly in God's eyes, she was going to share in the knowledge and bear witness. She happened to be working back late that night.*

Charles: *So what happened in this council?*

Clive: *Well the council was fairly informal. The Pastor had already told his colleagues about the dream. Initially the Rabbi and Cleric asked me many questions as if I had direct knowledge of who committed all of these events. It was ridiculous. As if I could create an earthquake?! They were sceptical of my dream with God, just as I and the Pastor were sceptical when I first had it. They thought I was in cahoots with Jean-Pierre in trying to trick them. Crystal, bless her soul, came to my defence saying that I was just a plain old teacher and that it was stupid to believe that an insignificant teacher like myself would try to pretend to be a prophet, or to believe the alternative that I could plan for a plane to crash thousands of miles away. She said that I had no reason, creativeness, foresight, money or means to even contemplate these events. Clive laughed at the thought. Crystal has a way with words—she defends you, and insults you at the same time. God bless her!*

Charles laughed, and then replied: So you were grilled heavily in this first meeting. Did they believe that you communicated with God back then?

Clive: *No. Even the pastor still didn't quite believe that I met with God in my dream. He just thought that he better have some witnesses if things prove to be different, especially from different faiths.*

Charles: *And they did prove different. The prophecies came true.*

Clive: *Yes. The Third Event happened.*

Charles: *Which was??*

There was a shuffling noise in the background as Clive arranged himself uncomfortably.

Clive: *In the dream, I was told by God that an Oil Rig would explode in the Gulf of Mexico on April 20 and that it would sink below the waves showing that man cannot control the earth and water.*

Charles: *Surely not that specific.*

Clive: *Yes... that specific! Ask Rabbi Peters and Cleric Yasin. Ask all in the council. They knew of the prediction three weeks prior to it happening.*

Charles: *Did they warn anyone?*

Clive: Well... No! They still didn't quite believe me, so they didn't feel the need or think it was necessary.

Charles: So, after it happened, were they convinced of your prophetic ability?

Clive: Not quite. They weren't quite convinced that somehow there was not some foul play in some of the events. It wasn't until the fourth and fifth events happened, that they started to believe.

Charles: Which were?

Clive: The fourth was the deposing of the leader of Australia which "will not come from the people"... this being the rolling of the then Australian Prime Minister Kevin Rudd by his own party. And the fifth was one which even I found it hard to believe that it would occur. This was to be an uprising "that will come from the people" near the then current heart of religion. This as we all know became the Spring Revolutions of the Middle East, the one that started at the beginning of 2011.

Charles: Wow... So these were all told to you by God in your dream. A rather small country's, population speaking of course... This small country's political turmoil? And then some rather major turmoil?? God told you all this?

Clive: Yes! And these were all told and passed on to all six at the council!

Charles: And what did the council think after the fifth prophesy?

Clive: They believed!

Clive steadied his voice.

Clive: They believed. They knew that it was impossible that I was involved in Australian and Middle Eastern politics, let alone earthquakes.

Charles: What about the rise and fall of Islamic State, ISIS? Was God involved with that?

Clive: No. We all know what eventually happened there.

Charles: True.

Clive: The subsets of ISIS started destroying each other as there was no one group that could decide what were the right teachings and interpretation. It was self-serving, it was chaotic. That set of events was not God, but evil set in man. And God has shown what he thought of such evil.

Charles: So please go on. Back to your prophecies. You were saying The Council knew it couldn't be you causing these problems

Clive: Yes. They kept in close contact with myself. They realised that God knew and created those somewhat terrible first set of events – the Earthquake, the plane crash, the oil uprising, internal government turmoil, external government turmoil. They became scared because of what the sixth event would do and what it meant.

Charles: What was that? And what did it mean?

Clive: The sixth and final prophecy from that first meeting with God – the dream as such – was that in the beginning of the Northern Autumn of 2011, the seas would rise in Japan showing that land and power cannot be protected from God. This will be his great warning of what would come.

Charles: Dear God!! You're not talking about the Japanese Tsunami of 2011, and the subsequent nuclear meltdowns.

Clive: Yes.

Charles paused, silent on the radio. Everyone was silent in the car, riveted to the story.

Charles: *And what were these prophecies supposed to mean? What did they foretell?*

Clive: *That God was returning and he was not happy. That the world should be prepared for more to come. The World would be made aware of his hatred of humanity's greed, corruption and abuse of power both in his name and the name of the people. Once the world had learnt and was ready, the second coming would occur.*

Karen broke the silence. "I always knew of his great flooding prophecies, but never knew the background story – impressive. It all makes sense as to why so many follow him. I wonder what Charles will do next? It should be interesting where he takes this."

"What do you mean?" responded John. "The interview has been crap! He's just let Clive have free rein."

"You'll see," smirked Karen.

Charles: *So what do you then say to your critics? They say that you just colluded with the Council, that this 'Holy Entourage' was invented to make out that you were a prophet?*

Clive: *What would The Council have to gain from it?*

Charles: *Fame? Notoriety?*

Clive: *I resent that inference. That's a massive insult to them. It goes against every grain for which they stand for. For a Priest to believe in what I said, let alone a Rabbi and a Cleric? It takes a major leap of faith to go against what their beliefs, and their culture have told them for over two millennia. They were risking their statuses in society, their positions in their churches... It was a huge risk for them to follow me. They could have been thrown out by their religious orders, excommunicated. Instead, their religious orders listened to them and now they believe too. Surely, that is proof enough.*

Charles: And Maria? Why do we hear so much from her and not Crystal?

Clive: Maria just wants to help spread the word.

There was a slight jar in Clive's voice.

Charles: Okay, now let's move on from your origins. The general public knows of your Major Predictions – the so-called "Great Prophecies". But what has been more controversial is what has happened on the side-lines both during and after these events. Many of these prophecies have gone parallel to the principles of science, and in fact many people say that science predicted many of these outcomes. At the heart of it you say God, not man is the cause of the world's current state. How do you justify your views?

Clive: Let me first say these are not my views, but these are messages from God. I have a great respect for science and its laws, and I thank God for providing such a framework. Science, however, can be wrong. Look, science tried to tell us that the globe was warming due to carbon dioxide, methane, et cetera, but this is not true. The level of human induced carbon output was miniscule compared to the amount put out by volcanoes, animals and the natural environment....

James was heating up. "It gives me the shits when people say crap like that. Volcanoes put out fuck all compared to what we humans have done. In fact humans emit a hundred times more carbon dioxide each year than volcanoes..."

"Shut up. We're listening to this," said Karen in annoyance.

Clive: ....In fact did you know that termites are one of the greatest producers of methane, another supposed major greenhouse gas. They put out more methane compared to the rest of farmed cattle and sheep combined. If global warming is partially due to our livestock production, then termites need to be made responsible too. But they have been around at large levels for millions of years, yet scientists claim that humans induced global warming.

Charles: *I vaguely remember hearing the story about termites, but that is just a distraction. I put to you the earth coped very well before the industrial age. From my understanding what is more important is the additional gasses that we are putting out compared to nature. Scientists say that fossil fuel use is the main culprit. Mankind has increased the level of carbon dioxide far more than nature has done. Your assertion on volcanoes is not quite true. Senior scientists that I have spoken to tell us that only a small fraction of carbon output comes from volcanoes, and this is countered through the equal removal of carbon within our oceans as this has been done for billions of years. So how do you counter this?*

"Told you," said James, still sulking at Karen's retort. Karen mockingly poked her tongue out at James.

"Okay. You're right. He's good!!" said John surprised at Charles' strong arguments. It was almost unheard of for people to argue back at Clive.

Clive's *voice was no longer relaxed: But did these scientists predict with accuracy when these changes would occur? No. Did God? Yes. God is almighty and does what he so believes fit, and can go around scientific principle if God so desires. God has created these types of rapid events throughout history and I'm not just talking about Noah's Ark. Let me give you an example where science has proven God's work. Your Lord Kelvin, in 1800—he was an eminent scientist who studied temperature scales and entropy – basically how heat and energy work. Lord Kelvin was a brilliant scientist and mathematician. He came up with the now famous Kelvin scale in temperature.*

Charles: *But we use Celsius and Fahrenheit?*

Clive: *Yes, but calculations in Science using temperature are done in Kelvin. Anyway, from his research, he was able to do calculations and measure when the earth was first born. He did this through his knowledge of heat loss and the temperature of the Earth, sort of like working out when a pie was cooked by measuring its temperature whilst cooling on a window sill. As the heat leaves, the pie cools at a steady rate. Working backwards, we can work out when it was cooked.*

Charles: *So he determined the age of the Earth?*

Clive: *Yes, that's right. When he did his calculations, he estimated that the Earth is only a couple of hundred million years old. Now, the really interesting thing is this; it flies against the so called fossil records that go back in some reports three and a half billion years. This is one of the many arguments that destroys Darwin's theory of evolution. Evolutionists think that the Earth is four and a half billion years old, and here is one of the most reputable scientists in history telling us it is different.*

"For Fuck's sake, he is a moron. Kelvin had no idea about radioactivity back then and the fact that radiation creates heat like an element heating a kettle. The Earth is full of nuclear material. That's why the earth is still warm and takes a long time to cool. So the fossil records can still work," said James.

Clive: *So we must realise that most of evolution is a falsehood. The Lord placed us here to care for his creatures, and God was creative in his design. God has recently explained many things to me... what he meant in the book of Creation... and more specifically being the first seven days of earth. This was not a true seven days, but an analogy for several hundred million years, not billions. There was design.*

Charles scoffed slightly: *Many eminent evolutionists smarter than both of us combined will most likely disagree with your arguments. We will certainly have to organise a debate with yourself and them to pursue these points further.*

Clive: *I look forward to it.*

Charles: *Okay, we'll move on... Some people now say that you have too much power, that you control the general populace and as such have control over governments and their policies.*

Clive: *I do not seek this control. God came to me to pass on his message and he entrusted me to be his messenger. I do not choose to speak to governments, but many do seek my counsel and where I see fit, I pass on my advice. They have no obligation to take my advice at all. I do not direct their decisions or policies.*

"But any that do go against your directions will have a backlash from your followers. Nice work," said James.

Charles: *Still, many people complain that you are overly influenced by your financial backers such as the Creative Institute of America, and the Vatican. What do you say to that?*

Clive: *We have many financial backers. They thought that this message that I have been blessed to receive needed to be heard and have generously given some of their funds. I might add that many different religious groups – past Jewish, Hindu and Muslim groups also donate to us so that this message can be heard by all, and yet you don't mention those groups. The message that God has told me to bring to this modern age should be praised.*

"Well dodged as always," said John.

Clive: *God now accepts and embraces many modern concepts – contraception, for example. God has deemed that a human is not a human with a soul until it has human form...*

Charles: *But gay marriage is still not accepted.*

Clive: *No....God deems marriage a religious sanctity for the procreation of children.*

Charles: *But what about single parents? Are their children then cast off from God's eye?*

Clive: *Children from single parents are still sacred in God's eye*

Charles: *I see.... I could keep going for much longer as we have so much that we didn't get to cover in this short time, but unfortunately, that brings us to a close. Your Holiness, Clive, it's been a great pleasure, and we thank you for your time.*

Clive: *Thank you, Charles.*

Charles: *This is the 'Long Talk Back' with myself, Charles Sekinger. You can hear this interview podcast on....*

James turned off the radio. "Geez... Clive is a dick, an influential dick, but a dick nonetheless."

John smiled as the van continued driving eastwards sliding past the busy metropolis of Bristol.

CHAPTER 6

THE WHITE VAN journeyed northwards over the large concrete spans of the New Bristol Bridge as the warm sun beat
down. The surrounding countryside had been transformed
over the years from fertile farmlands to vast swathes of wetlands, rivers and small islands as a result of the modern ocean levels. Waterbirds
waded through the marshes picking out bugs and insects in the long
reeds. Occasional ruins of buildings dotted the wet landscape giving a
reminder of what once was.

John peered out at the scenery, fascinated at the modern expanse.
*Amazing. I always wanted to check this area out. Lucky, though. Don't
see this good weather here too often,* thought John. *It makes the vast
waterways and paddocks look stunning.*

Everyone in the van was once again quiet in contemplation. James
stared out the front window as his olive skinned hands held the van's
faux-leather black steering wheel. He occasionally looked into the
rear vision mirror, often flicking his gaze at John showing signs of his
distrust after the shopping centre incident. Jenny was sitting back in
the front passenger seat checking her emails and the latest news on
her smart-phone. Ahmed, Karen and John sat cramped up next to
each other in the back seat. The van was fairly sparse in its interior
besides the rear which was stacked with various hard cases and bags.

John, trying to pass the time, pulled out his phone and flicked it on. The screen flashed up with its various multi-coloured icons, and to his relief and more importantly with a small plane symbol in the top right corner. He smiled at the thought that people were still paranoid of mobile phones disrupting a plane's flight. He had talked to a flight engineer one time and apparently it would take all the phones of all the passengers turning on at exactly the same time to even cause a slight blip in the plane's electronics. The flight engineer said the reason for forcing flight mode was more about stopping people talking on phones and annoying other passengers than flight disruptions. Mobile phone companies still made sure that their phones carried flight mode to turn off all transmissions from a handset. John had now discovered that flight mode had more uses than just on a plane.

Ahmed looked over John's shoulder to see what he was doing. Ahmed was restless and getting tired of the silence, so he decided to intrude.

"I've tried to be patient, mate!" said Ahmed. "Jenny wanted us to let you recover more after your plane ordeal, but frankly I can't wait any longer. What was it that *Them* wanted from you so badly?"

Jenny turned and glowered at Ahmed in annoyance. Ahmed responded with an innocent shrug and a curt grin. She returned back to her activities on her phone with a huff.

John ignored their silent conversation. "I'm not entirely sure," he calmly replied. "However, I reckon a certain email that I stumbled onto had something to do with it."

Jenny reacted with a slight lift of her head, ensuring she could hear the conversation a little better. Her long red hair fell over her shoulder as she arched her neck. John looked up at her, noticing the beauty of her profile and her full red lips. He quickly diverted his gaze back to Ahmed so as to not be noticed.

John looked at his phone. He decided he should lay his cards out. It was time to try to gain their trust.

"Here, I'll show you."

John flicked the phone's screen to the emails section. Several new unread messages stared back at him. *Forgot about those. Must have downloaded when I turned the phone on.* Most were just junk. He quickly scanned through them until he found the one he wanted dated 10.13am, March 15, 2017. He handed it over to Ahmed who read it out loud. Karen looked on with curiosity.

Dear Frank,

This email is of the utmost importance; hence we sent it through the usual security.
 Operation Warmth will continue and more funding is needed for the Delugionist Foundation. It is absolutely vital that the funding is to continue as we have so much still at stake. Them and the others have so far agreed. Stage 4 will start soon.
 Please reply using the correct procedures.

 From TG!

"Well we know what disobeying the 'usual security' resulted in..." said Ahmed.

"What?" interrupted John.

"Do you think it might have something to do with why you are now here?"

"Oh."

"You were really stupid with that email, you know."

"Come on," replied John. "How was I to supposed to know that sending an email to myself would lead to murder, let alone my kidnapping?"

"Well…"

"Look! As far as I knew, Frank was an innocent minister of the Australian parliament, and was not part of some global conspiracy. I am not a bloody secret operative that looks for extra meaning in every comment. I was just wondering what the *Delugionists* had to do with Frank, that's all, and I was going to do a little research at home."

"Okay. Fair enough," said Ahmed. He was now a little bit more demure after John's reproach. Ahmed looked back at the email. "Operation Warmth, Jenny!!!"

"Yeah, I heard!" replied Jenny, still not lifting her head as she read more of her mail messages.

"What's Operation Warmth?" asked John.

Jenny put her phone down. "We don't really know for sure," she replied. "It's appeared a few times in various correspondences that we've come across. Some have been from your minister's office, others from foreign government officials and one was from an oil company. Obviously, we've never forwarded it on like you did. Normally we just take a photo of the screen, and send that on to our group. Even then, we're careful nowadays with text recognition software intercepting mail and other messages. It's getting more and more difficult. Does Operation Warmth mean anything to you John?"

"Not entirely," he replied. "Frank was often secretive on some issues, but never mentioned any Operation Warmth. What about those other messages that mentioned Operation Warmth? Did they say anything about the *Delugionist Foundation* in them?"

"No, this is the first time that they mentioned the DF," said Jenny. "We've often wondered if the DF had anything to do with *Them*." She put down her phone and turned to the three in the back seat. "What about the letters T.G.? Does that mean anything to you?"

"Someone's name perhaps? Their initials? Not anyone that I know of."

"We've seen it a few times, always the same letters. There's no one important that we can match it to. It's probably a pseudonym anyway."

"Okay. I understand that *Them* kidnapped me and are very willing to kill. So, what is it exactly that *Them* have been involved in and why? Who are they?" asked John.

"It's taken us a while," replied Jenny, "but what we've managed to work out over the years is that *Them* is a close-knit powerful, infiltrative, yet secretive organisation. They appear to come from and interact with various power groups like oil companies, mining conglomerates, government officials, and so forth. Those who want to try to keep control of the world market. We know that they want to maintain the status quo and power structures, and they do this we believe by using people like your Frank to control the debate. I don't think Frank was necessarily one of *Them*, but he must have been under their influence.

"Who are they specifically? Frankly, it's been too hard to determine exactly and definitely too hard to pin down, but we know they have their claws everywhere. *Them* aren't afraid to use brutal tactics. And for the past twenty years, we believe their main focus of control has been the global warming debate. They deem any action along these lines, a danger to them."

"John. They are basically a bunch of fucking control-freak denialists who are trying to control the world," said James all of a sudden.

"Well put," said Ahmed.

"Piss off Ahmed!! You know what they did to us!"

John was surprised at James' outburst.

"James..." said Karen looking concerned.

James ignored Karen's plea. "It was their fucking influence that destroyed everything that Karen and I stood for..."

"James, it's okay!" said Karen. She leaned forward and put her hand on his shoulder in reassurance.

"No, it's not!!" retorted James, brushing Karen's hand off. The van swerve towards the next lane. James grabbed hold of the wheel and redirected it on track. "You and I used to be highly respected scientists. Our work was ground breaking! We had our lives ahead of us... Our career, our friends, our family, everything!!! Don't tell me it's fucking okay!! *Them* fucking destroyed it all!!"

CHAPTER 7

THE TENSION IN the car was apparent. John looked over at Karen. She turned away and looked out the window wiping away a tear. James was digging his fingers into the wheel.

"What happened?" asked John.

"Don't get him started," said Karen under her breath. Even distressed, Karen had an aura of strength about her.

James looked through the rear vision mirror at John. "A few years ago, Karen and I were based at East Anglia University doing research. Karen and I were just finishing our post graduate doctorates in climate science. The research we were doing had some pretty big implications. My thesis was looking at carbon dioxide in the atmosphere and what proportion that could be definitely proven had come from fossil fuels. I had worked out that we could do this by looking at carbon isotopes, their forms in nature."

John looked a little puzzled.

"You see, carbon has various forms," explained James, "what we call isotopes... Carbon 14 and Carbon 12. I like to call it new carbon and old carbon. Most people think Carbon 14 is old carbon, but it actually is new because it's created in the atmosphere all the time by cosmic rays and normally the amount in the air is fairly steady. Well we can age many things by working out the ratio of old carbon to new carbon, as it gets sucked into their structure and slowly decays. Most people know this as carbon dating. It's been used to age objects antiquities that are thousands of years old.

"Anyway I digress. For years we thought this method could help us tell what carbon in the atmosphere was released from the burning of fossil fuels such as petrol and stuff like coal. Basically a lot of old carbon was released because cosmic rays couldn't penetrate the ground.

"Well the theory worked okay except for the fact that open air nuclear bomb testing in the twentieth century had changed the atmosphere by converting a lot of the old carbon back to the new type. Nuclear testing had stuffed up the carbon ratio in the atmosphere quite considerably and then we discovered various other blips. It was easy still to work out carbon dating in ancient structures by comparing objects, but it was hard to get things right in modern times. It was thought that the atmospheric carbon ratios in modern times couldn't be used to work out human's fossil fuel carbon imprint. And climate denialists used to pump out the old rhetoric that the increased carbon in the air was mainly from volcanoes. What we had worked out in East Anglia, was a way to account for all of these changes and do it in an incredibly accurate way."

"So you could definitively say where the extra carbon in the atmosphere had come from?" asked John.

"Yes. From man!!" replied James.

"The implications would be huge," said John.

"Yes. It made a lot of big business nervous worried about potential law suits, and not only just from my work. There were several different projects going on in our department looking at various parts of the recent global changes. The work linked all of the Earth's changes that had happened over the past decade together. For example Karen was looking at ocean rises and the destabilising effects on tectonic plates," said James.

"So... the recent earthquakes?"

"Yes," replied Karen, still upset with James' outburst.

"So you guys had worked it out. How the set of events in the past decade actually happened," said John in amazement.

"Yes!! Basically, what the team at East Anglia had shown was that the Great Global Flood was not due to Clive's God, but due to human's greenhouse gas emissions," replied James.

"And you could prove that it was from the burning of fossil fuels?" asked John.

"Without a doubt!!"

"That would piss off the *Delugionists*, disproving that God did it. So why didn't we hear of this research?" asked John.

"It was unfairly discredited and buried," said Karen. "What James and I didn't realise, was the levels that people would take to destroy our work. I guess we didn't think of the implications."

"Well that's not quite true. We did understand the implications to an extent," said James. "We knew it meant that people and even countries affected by the floods and earthquakes could potentially sue the oil and mining companies for all that they were worth. We were always ready for the backlash from that. What we didn't know about was what *Them* would do. We never even knew that *Them* existed!"

"Hang on!! Now I know who you are. Yeah!! East Anglia!! It's starting to come back," said John. "I remember hearing about this on the news at the time. Is this the infamous East Anglia Scandal – 'Angel-Gate'?"

"Yes! I want to kill the person who decided to put 'gate' on the end of every supposed scandal," retorted James.

"Yeah, I remember the news articles," said John. "From memory, you guys had paid off people to falsify data. Apparently one of you even... what was it? ...had 'sexual relations' with another researcher so that you could get close to their data and alter it. You know... to make it more prominent and get you more money to fund your work."

James sighed and gripped his hands tightly on the faux leather steering wheel. Karen glared at John at the insinuation.

"That's what those bastards in the media were led to believe," said James, "but that's not what actually happened. Yes! Karen and I were seeing each other, but that was from the time when we first started our PhD's together, several years earlier!! Our relationship had no relevance whatsoever.

"And No! We did not falsify or forge any data. Far from it! You see, at East Anglia we tried to make all our work as open and honest as we could. We had been blogging about our research and were getting really exciting results. All climate scientists now blog, especially at East Anglia. It was something we had learnt from that other supposed scandal at the uni back in 2009–'Climate-Gate'.

"The idea of blogging was the more open we were about our work and the more transparent we were, the more honest and open for scrutiny we would seem. It was university policy. Personally I think it backfired on us."

"Why?" asked John.

"I'll get to that in a moment. Well, I'd finally submitted my key paper to Science, *the* major scientific journal and blogged about it online. Everyone in our team and everyone who had followed the blog knew of the importance and the revelations in all of our work. We were really excited.

"And remarkably quickly, it was accepted. Science was going to publish it. We knew it would take time for it to be fully scrutinised and vetted, for it to come back with the usual checks and balances, the usual reviews, and it still could be disregarded. But still, I was over the moon.

"What happened next…? We never saw it coming."

James took a deep breath.

"After I found out about my paper being accepted, I had a massive blinder. It was a big night, one for the records. The next morning I desperately needed to get some grease into me. So, I went to get some food. I realised I was out of cash and went to get money out of the a.m. When I got my receipt out of the machine, it said I had over £300,000 in the bank. Even in my state, I knew there was something pretty wrong. I thought *'How the fuck did I get this much money? It must be a bank error, or the uni has majorly lifted my wages from borderline poverty to fan-fucking-tastic.'* With the huge hangover, I thought it best to wait and call the bank later that afternoon to sort it all out.

"So, I checked my account online later that day and it was still over, but now down to £180,000. I was even more confused. I thought, *'Stuff this!!'*, and called the bank.

"They said that my account was fine and that it had the £180,000 as stated and that there were no unusual transactions over the past few months. I tried to convince them there was some terrible mistake. They said that the bank statements checked out, but they would look into it and if there was any real concern to check my bank records and send them through.

"It started to freak me out. So I went back to my computer at home and opened up my old email bank statements. It was bizarre. It showed that I had all these payments going in and out of my account for the past year for large sums of money."

"Were the statements on a cloud network?" asked John.

"No, I've never trusted the cloud," replied James. "I always thought that someone could hack into it, but I was naive. Apparently they can easily change the data on your computer too. I mean, my quarterly statements had literally changed on my laptop. Someone had somehow got in and changed it on my laptop... on my emails... without me even knowing!

"I was freaking out. So I called Karen and got her to come over. She had a look through my computer and it freaked her out too. We then found some weird emails that were on my computer from way back talking about these payments and forging data to people we knew, even to Karen."

Karen was staring out at the countryside. She turned when James mentioned her. She had several tears rolling down the pale freckled skin of her cheeks. She quickly wiped them away, and dejectedly gazed at James with her dark brown eyes.

"James was panicking," she said. "I guess so was I. Someone somehow had gotten into James' computer, his bank account and made out that he, myself and our team had forged data, and that James was the ringleader. We all checked our computers and there it was, forged emails and other correspondence that matched up. We were being set up. It was amazingly detailed."

Karen took a deep breath.

"And then we got the phone call."

James sighed. The van's tyres continued to whir in a low hum along the bitumen freeway. James looked through the mirror at Karen. It was obvious he was concerned for Karen, upset at the distress he was causing her. She wiped away more tears smudging her mascara. Karen reached into her bag and pulled out some tissues.

James looked forward and set his gaze back on the road. As he spoke, various emotions of sadness and rage quavered in his voice in the recollection of the events that had passed.

"Yeah! The phone call!" James continued. "It was the Dean of the faculty. He told me that he'd been contacted by someone in the media. The Dean said that someone had made allegations that we had falsified our data by paying off various groups and researchers so that we could secure more funding for our work. I told the Dean it was all crap. He said he had seen some pretty convincing material including emails that implicated me and as far as he could see, it looked like I was guilty of research fraud. He was withdrawing our paper. I protested. I said that he's got it all wrong. That it was a lie. I asked him how did they get our emails.

"He said that a group of *Delugionists* hackers who believed that we were falsifying our work had decided to hack into our computer and found the relevant emails. They were sent on to the media.

"I told the dean that the emails weren't true. I told him that I believed that someone had hacked into my computer and placed fake emails into the system.

"He didn't believe me. He said he had more evidence of financial misdealings. And in any case, if what I said was true, I should be able to prove him this by showing him my banking records to disprove any payments.

"I was starting to panic. What was I to do? So I told him. I told him that my bank accounts had been hacked into too.

"He said that I should stop coming up with crap and excuses, and come clean. To him, it was simple Occam's Razor – the simplest solution is the most likely. The excuses... No. The truth I was telling him was starting to make me look like a liar.

"The Dean told me that he had all the evidence he needed. He said that it was unlikely that hackers would be so elaborate to break into the banking system and forge financial data. They were going to look at everyone else who was involved, as there were more implied. If what I said was true, their records should prove me innocent.

"I was gutted. I even thought I was starting to sound like a liar. I needed to clear my head... to think... So I asked him if I could call him back later. He barely agreed."

Karen looked up. Her mascara was smudged down her cheek. "James came back to my office stressed out of his mind," she said. "He told me everything. I straight away checked my banking. It looked as if James had been paying me off for years. It was fucking freaky!"

"We thought if both of our accounts had been hacked," said James, "then everyone at work had probably been hacked too. I called the Dean back and tried to explain everything again. By that time, he just said that I was to be suspended and was to leave University grounds until a full investigation was completed. I tried to protest. He said that the police were now involved and they would take over matters from now. He also said that everyone in our team was also under investigation and appropriate actions would be taken."

James rapped his fingers over the steering wheel. "By the next morning, it was all throughout the media – *Angel-Gate*." He laughed. "Everyone's reputations in the department were ruined. Our scientific work was considered baseless... a work of fiction. And on top of that, we were now the target of a massive hate campaign for being anti-God and anti-*Delugionist*. It was awful. The newspapers called us *The Deluge Denialists*.

"The public was out ready to lynch us, all of us, our whole department. The amount of hate mail and threats...

James looked in the mirror at Karen.

"That was all we needed, to have some bloody *Delugionist* nutter come and beat us up. And they succeeded.

"Someone had managed to publicise our personal details. Our phones started being rung constantly. We were sent abusive texts. Our blog had been hacked and was full of death threats. Our homes had even been graffitied. Every essence of our lives, our family's lives, was being destroyed. Karen and I started sleeping away from home for peace and safety."

James paused remembering those awful moments. He lowered his voice in sorrow. "It was too much for one of our research assistants, Christine. The pressure got to her. She hung herself one evening. It was awful. Karen found her in her apartment hanging from the light fitting. There was nothing we could do."

Karen wiped away a tear. She was visibly upset at the memory of Christine's hanging body. "I just wish I could have done more," said Karen. "She could have called me. I would have come over... I could've..."

Jenny reached over and held her hand in comfort.

"That's terrible!" said John. He saw the grief Karen felt sapping her strength within. "Do you know if it was the original hackers that were harassing you on the blogs and at home?"

"No. We don't know. Probably not," replied James. "The public outrage against us was so huge. There was a multitude of people who wanted to hurt and destroy us. Any one of them would have been petty enough to target us. It was generally all minor..."

James looked in the rear vision mirror at Karen again. John saw his face etched with deep anger.

"...except for one night..."

Karen reached over and gave James' shoulder a reassuring touch.

"...one night, when we were on our way home, and it was raining heavily. I was driving us back from one of the many disciplinary hearings that we were made to attend. Well, we were waiting at the traffic lights by a fairly big intersection when suddenly from behind us, a big four wheel drive came racing out of the dark and slammed into us. It had no headlights on."

James paused and took a deep breath.

"We had no idea it was coming," he said. "It smashed into the back of our car throwing us straight into the traffic. Fortunately for us, the road was slippery that night and it pushed our car past an oncoming lorry. Thank God! But the four wheel drive that hit us wasn't so lucky. It slid into the traffic and got collected by the lorry meant for us. The lorry dragged it over a hundred metres down the highway. We, on the other hand, kept sliding and hit the road divider.

"Even though my seat broke, I was okay. I quickly checked on Karen. She was fine... a little shaken, but fine. Our car wasn't too badly damaged.

"I got out to look at what happened. The lorry was stuck on top of the demolished four wheel drive. I ran over to the lorry. The driver was a little stunned, but okay. I then went over to the four wheel drive. It was a wreck!! The windows were smashed! The roof was caved in! The bonnet was crushed beyond recognition and the engine was starting to smoke.

"I tried to open the driver's door and managed to get it half open. The driver was slumped in his seat struggling for breath. His chest had been crushed by the steering wheel which was pushed up against his body. I quickly released the back of his seat, undid his seatbelt and pulled him out. Don't ask me why? I didn't know if I was doing the right thing at the time, but the vehicle was starting to smoke and it scared me that a fire could start at any minute.

"I dragged the driver onto the road, and noticed some familiar numbers and letters written on the back of his hand. I ignored it and started to give him mouth to mouth, but it was useless. He started to cough up blood and was unable to breathe. There was nothing I could do. He died shortly after.

"The numbers and letters continued to bother me. So I looked at the back of his hand again and realised what they were. It scared the shit out of me. It was the number plate of *our* car. That guy had purposely come after us. He had meant to kill us."

John breathed deeply. The style of the accident was all too familiar.

"I thought about going to the police," James continued, "but realised that our credibility was non-existent, especially after the university scandal. So, I did what you'd probably think was a really stupid thing. I wiped the numbers off his hand.

"I decided there and then that I didn't want any more trouble from all of this shit. Karen and I had had enough.

"The lorry driver by then had gotten out and was looking after the scene. A crowd was starting to gather. So, we left."

James paused. He bit his lip. "For someone to try and kill us, to go to that effort, to go to that level of planning, that... that was going too far! When was it going to stop? Don't get me wrong, I loved the research that we were doing, but not at the expense of our lives. We needed to get out. We needed to get safe. Karen contacted one of her mates and he got us in contact with Jenny and Ahmed, and the rest is history."

"*Them* had succeeded," said James. "*Them* had destroyed our reputations, our lives and our livelihoods."

"How did you know it was *Them*?" asked John, sympathising in all that they had been through.

"From an email," replied Jenny. "From one of our European members. She had a fortuitous intercept while this was all going on. We discovered that *Them* had planned the original hack into their system. The hit on their car was very much in their style... make it seem like an accident... though it doesn't always work."

"The same thing happened to Rebecca," shared John. "She wasn't so lucky."

"We know," replied Jenny. "We're very sorry."

This irked John. "So then, one question. Why didn't you warn James and Karen? Before it all happened? Why didn't you go to the police?"

"You already know the answer," replied Jenny. "If I brought myself into the open, I would've been caught for a variety of reasons, some I've done, some I haven't. They've been monitoring all emails in and out of James' and Karen's systems, to make sure everything was in order and to plan. It would have been impossible to contact them without *Them* knowing. It would have put everybody's lives in jeopardy."

"You could have been anonymous!"

"Really?? You think?!"

John knew she was right. Still, he didn't like it. John looked to James. "So why haven't you publicised this before?" he asked, "Everything that's happened to you... You could have gone to the media? Put it out on the internet, like YouTube, Facebook... you know... put it out there?"

"They watch and track us," replied James.

"What?"

"Not physically, but on the internet and media," added Jenny.

"How?" asked John.

"You are so naïve John," said Karen in disbelief.

Jenny turned to face John directly. Her olive green eyes were piercing against her flawless pale skin. There was a deep sense of sadness and fragility behind them. "Did you ever notice the amount of stuff coming out from our group, tERROR, has been sparse?" she said. "Have you noticed for the past fifteen... twenty years, whenever we've posted things on the net, it's been very generic and non-specific?"

"Yeah!" John replied. "But I always thought..."

"That we aren't organised? That we are chaotic in our words and actions? That we are dysfunctional?"

"Well, not exactly..." said John. He was trying not to be rude, but it seemed a ruse. He thought it better now to be honest. "Actually... well...Yeah... It was something that I could never work out why an organisation like tERROR wasn't more persuasive in their arguments, more vocal. You guys are really very quiet."

"We have to be. *Them* monitors the internet like no Government or group has ever done," said Ahmed. "They look for us. They look for linking statements and keywords like *terror, climate, Jenny* and so on, on websites and blogs. They look for speech patterns, face recognition and voice imprints, and can pull material off video sites, social networking in a matter of seconds if they want. They monitor

Facebook, Twitter and any on-line social accounts that we may be associated with.

"Basically, anything that is flagged as a problem gets deleted almost immediately along with any links or information to identify it. We don't know how they do it so quickly and without detection. But what we do know if they then follow the IP address, hack into computers and eventually find out the source and where it came from. Ever since the embarrassment that Julian Assange, Edward Snowden, Samantha Serrano caused the world through Wikileaks and leaking of classified documents, governments and organisations have invested huge amounts of money and resources into internet tracking and control. There is no longer any true privacy, but at *Them*'s level, it is something of a phenomenon."

Ahmed looked directly at John as if he was about to lay a heavy truth. "We get around it internally by using the dark web. But even then we only use disposable phones to access it and no more than for two weeks at a time before we turf the phone. *Them* have only allowed selected materials from us to stay on the open internet to make us look like a bunch of deranged zealots. For us to be safe, at any time we've sent stuff or put anything up on the open 'net, we've had to immediately move on. And whenever we've checked back on the stuff we put out, it's been heavily edited or removed. Friends also tell us that strange people come by to where we were, often asking strange questions. *Them* don't need a huge army. They just need control, and they have it."

"Jesus!! That's scary!" whispered John.

"Yeah! I know!" Karen whispered back. "I'm sorry you're now caught up in all of this."

"Thank you," said John. He appreciated the thought. The predicament he realised he was now in was far more complex than he first anticipated. He thought back to his time working in parliament.

It disturbed him how much *Them* must have manipulated his life's work through Frank through all of their control and subterfuge, but to what extent? The thought angered him, but none more so than Frank's betrayal. And yet, still John was wary of his captors, and to what extent they would go to seek their truth.

John looked out onto the road. The traffic was starting to bank up as swarms of parents descended onto the freeway, ready to pick up their restless kids from school.

"Hey guys, we're almost there," said James.

Ahmed turned off John's phone's screen and handed it back to him. He looked at John and smiled in sympathy. Any angst that was there before had now settled. At least that is what appeared.

"Okay. Time to get ready," said Jenny.

John took a deep breath, nervous at what was ahead. It had been a while since he had seen the minister. They had been good friends, but that was before the knowledge of the true state of affairs. Hopefully he would be there. Hopefully their questions would be answered, otherwise John was truly lost and his new so-called friends would have no reason to continue to protect him.

CHAPTER 8

THE WHITE VAN turned off the M5 freeway and headed east towards the sleepy town of Cirencester. As the afternoon progressed, the Cotswolds' traffic started to build up as people headed home from their various workplaces. The sun started to dip towards the horizon giving the scenic golden valleys a warm earthy feel.

John and the four members of the British arm of *tERROR* were on the final leg of their journey to the minister's house within the heart of the district. Over the next half hour the cramped vehicle travelled through small windy streets of small close-knit houses, often opening up into lush green fields and treed paddocks on rolling hills.

As they neared their destination, Karen and Jenny told the group of the plan for when they arrived. It wasn't complex, but John was concerned that they were going a bit extreme. The only part of the plan which he thought was sensible was moving in after dark. Karen had explained it, saying it was more important that they used the dark as cover. That didn't bother John. He just figured it was simply more likely for the minister to be home at night rather than day.

Karen seemed more paranoid than before. She was still somewhat shaken that they had such a close call in Taunton. It appeared that she wanted to make sure that nothing would go wrong this time, and that all factors were accounted for. She repeated the plans again.

By the end of the third rundown, they were only a few minutes away from the minister's house. It was still light, so James pulled the van into a small empty paddock off a side street. They all decided to get out of the van to stretch their legs and kill time whilst the sun set. A large copse of dense trees shaded the group and gave them enough of a cover from the main road so as to not arouse suspicion. The evening was setting in and it was not long till dark.

Jenny gathered everyone by the van to give final instructions. Everyone seemed relatively calm and relaxed, except for John who was feeling somewhat nervous. Karen realising this, came up to John and whispered quietly into his ear, "Don't worry, John. We'll look after you."

John smiled in appreciation. He needed all the comforting he could get. He was worried about what potential disasters lay ahead. He still didn't trust that they wouldn't go overboard, but he had no choice. He had to await and see what laid ahead.

Jenny cleared her throat. "Okay! We're going to wait here for a little while. If anyone, by chance, asks us what we're doing, just say we're having a picnic."

"Yeah, right... Okay... Setting up for an evening picnic? Uh huh!" said Karen with a slight grin. "And the guns in the back are to hunt rabbits?"

"Yeah some really, really big rabbits... and lots of them," said James joining in. "Maybe they're zombie rabbits? And the smoke bombs are to confuse the vampire foxes."

"And what about the werebadgers?" asked Ahmed.

"Yeah. You've always got to be careful of werebadgers. That's what the tranq' gun's for," replied Karen. "You see, they're endangered. So we can't use bullets because the animal libbers will then target us enviro groups, and if that happens, that's when all chaos breaks loose. And we don't want that!!"

John couldn't help but laugh.

"Alright you guys," said Jenny in an amused exasperation, "that's enough! You know I like to be well prepared. Anyway, it seems we're on the same page. So, go on then. Piss off! And be back in fifteen minutes."

"See ya!!" said Karen as she walked off laughing with James.

"Idiots," laughed Jenny.

Ahmed walked to the van, reached into the back and pulled out a rolled up mat. "Might be time for me to have a pray to Allah," he said.

John raised his eyebrows in surprise, not seeing Ahmed having any earlier religious inkling. Jenny smiled.

"Look," laughed Ahmed registering John's surprise, "I might not be a good Muslim, but I try to pray when I remember... that's if I remember. But really, five times a day, I'm sure Allah understands if I miss one or two... occasionally more... well a lot more."

Ahmed looked around slightly lost.

"Which way is Mecca?" he asked.

"Ummm... Shouldn't you know that?" asked John.

Ahmed shrugged it off and seemed to find his bearings. "I'm pretty sure it's that direction..." he said. "Must be! There's a good spot. I'm off. I'll let you guys be." Ahmed wandered off to a small clearing to have his peace and privacy.

"He's got the wrong direction, hasn't he?" asked John.

"Completely!" replied Jenny with a big smile. John laughed.

"Still, he's trying," she said. "He's just only recently rediscovered his Muslim past."

"They're a nice bunch," said John, "the three of them. Young and enthusiastic."

"Yeah. They're a challenge sometimes, but their hearts are in the right place," replied Jenny.

John and Jenny sat back on the van's bumper looking out over the green expanse. It was quite picturesque. The large field was edged by a small rambling creek with ancient grand arched trees giving a glimpse of the country's past. The new weather systems had spared this area. John could just see Karen and James disappearing into a small thicket in the distance.

The sun started to set on the horizon turning the now ashen grey sky to a bronze hue. A flock of starlings bobbed and ebbed in the sky like an amorphous speckled disc being stretched and turned. A flash dashed the sky and the ground rumbled. A storm had been brewing in the far off distance and was slowly moving in from the east.

"How are you doing?" asked Jenny. "You have been through a lot."

"Yeah, I'm okay... I think," replied John as he rubbed his eyes. He took a deep breath and looked up at Jenny's hazel green eyes. "It's been a big few days."

"I know. It can be hard when you find out that someone you've been close to might be involved in something you've been fighting against your whole life. I know you worked hard for environmental reform." Jenny looked across at John. He was tired and stressed. She touched him on his shoulder. The warm touch gave John a sense of relief, that someone was there, ready to help.

John sighed, "Yeah, and now Frank's dead. Whatever he was involved in was enough to get him killed. I guess it was enough to get Rebecca killed too."

They both sat silently as the storm slowly moved in closer. The leaves of the trees started to stir as a slight breeze whipped through the air.

"And on top of all that, I'm now also worried about my family back in Sydney," said John thinking about the phone messages he received earlier. "Jenny, I've got to know. Will *Them* go after them?"

"Generally friends and family get left alone," she replied as she looked off into the distance. She tried to avoid eye contact. "From personal experience, their phones and emails are monitored, but *Them* generally wants to avoid killing family. It brings up too many questions from the authorities, particularly when multiple members from one family die or go missing. Easier to just get rid of one random individual person at a time... especially if you make it look like an accident."

"That's good.... I guess," said John. The realisation suddenly dawned on him with a sinking feeling, "So you haven't seen or heard from your family for years?"

Jenny wiped a tear away. "Seventeen years five months to be exact."

"Wow!! I'm so sorry."

Jenny broached a smile. "Don't be. It's the path I chose to go on and it's important what we're doing."

"So if everyone who has been murdered by *Them* is killed in an accidental fashion, why make my disappearance and the minister's murder so public?"

"Good question," said Jenny. She paused in thought. "Maybe Frank was now too much of a risk to them, and you were in theory feeding us information for over ten years. Maybe your abduction was the only way to get you out of the country so they could interrogate you without arousing too much suspicion. Kill two birds with one stone. Who knows?"

John pondered the situation.

"Or maybe it's a warning to us all," she said.

John didn't like the idea of being used as a sacrificial lamb on its way to the slaughter. He shivered at the thought. "So, why did you get involved in all of this in the first place?" asked John. "Especially if you had to abandon everyone you love."

"Ultimately, I did it for them, but... another time..." said Jenny sadly, but with a resolute smile. The sky flashed again and ground rumbled louder and stronger. The storm was moving closer.

"Then why save me? Why use me?"

"Because you're halfway between us and them," said Jenny. "You know many involved. You may not know who directly, but you have seen what has happened. You are key to helping us. We need evidence. We need proof to expose *Them* and to give people like James, Karen, yourself, your lives back. There are many more like you three. I just hope we're on the right track. You really believe Phillip Cudsworth knows what's happening?"

"Yeah. I think I know when it all started," replied John. "Like you said, it all changed at Copenhagen. Frank had somehow changed... and Phil was there. He's gotta know."

"And you reckon Phillip will be willing to talk?"

"Well, we'll soon find out? Won't we?!"

James and Karen appeared out of the thicket of trees and started to wander back.

"Those two sound like they've had a tough time," said John.

"Yeah. It wasn't easy for them. When they arrived back two years ago, they were a mess. We took them in, helped them along. That's all we could really do."

"And Ahmed?"

"He's helped me along since I first started. I trust him with my life."

"So are you two...?" John asked with a wry smile.

"Us??? No!!" laughed Jenny still a little bleary eyed. "Let's just say it would take a very unique woman to keep Ahmed. Besides, I think he enjoys the single life a little too much."

John laughed. "I understand."

Ahmed stood up in the distance finishing his prayers. He bound up his mat and ran to catch up with Karen and James. By the time he caught the pair, they were almost back.

"So why base yourselves at *The Reform*?" asked John.

"Some friends of mine grew up around there. With all the alternative culture and lifestyle, it was the perfect place for a safe house. Many are sympathetic with our cause and are paranoid enough about any authorities to be over-vigilant. It's really helped us a lot in the past."

"And you really think we can actually beat *Them*?"

"I don't know," replied Jenny. "I really just don't know." A look of helplessness crossed her face. "But we've just got to try, otherwise who will?"

Karen and James had a big grin on their face as they meandered back. Ahmed whispered something quietly. They both laughed.

"Hey, you two!" yelled Karen. "Didn't get up to anything naughty whilst we were gone? Get to know each other that little much better? Jenny, you did say he was pretty cute."

"Okay, that's enough," replied Jenny blushing a little. James elbowed Karen in the ribs.

"Sorry," replied the chastised Karen with a grin.

"So stretched enough?" asked Jenny in mocking revenge. "You both look a little out of breath. No frenetic exercise?"

"We're fine," replied Karen not rising to the challenge. "We actually came across a pretty little gully down the bottom of the paddock... small stream, mushrooms.... really pretty. James wanted to try the mushrooms. I wouldn't let him."

"Yeah little Miss spoil my fun," said James.

"Well, I can't tell the difference between the poisonous ones and the good ones, and I know that you are no mushroom expert. I didn't want you to get hurt."

"We used to pick them when I was a kid in Wales," argued James. "I've done it thousands of times."

"Save it for the bedroom guys," said Ahmed smiling as he put his arms around them both. "With the way you clean your house, I'm sure there will be plenty of mushrooms to pick there."

Karen pushed his arm off. "I'm going to hit you one of these days Ahmed Johnson."

"See Jenny, I told you," protested Ahmed. "Violence against Muslims! I always knew Karen had it in her."

"Fuck off!!" replied Karen. Ahmed continued laughing as Karen tried to punch him in the shoulder.

"Enough guys," said Jenny. "No more joking around. We have work to do."

Jenny opened the van's back door and pulled out several moderate sized bags. The four grabbed a bag each, opened them and started to change into the evening's attire. John stood back letting the group ready themselves impressed at their level of organisation. He had no special clothes for the occasion, but he really didn't care.

A drop of water thudded on the ground sending up a small cloud of dust. The smell of moisture pervaded the air as several more followed. Suddenly, a cascade of rain started pummelling down. Everyone dashed inside the van.

Extra cover I guess, thought John, *Never hurts.*

James, now dressed in black, started the van and slowly drove off into the rapidly developing dark. The rain continued to pummel the van drowning out all other noise. Their operation had just begun.

PART 2
DISCOVERY

JAMES TURNED OFF the van's headlights as they approached their destination. The heavy driving rain continued to fall incessantly creating a bleak shroud to the surrounding world. The dying dusk light was just bright enough for James to slowly navigate the van through the small unlit cobbled streets. He turned the corner past a high set two storey house surrounded by large lush green hedges and slowly drove under a set of tall Roman-styled aqueducts. Sheets of water poured off the aqueduct's edges forming a cascading curtain.

Just below the aqueduct, several houses were lined up facing the edge of a large green field. Curved streams of smoke flashed solid with every lightning flash as they slowly billowed out of various bricked chimneys.

It had been over two years since he had visited Phillip at his Cotswold home, the last one being with Frank. In the rainy night, it made the place seem far and distant, not the warm hearth that he had remembered.

"We'll park under here and move in by foot," said James pulling to a stop next to one of the aqueduct's arcades. "The Minister's less likely to notice us coming in from up here. So, John, he's the first house on our left?"

"Yeah," replied John as he looked out the van's window towards the large converted barn. "I've been there only twice before, once for dinner and another time for his fiftieth. Stayed overnight. Nice place, but not overly secure from what I remember."

The building in question was a large eighteenth century Renaissance stone barn that had been converted into a lavish dwelling whilst preserving its grand structure. In addition to its restoration, the side facade had been expanded to include a large glass conservatory interspersed with rough rendered white walls. The extensions, in John's view, were too modern for its archaic structure, but its main saving grace was that ivy had started to grow up the rendered sections letting the conservatory blend back into its green surroundings.

John looked over at the building wondering what the minister was doing or even if he was there. His thoughts were soon answered. One of the conservatory's lights flickered on and a person moved into the glassed room. Through the blurring of the rain covered windows, John could just make out the distinct silhouette of a figure he knew. It was the British government's minister, Phillip Cudsworth. The figure sat down on a large lounge suite as music started piping from a house down the road. John hoped that Phillip was alone. Nerves started to creep in as he contemplated what the team's moves would be.

They exited the van. James, Karen, and Ahmed were all dressed in thick black uniforms with balaclavas pulled back on their heads. They each carried a pistol and Karen had various explosive devices attached to her side. She also had a night vision mask resting on top of her head. Karen tucked her pistol under her belt and padded her side making sure everything was safe and secure. Jenny, unlike the others, was dressed more casually with denim jeans and a khaki green shirt, but still carried a pistol. Everyone, besides John, wore an earpiece transceiver for communications.

"Jenny, you are going overboard," said John quietly in protest.

"You still don't know what we're dealing with yet, John," replied Jenny.

Karen gave the orders. "Okay, we'll head to the house. John, you stick with Jenny and go no further than the driveway until we give the signal that all is safe. James, you mark the front door. Ahmed take the side entrance and I'll take the conservatory. Once Ahmed and I have gained access, we'll restrain the minister, make sure the place is clear and that's when everyone can come in. Everyone got that?"

They all replied in confirmation, except James. He said, "But I could take out..."

"No Sweetie," said Karen. "Ahmed and I have more experience in this and besides, I couldn't bear you getting hurt."

Karen fidgeted with her explosives holster at her side. She looked over at John. "So John, you're sure that there will be no one else?" she asked.

John let out an exasperated breath. "Well, yeah, as far as I know," replied John. "He doesn't use a body guard and he recently split with his wife. So unless his daughter and family are here to visit, it's unlikely that there'll be others." John was bothered about the plan, but even more about the amount of munitions they were taking. "Is it really necessary to go this covert and use force?"

"You don't understand yet," repeated Karen. "We have to be careful, especially with the tactics and force that *Them* can use. They are very cunning. We're even wearing heat reflecting suits which we do so, not for practicality, but from experience. It's so they can't detect us with infrared goggles. Something I managed to score off some mates back in the IDF."

John was dumbfounded with all the military grade gadgets and weaponry they carried. "He's just a plain minister," he said. "I've worked with him for many years. Everyone I've worked with in government is boring and frankly inept. They have no secret ops training, no hidden martial arts skills, perhaps maybe Jim, the Australian Greens' leader.... but that's irrelevant. This is stupid. We don't want to scare Phil unnecessarily."

"John, Karen's right!" said Jenny. "We don't know what traps or protections that the minister or for that matter *Them* may have set up. We need to be careful."

John gave up trying to fight. "Yeah. Whatever," he said. He shook his head in exasperation. Karen gave John a reproachful look.

Phillip Cudsworth was a gentle family loving man. Even though he had several slip ups that led to his divorce, the idea that he would be willing to hurt or kill seemed completely absurd to John. It was the last thing John ever imagined that he would do.

Karen returned her gaze to the others as she pulled her balaclava over her head. She checked the rounds in her gun and placed it back in her belt.

Jenny said to the group, "If anything goes wrong, if we're split apart, remember our usual contingency plan."

"Absolutely!" said Ahmed. The others indicated the same. John had no idea what the plan was, but suspected he was kept out more on a trust issue.

Karen gave a quick nod to Ahmed and James in a silent agreement. They followed her lead and quietly made their way down to the front driveway. It was a dead end street, and the grand house was shielded in one section from the main road by a strip of large pine trees in front of a small low stone fence. John and Jenny hid by the trees using them as a dense cover whilst the other three carried out their plans.

The three slowly made their way to their respective positions around the house making sure they weren't seen or heard. The rain and darkness aided their approach.

John sat on the edge of the fence. He looked at Jenny. She seemed troubled and was deep in thought.

"Geez, you guys are very well set up," said John breaking Jenny from her thoughts. "Have you always been that way?"

"It always pays to be well prepared," replied Jenny.

The rain continued to stream down. John looked down at the corner of the house. He could barely just see Karen as she gave a quick wave to one of the others to move on.

"It seems bizarre," said John.

"What do you mean?" asked Jenny. She had been checking her phone as some emails flashed up. She was slightly annoyed at the distraction.

"Why did Karen leave the IDF, of all things to go and study climate change?"

"Oh, Karen?" Jenny replied. "Yeah, I know it seems bizarre for ex-military to go and study climate science, but the reality is sadly more mundane. Basically, in Israel, they still have conscription for people over eighteen years. They have to serve for at least two years and Karen was one of those. She had just finished her degree in Climate Science in Tel Aviv and was conscripted to the IDF. She served her time there. Apparently, she was a particularly talented marksman and leader, and made her way up in the ranks quite quickly."

There was a buzzing in Jenny's ear. She turned away annoyed and spoke into her mouthpiece. "Just keep going, I don't care if James cut himself on some thorns."

Jenny turned back to John. "The idiots... Sorry, where was I? Karen, that's right. Anyway, she made her way up the ranks in her various roles and stayed in the IDF for about four years in total. Eventually she became disillusioned like most of them do with the ongoing sexual harassment, flawed policies and incompetence from her superiors. So she decided to go back to her original passion, science. She wanted to get away and came across to East Anglia University to do her doctorate which had one of the best reputations for climate science. The rest you pretty much know."

Another crackle went off in Karen's ear.

She replied to the mouthpiece, "I don't care if you can't see him. Just wait for him to come back, then go in and restrain him. Bloody Hell!! Use force if necessary."

"This is stupid," said John.

"It's necessary," replied Jenny in frustration. "It's the best way for..."

"No... Fuck this," said John, as he dashed off to the front entrance of the house before Jenny could stop him.

Jenny yelled into her mouthpiece as she ran after John. "Change of plans guys."

"What!?! Oh fuck!! Don't tell me!" replied Karen. "Where's John?"

"He's on his way," said Jenny very much annoyed.

"Can't you stop him?"

"How? The commotion will set off the neighbourhood."

"Well you could have.... fuck... We'll be there soon. Ahmed, James. Meet you guys at the front," said Karen over the radio.

John reached the Barn's wooden front door just as Karen and Ahmed rounded the corner.

"It's easy!!" said John as he knocked firmly on the door.

A few seconds passed, and James finally caught up. He was clutching at his leg where there was a small tear in his pants. A light flashed on inside and a voice yelled in the background, "I'll be there in a moment. Let me find the damned key. Where the hell did I put it? Ah, here it is." There was a rattling in the lock and the door opened revealing a tall balding man dressed in a light green and yellow tracksuit. "Hello, who is it?"

The blood drained from Phillip Cudsworth's face. "John? What the hell are you doing here? How are you here? Why? The murder in Australia.... Frank..."

Phillip looked around confused. Three black balaclava covered faces stared back. Jenny wandered up the porch. The rain continued to soak everyone.

"Are you being held hostage, John?" Phillip asked in concern.

"Guys take them off," said John.

"But he'll recognise us," replied Ahmed.

"You don't think that he's recognised Jenny and me already?"

Ahmed hesitated for a second. "Fair point," he replied.

Ahmed and James took off their balaclavas. Karen just lifted hers a little, as her night vision mask held the rest of hers down tightly on her head. Phillip stared dumbfounded fixed to the spot.

"No Phil, I'm not being held hostage," replied John. "But right now I am wanted for the murder of Frank. So if you could be kind enough to let us in, I'll try not to kill you too."

Phillip's face flushed white again.

"Phillip, I'm just kidding!!" said John. "God!! You look like you've seen a ghost."

John walked in through the front doorway brushing Phillip on the shoulder on the way past. Phillip remained motionless, just holding onto the door's handle in shock, not knowing whether to run or to shout out for help. The rest of the group stood fixed blocking any exit out.

"Don't be a dick Phil," yelled John from the hallway. "We're not here to hurt you. Just come back inside and we'll explain."

CHAPTER 10

D ESPITE BEING INITIALLY surprised and shocked by the sudden appearance and make-up of his new guests, the Secretary of State for Energy and Climate Change, the right honourable Phillip Cudsworth MP still grabbed towels for everyone to dry themselves off. The motley crew had all trudged in soaked to the bone, and looked completely dishevelled.

Phillip felt it was still important to keep up appearances, and as such look after his guests. He sat down by the large oaken table inside the confines of the entertainment room of the converted barn, whilst contemplating their actions and his fate.

John took a seat and started to dry himself off, oblivious to Phillip's concerns. He looked around the once familiar room. It was quite a grand and spacious room with a high vaulted roof supported by heavy oak beams. Two chandeliers made of an early twentieth century wooden carriage wheels hung from the ceiling by wrought iron links and lit up the room showing off its firm angular structures. The rough sandstone walls gave the room a rustic rough earthen feel bringing back forgotten memories of a time that once was.

John lay his towel on his lap. There was a large white flash from the room's large glass vaulted windows followed by earthen rumbles. The rain pummelled the ground and the roof with ever heavier drops blocking out all noises from beyond.

Phillip surveyed his guests as they all sat towelling themselves off.

"Thank you," said Jenny.

"I can't let John's friends catch a cold from the wet," replied Phillip, "even if they do wear balaclavas, carry guns and explosives, and are wanted for terror charges for that matter."

Jenny curtailed a smile. Karen just ignored him and continued to dry off. She rested her gun on the table never leaving a hand too far. Ahmed decided to leave the table and check the other rooms of the house. The tension in the room was quite palpable.

"So for what do I owe the pleasure to have your group rock up unannounced on my front doorstep?" asked Phillip.

"John?" said Jenny.

"Yeah. Ummm... Phil. Frank's dead," said John.

"Very eloquently put. Yes I know he's dead. You killed him!" replied Phillip.

"Um... No. No, I didn't."

"Well the authorities believe that you did as such."

Jenny interrupted. "Does *Them* mean anything to you?"

Phillip froze slightly, only for a moment. "I don't know what you're talking about my dear," he said. He tried to hide his recognition further, which unfortunately for him was not very well. "Your grammar is terrible. Do you mean to say *'Do they mean anything to you?'* and even so, to whom are you referring to?"

"Listen you snot-nosed prick!!" Jenny's temper was starting to fray. "You know exactly who I mean. *Them.*"

"Jenny!" scolded John. "Listen Phil. What I've been through over the past few days is pretty damn serious. Three days ago, I came across an email on Frank's desk that apparently I shouldn't have seen and because of that email, Frank has been killed, I have been framed for his murder, and I was supposed to be interrogated in Egypt by God only knows who for God only knows what. Somehow, I think you'll be able to tell me why Frank is dead and why all of this shit is happening."

"And why is that?"

"Because of Operation Warmth and whatever that means."

John slid his phone across the table with the email spread across the screen.

"And mainly because of Copenhagen. You were there and so was Frank. Everything changed after that, including yourself. I reckon that's when it all started. I think you know exactly what I'm talking about. That's when it all changed. You and Frank changed after the white room meeting at the Accord. And I believe whatever happened there was important enough to change government policy and important enough to kill people including my Rebecca and Frank..."

Phillip lifted his head in surprise at the mention of John's wife.

"...and somehow this has something to do with the *Delugionists* too."

Phillip picked up the phone and scanned the electronic document. His eyes widened as the blood rushed out of his face. "John, you shouldn't have seen this. I'm so sorry. You've put us all in danger." He put the phone down with a trembling hand.

"No minister," said Jenny. "We're already *in* danger. Don't worry! The phone can't be located right now. However, I think John's kidnapping and the various murders have more than shown the dangers that John's faced. We've put ourselves in danger after taking him from his abductors, and now I guess you are now in danger too with us being here. So come clean and tell us what happened."

"My dear, they'll kill me," said Phillip with a slight panic in his voice.

"Well, you shouldn't worry about that," said Karen. She pulled out her gun and pointed it at his head. "...because I could kill you too! Right here, right now!"

"Karen, stop this! Put that away!" demanded John. "This is..."

"No, Karen. Keep it there," interrupted Jenny, unphased by Karen's actions. "Let him understand the position we've been put in. Let him appreciate how far we are willing to go."

Phillip turned to John for help. "Look John," said Phillip with panic. "This is ridiculous. I cannot help you or they will kill me."

"As far as I can see, minister," replied Jenny, "you have two options. You can either help us and we'll hide you, or we'll just put a video on YouTube saying that you helped us. Of course, come to think of it, there is a third option. Karen can end things quickly for you right now if you prefer."

"Jenny!!" protested John, somewhat shocked at the evening's progression.

Phillip was highly distressed. "My dear, you have killed me nonetheless," he said. Phillip looked pale and withered at the options presented before him. "*Them* monitor YouTube and all social and video networks. Any internet video, post or photographic material that is put out by your group, especially if it is referring to *Them*, is immediately pulled off the internet in less than a minute, sometimes within seconds. It doesn't matter if it's your photo or your voice, or for that matter any of tERROR's material. *Them* delete or release the material depending on what they want or when they want it released.

"You see, *Them* approves what you at tERROR put out. You have no choice. You never had any choice. *Them* will see. By putting that material out, *Them* will immediately see what you say about me.

"My dear, you are basically signing my death sentence." Phillip started rubbing his temples in tension. He was stressed. He was struggling to work out what to do in his situation.

"Don't call me dear!!" responded Jenny. She was unmoved by Phillip's plight. "You must think we're blithering idiots if you think we didn't know that. Of course we know that anything we put out on the net never makes it to the public without being heavily edited. We know it's *Them*, and frankly that *is* why you have the options in front of you."

John didn't like their tactics, and felt he should take some control back. He knew Phil better than the others. "Listen Phil," John interrupted. "I can no longer go back to my old life. Well... not any time soon. Even if we do nothing, sooner or later they're going to work out that we've contacted you. Tell us what happened. Let us get your story out. The truth will help us fix everything. I have already had ASIO contact me."

Jenny looked up surprised at John's revelation. John realised he probably should have kept that one quiet. He quickly let it pass. John continued, "With your story, we can get them to help us to get somewhere safe, to get us all in the clear. Tell us. Tell us everything. Tell us what happened."

"I don't know," said Phillip somewhat dubious. He briefly pondered the situation laid out in front of him. "You'll look after me?" he asked.

"Yes," replied Jenny. She waved at Karen to put her gun down. "We'll make sure that you are safe and taken care of."

"How?" laughed Phillip nervously.

"We'll get you to a safe house," said Jenny, "one of many that we have around the country."

"Like that will work," he scoffed.

Karen sat back down next to James. He had been quietly studying the progress of events. James put his hand on Karen's as she gently lay back the gun on the wooden table. Phillip stared at the gun, uneasy with its presence.

"You know that *Them* will stop at nothing to keep this from going public?" said Phillip emphatically.

"We know," replied Jenny. "We all have had personal experience in this."

Phillip bit his lip with uncertainty. Meanwhile, Ahmed wandered back into the room. He gave Jenny a nod to let her know that everything was safe. Ahmed sat back down on one of the lounges near the windows, and rested his long legs on a nearby pouffe.

As Phillip contemplated his position, John surveyed the scene. It was a surreal experience with half of the people sitting around dressed in black with towels draped around their shoulders whilst the key member was dressed in a bright green and yellow track suit. It reminded John of an Australian – New Zealand sports training camp, except the stakes were much higher and a lot more deadly.

"Okay," said Phillip begrudgingly. He sank his shoulders in defeat. He knew he had no out. "I'll tell you. Just promise to look after me and protect my family."

"We will take care of you. Your family will be safe," promised Jenny.

Phillip looked dubious. He shook his head in slight disbelief at what he was about to say. "Okay, okay. John!!" he said. "You are right... about it starting in Copenhagen!"

CHAPTER 11

"I THOUGHT SO," MUTTERED John quietly. He realised that he had been truly hiding from the truth all of these years.

"Well," said Phillip, "it all started at the start of winter in 2009 at that summit. Even though I started later in life in politics, I relatively junior as a minister at the time and was there to help assist Wayne McMahon, the then UK secretary for climate change. I was basically there to help with the talks and negotiations. Of course as we both know, you John, and Frank were there to help with the Australian delegation."

John stared quietly back. He remembered the stress of the meetings as if it occurred only yesterday. It was his first big foray into international politics. Phillip looked over to Jenny and the others.

"The idea was, as we all had naively hoped, was to broker a deal for what was meant to be the successor to the Kyoto Protocol. The Kyoto Protocol, you might remember, was one of the first big international agreements that set binding targets on capping greenhouse gas emissions to help prevent climate change. The big problem with the Kyoto Protocol was that when it was created, it only focused on the developed countries like the US, Europe and UK, and ignored the developing countries like China and India which soon themselves became major emitters. As a result, the Kyoto protocol never made any real major impact.

"Don't get me wrong, it was a start, but a proper successor was needed and that was to be developed at that convention, the UN Climate Change Conference. It was supposed to be the big one, the one meeting that would make a difference, or at least set up a process to get real action on climate change. All the major leaders from around the world were there–the US, China, UK, France, South Africa. With all of these people in one room, there was hope that something real could happen.

"Anyway prior to the conference, we had been involved in several meetings and complex negotiations with various groups and countries about global climate action. We were very excited with the efforts from within Europe and other nations in setting up a CPRS. And Australia finally coming on-board with their signing of the Kyoto Protocol back in 2007, it looked like that we would have some good pressures on governments from all sides for unilateral efforts."

"Why was Australia so important?" asked Karen.

"You see, Australia was seen as a special case," replied Phillip. "For ten years, Australia had held out from ratifying Kyoto. Australia and the US were the last major developed countries that had avoided joining the Kyoto Protocol. And just over a year before the summit, Australia had changed its mind, and joined the fray.

"Naively it was hoped that by Australia explaining to the other countries why they had such a big change in their country's policies, hopefully the antipodeans could influence the newly developing countries such as China and India. Australia was developing quite strong trade relationships with these two, and more importantly they were seen more as friends than as an aggressive military threat. Australia's delegates were to be key in many negotiations."

"I didn't realise the Aussies were so influential," said James.

"Absolutely! Back then, they were! At least to many of the Asian countries," Jenny confirmed. "We all had great hopes with Australia being key negotiators. Sadly, it didn't pan out. Australia lost a lot of credibility with their internal government conflict and turmoil. And then there was Snowdon's revelations…"

Phillip, annoyed at Jenny's interruption, avoided her gaze. "Yes, well, we'll come to that shortly," he said. "So, during the summit, to help move negotiations along, the UK, Australia and other Western country delegates often worked hand in hand on many issues. We had many small quick meetings to iron out problems whenever they popped up. So when there was another opportunity for our five countries: Australia, France, Germany, South Africa and us, the UK, to meet to strategize further, we thought it was important that we should attend."

"The White Room Meeting?" asked John.

"Yes. The White Room meeting…" replied Phillip. The words seemed to reverberate around the room with a heavy resonance. "As John probably remembers, the meeting happened late at night in the White Room of the Marriott Hotel. There were some important key summit sessions happening the next day, so our key ministers decided to delegate this planning group to us junior ministers. The French were the ones that organised the meeting. It was ultimately the idea of their junior minister Francois Maury. It was made clear to all the groups that as it was late, and to ensure the meeting was quick and succinct, only one person from each delegation could attend. It was unusual, but no one questioned it. We were all getting pretty tired by that stage."

"So who was there?" asked Jenny.

"The names of those who attended, you will know quite well now, especially to you, John. Of course, Francois was there, and then there was also Dr Freijda Stodden from Germany, Henry Kroezen from South Africa, your Frank and myself."

It dawned on John as to who they all were. A cold shiver of realisation travelled down the base of his spine. He now realised, unknown to everyone back then, that this meeting must have held a high level of influence.

"You've got to be kidding me," said Ahmed leaning forward on the couch. "Surely not."

Phillip nodded.

"But they're all environment or climate ministers now!" said Jenny.

"Absolutely," replied Phillip. "These people were all in the pipeline for higher positions. Their political parties had seen great hope in each of them, hence why they were in Copenhagen. For them to go to international negotiations, it was a great honour. But for them to all be made climate change ministers and never move any further? To never to go onto other portfolios in ten, sometimes fifteen years? I have always wondered why no one has ever picked that up on that. I guess we're all probably too boring."

There was a large flash followed by a deafening crack of thunder that rumbled for several seconds causing the windows and the wooden chandelier's chains to rattle.

"Anyway," continued Phillip, "we all met in the White Room and discussed the next day's coming events. It was quite productive and a little bit vocal at times. One thing was strange though. Francois was not being his usual self. He was being unusually quiet and surly, and sat back for most of the discussions. But that soon changed.

"At one in the morning, Francois stood up and told everyone to be quiet. We all were taken quite aback. I thought typical bloody French, but he had caught our attention. Then Francois leant forwards and told everyone that he had some important information *that would change everything*. We all thought that he was just being arrogant trying to big-note himself and take control of the discussions.

"I asked him, *what sort of information could be so bloody important that it hadn't been presented to the IPCC by now*. Francois told me to shut up. He said he had a guest waiting outside and that we needed to listen to what his guest had to say.

"We never expected anyone else! We all protested saying that this was a closed meeting and was against all protocol. It threw everyone off guard. Francois made his case and convinced the others in the group to let this person in.

"I was extremely annoyed. This shouldn't have been allowed. But, as always, we went with the group majority and accepted the guest in.

"And in he came. He was actually quite a sight, almost caricaturish in a way. I can remember this almost as if it happened today. In came this man, a slightly tubby man, I will add. He was dressed in a taupe brown pleated suit with a bright crimson bow tie. Half of his face and neck was severely scarred from what seemed to have been a chemical burn. One of his eyes was opaque white from which I believe he had no or very little vision. Even though he appeared to be in his mid-thirties, he required the use of a cane to support himself as he walked in.

"We asked Francois to introduce him, and he said it was better that we did not ask this sort of thing. I told him that this was unacceptable, and demanded that we should be told immediately who this person was.

"The guest spoke up. He said that it did not matter who he was, but only that he represented a group of key individuals from various oil and mining companies that he would not name.

"Freijda protested. I mean, really, why bring someone from this group? Why should we trust and believe him? Especially in regards to climate science and negotiation. Freijda pointed out what we all knew, that the oil and mining companies had funded climate change denial pseudo-science and propaganda for many years. These companies had vested interests in keeping carbon pollution going, and keeping the truth from the public. They had no interest in addressing climate change.

"For us to listen to them, given their track record, was like asking a fundamentalist Christian to talk on the finer points on the science of evolution. It just didn't hold water. Despite the fact that the science was irrefutably telling us the world was definitely warming, that the oceans were rising, and the evidence showing that his bosses were a big part of the cause, these people kept on irreverently saying that global warming wasn't real. So Freijda put it to him. Why on earth should we believe him when their companies have been propagating and feeding us lies?

"What he said next took us all aback. He agreed."

James interrupted in disbelief, "What? He agreed that they propagated lies? Did those dickheads in oil and mining then finally admit that it was them causing climate change?"

"Actually, yes!!" said Phillip emphatically. "We too, couldn't believe his response. He agreed, but he then said that the group he worked for would never admit to it."

"Of course!" said Ahmed. "Why would they? It goes against what they are. It would have been suicide for their companies."

"Absolutely! That's what we thought too. He then said something that really shook us. He said that we should change our stance too and not admit to man-made climate change."

"Really!?!" said Ahmed.

"I know," replied Phillip. "I asked him why on earth would we do such a thing? I couldn't possibly understand the ridiculous stance he was asking us to take. He just said that the global situation was a lot worse than what we anticipated. The guest said for us to truly understand, he would have to explain everything."

"Sorry!" said John. "You keep saying the guest. Did he have a name?"

"No," replied Phillip. "Well, not that we were given one. We had no idea who he actually was, but it was someone Francois knew or probably a better term was acquainted with. It will make more sense later."

John was frustrated, feeling that Phillip was holding out on the information.

Phillip, realising this, explained a bit further. "Look! Francois, interestingly, had kept quiet during the whole discussion. Obviously he knew this person well and he seemed to have heard it all before. So I believe there most likely was a reasonable connection between the two, but not one he was willing to divulge. Anyway, where was I?"

"The guest said he would have to explain everything," replied James.

"That's right," said Phillip. "Thank you. Everything..." Phillip pondered the point momentarily with a sardonic smile on his face. He shook his head with incredulity. "You see what he said was what we all knew and suspected of these groups, but more... a lot more. He gave us the whole background of what these companies had been up to, especially in sabotaging our efforts in Government for, I guess, the past decade. He admitted that his employers had been manipulating public opinion for a long time... a very long time.

"You see, for the previous decade, these companies had done a lot of subversion. They had funded grass roots movements, media organisations and political activists who were sympathetic to their causes. The aim of course was to try and derail various governments' policies and worldwide efforts in combating climate change. On top of that, they had funded the work of climate change sceptics like Viscount Riley, Dawn Rogers and many others to speak at major conventions about how climate change was a farce and that man was definitely not the cause. They even-created and funded some of these conferences entirely on their own. They got the media to attend and report on it like it was a legitimate annual event of international experts on the field, instead of the reality of cherry picked likeminded individuals whose expertise were never questioned.

"On the political front, they met with world leaders and other politicians. They bankrolled their campaigns to ensure they would be listened to. They funded climate sceptic protest groups. They had to do it often through secret charities to hide any links. Sometimes they even paid for individuals to rouse up others to make sure that the public would protest about combatting emissions. Through selective media advertising and putting financial pressure on media companies to rally in their favour, they helped fund radio shock jocks, right-wing commentators, and TV presenters who were sympathetic to their views and made sure they were given key time slots. They even funded certain climate research to try and disprove the then current beliefs in climate science. The guest showed us all.

"These companies didn't actually make things up. They didn't have to. Really, all they did was fund groups and individuals whose beliefs matched their own, and the rest worked in their favour."

The whole room was engrossed by Phillip's revelations except for Jenny. She seemed to be lost by a different thought, but even so, some of the revelations made her take notice.

Phillip continued on. "Really, the most significant point to us in their whole smear campaign was their research. The guest said that the research was the most frustrating part in trying to get material to support their views. In the mainstream media, they were having good success in getting what they wanted, i.e. doubt from the public, but they weren't getting the research results that they needed. In fact, every research project and group that they had funded had either had minor questionable results that supported their denialist cause but actually did not hold up to scrutiny and so was easily shredded; Or it, even more concerningly, proved to a greater extent the man-made effects on climate were real."

"Surely you didn't find that surprising?" asked Jenny.

"No," replied Phillip. "Not really. What the guest told us wasn't news to us at all. This had happened time and time again. What was news to us was what he said next. There was one research project that they had all pinned their hopes on. It was the project that was going to be the coup d'états, the one to change it all. It was going to be so big, so accurate and so strong, it would supersede all other research. Only a very few knew. They had kept it secret for many years so that it would be well tested and irrefutable. They wanted to fight with a new credible, yet powerful scientific weapon to show that they were right and that climate change was not manmade."

"But that would never happen!!" said James. "Because man-made climate change is real."

"I know. Their project backfired in an amazing way. Their results scared them beyond their worst dreams. It was something that even they were struggling to deal with. And when the guest told us, we dared not believe him. In fact we didn't. We thought he was stringing us along, trying to bluff us. So he handed us a document showing some of the research, its proof and more scaringly what was to come."

"What was it?" asked Karen.

"They had created a climate model that was far more accurate than any climate model than we had ever come across. Now we've seen many models showing us predictions of what can and might happen. A lot of them helped underpin the IPCC reports in the past. This model however was different. In fact, it was remarkably different. It was detailed, more detailed than any model we had ever seen. It predicted *exactly* when ice sheets would melt, when oceans would rise, even when large earthquakes would occur. It didn't give a range of decades, not even years. It could predict things in a matter of weeks to months. It seemed almost too detailed and too exact to be real.

"I asked him how did they come up with this model to be so detailed, so exact? He refused to go into too much explanation of how they came up with it or how they used it, but he said that every detail had so far come true.

"Back in 2007," Phillip paused briefly looking each one of them in the eye, "this man had told us that the world had gone beyond the point of return. The snowball effect on climate was well and truly on its way and not only that. It was going to happen very quickly."

"You're kidding!!" said Ahmed. "So they knew? They knew back then, fifteen years before it even happened? They knew of the changes that we would see? That the oceans would definitely rise?"

"More than that," replied Phillip. "Their model was that accurate, that it said that in approximately the next ten to twenty years, the world's oceans would rise by between five to ten metres... and there was nothing, absolutely nothing that we could do about it." Phillip still seemed to be amazed at the revelation he told. He sighed deeply. "This, as you now know, was going to have a devastating effect worldwide. He showed us all the different efforts that could be made to try to stop it, converting to renewables like solar, using nuclear power, reforestation, et cetera et cetera and sadly these efforts did nothing to alleviate it. According to their model, there was absolutely nothing that we could do."

"Surely not! Did you believe him?" asked James.

"No," replied Phillip. "Of course not!! We all thought he was mad, that his model was a ruse. Of our group, Henry and Frank had both had enough and were about to storm out of the room, until Francois spoke up. He addressed us calmly and sombrely. He told us to stay and listen. He promised us that what his guest had said was true. He explained that the guest had come to him with this model twelve months prior and for the past twelve months, every climate prediction, every single one that had been made had come disturbingly and accurately true. Francois was emphatic about it.

"We all sat back down. We all knew Francois well and trusted hm. For him to say that was putting his head on the line. He explained all the events that had happened and how they had followed the model. The guest now had our undivided attention."

"So you all knew?" asked Jenny, bare able to comprehend the confession.

"Yes," said Phillip.

"Why didn't you come to us back then?" asked John in disbelief. "Come back to our delegations? To Frank and me, or at least to Wayne? Tell us what had happened. We all could have worked something out. At least let the world know."

"Really?" asked Phillip, now slightly red eyed. "Do you think this knowledge was useful? Was good?"

"Well..." replied John, somewhat confused with Phillip's response.

Phillip stood up, walked over to the bar and poured himself a whiskey. He slowly ambled back to his chair. "What good would it have done to have everyone know that the world's oceans were going to rise massively and quickly no matter what we did? To know that the pollution put out by our countries over the many decades was going to ruin the world as we knew it? It wouldn't have done any good. Instead it would have ruined all of our economies, far worse than what happened back in the Global Financial Crises. Our governments would have fallen. The world at large would have blamed us, the western countries. There would be hate. There would be retribution. Situations like ISIS would have been far worse and more widespread. Tell the world what was going to happen? No. We couldn't let the people know the truth. We all knew that."

Phillip took a deep breath. He took a sip of his whiskey and sat himself back down. "What we wanted to know was why? Why tell us? Why now?"

Everyone sat on edge, looking at Phillip, waiting for the answer. The rain continued to thunder around them.

"Stability!" said Phillip. "They wanted stability. Their group saw this rapid global change being their greatest risk not only to them, as everyone would blame their companies, but also to global national and financial stability. The guest said that his employers couldn't achieve this on their own. They needed government assistance.

"I asked him what sort of assistance? He explained to us that as there were four things, four stages that needed to happen, and we would be implicitly involved."

Phillip took a sip of his whiskey. "First, they needed a scapegoat. They had devised a plan for that. The idea was to support a new religious cult, one that they could control. A group that, at the right time, would blame people's desertion of God for the global flood and convince the world to follow them. But it had to be convincing enough to convert as many as possible to them. It seemed mad, but it sort of made sense at the same time."

"What do you mean?" asked Ahmed.

"You see, with the rapid massive ocean rise, the world's social order would be on the brink of collapse. Slow rises over many decades… fine. Fast ones? A different matter. Some could consider it divine retribution. We believed that if a massive catastrophic climate event occurred worldwide quickly, different faiths and religious groups would blame the governments and even each other. They would say it was due to our desertion of God and their religion was the way. There would be fights between the groups and eventually they would start warring. Chaos would occur, and eventually a war, a new world war, a climate war would happen. What was needed was something to bring everyone together, to bring a world rule as such, especially to remove the influence of different faiths and leaders. And a popular undeniable religion that would bring in the new climate was the best way to control this problem."

"*Delugion*?" asked Karen.

"Yes… well… sort of. The guest said they were devising plans for a group that would fit the bill. They were monitoring several fledgling religious cults, but if needed, they could create their own. He said that *somehow* this group would pick a similar accurate forecast and if we and his employers helped fund and promote this group, then this group would make sure that our ideals were best maintained. We asked what if this group lost control. The guest said if necessary, his employers could and would destroy the group.

"So did they actually create Clive?" asked James.

"I don't know," said Phillip. "I always had my suspicions, but never really knew for sure if they actually created *Delugion*. Let's just say we have a lot to do with them now. The guest's preference was for us to have no real links to the religion. It was better to have the religious group independent, but easily influenced.

"Francois worked closely with *Them* and Delugion for that matter, but never told me any more than that. We were never told the full dealings. Basically we were told never to ask more than we needed to know, and that worked out well. Plausible deniability is a politician's strongest weapon."

"So what was the second stage?" asked Jenny.

"The second stage was our part," replied Phillip, "and to be honest actually started roughly at the same time as the first stage. The second stage was to delay world climate change mitigation actions. You see, by slowing these actions, we would make sure that the *supplied* predictions to the new religious group occurred sooner than later. More accurate and convenient!

"All they had to do was create general public denial of climate change and that, in a way, was quite easy. The oil and mining companies were well on the way in achieving this through their early efforts. These companies were quite effective. They had learnt a lot about ways of creating denial interestingly from the smoking industry."

Everyone looked slightly confused.

"What do you mean?" asked Karen.

Phillip took another sip of his whiskey. "Throughout the twentieth century, the smoking industry attempted to create doubt about smoking causing lung cancer and other diseases, but they never actually denied it completely because that would backfire. See, doubt was their product. By creating some doubt in people's minds, they created controversy. The idea was that if they could create controversy, then they could delay or derail government anti-smoking policies, and that's what happened in many countries. The smoking industry was very successful. Well, at least for a while.

"So, it was the same theory with climate change, except we had it easy. Instead of some of the population being hooked on smoking, everyone was hooked on carbon through their use of fuels and the supply of cheap electricity. So it was far easier to create doubt in the public's mind. People want it. And human nature is predictable. When you are hooked on something, you are happy to latch onto whatever insignificant article or evidence that may affirm your addiction being good for you. It's known in the psychological circle as cognitive dissonance. Ultimately deep down you know what you're doing is wrong, but regardless you choose to ignore the evidence, and will fight anyone that tells you what you are doing is wrong. No one wants to think that their lifestyle could hurt themselves, let alone cause global calamity.

"And that's what the oil and mining think tanks had been doing, making out that there was some question to the reality of human induced climate change. So for us in that group that night, what we needed to do was to get our governments to go for the least effective easy options in combating climate change. With the artificial doubt already sewn, it would be easy to push for half-hearted measures. The world would happily follow. And most of the public wouldn't even bat an eyelid as we were still seeming to care and fight the global change.

"I asked the guest why ask only our countries? There would need to be more countries involved. It would be far easier and more effective. He said the less people directly involved, the better. His employers had good influence in the Americas. Over there, the political parties are very reliant on donor funding, and hence the oil companies held a lot of sway. His employers just needed more influence over other key regions – Europe, Asia, and Africa. That's where we would be involved as it was seen that our countries had good influence in these regions and his employers trusted us."

Phillip took another swig of his whiskey. He studied the glass for a moment and placed it down on the darkly stained oak table.

"Stage three... Stage three was to let the changes occur and allow the majority of the public blame to fall on God. And that's what happened. *Delugion* by then was being noticed, and when their predictions came true, everyone payed attention. They all saw that this man Clive had predicted these changes pretty much to the date and that apparently God had created it all. Everyone around the world was confused as to what to believe. And so came the rise of Delugion. And by creating that confusion around religion, we in government were safe."

"And stage four?" asked Jenny.

Phillip looked up. "He wouldn't tell us exactly what was going to happen, but would let us know closer to the time. He basically said that it was to conclude the plan, and that would vary depending on what had happened through the other stages."

"But according to Frank's email, stage four is about to happen," stated Jenny.

"I know, and that makes me a bit nervous," replied Phillip.

"Why?"

"Because they still haven't told us what's going to happen!" Phillip's hands started fidgeting at the thought. He grabbed his whiskey and downed the rest.

"So was that it?" asked John.

"No," replied Phillip with a sense of remembered dread.

"Well, what happened next?" asked John.

Phillip continued, "Everyone in the room was quiet. They were all stunned. They really didn't know quite what to say. Frank, your Frank from Australia, then asked the question that everyone else dreaded to ask. Why tell this *only* to us junior ministers?

"The guest's reply horrified us and he did it so coldly. I remember it word for word. He said *'Because it is highly stressful in your first few years in politics. So often you hear of a junior minister committing suicide from the stress of the job. There are also a lot of angry climate change sceptics who have sent death threats at one time or another, and who knows when one might actually carry out their actions, might even target a group or a family. When a senior political figure dies, the country mourns; when a junior politician dies, the country only blinks for a second.'*

"That was our warning. I looked at Francois. He just gave me a terrified nod. Then I remembered that his secretary had committed suicide only months earlier. We all had thought she had been suffering from depression. For that, we were wrong. I wanted to run. I could see my political career crumbling before my very eyes. Everyone around the table had a sense of despair. Francois just looked despondent that he had put us in this horrible situation. Obviously his hand, too, had been forced.

"The guest then said for us not to worry. He would look after us. His organisation would make sure that we would get our dues and move into appropriate areas of our new expertise when the time was needed.

"I asked him who else knew about this. He said no one else in our governments. Influence was all that they needed and that was us.

"It made sense. The first lesson of conspiracy class 101 is the less people know and are involved, the less of a chance of it being found out. Governments leak like a sieve.

"He then said he had to go, but he would be in touch. Henry asked what we should call him and his group. He replied, *Francois introduced me as 'The Guest', and 'The Guest' is what you can call me. As for our group, we preferred to be known as 'Them'. It removes any direct recognition.*

"The guest then left."

CHAPTER 12

THE VIOLENT STORM continued to rumble around the converted barn. Claps of thunder echoed through the heavy wooden eaves as the lights dimly flickered bringing an ominous tone to the evening. The congregation within the confines of the walls were dumbstruck with the revelations that had been given to them, by of all things a balding man dressed in gaudy green and gold.

Jenny stood up and walked to the window staring off into the dark heavy rain. The revelations had given her answers she had been looking for for many years, but it didn't make things easier. She shook her head in disbelief. It confirmed her worst thoughts of what had happened and it scared her of what else had probably occurred. She took a deep breath and tried to calm herself. She knew she needed to be strong.

Phillip walked back over to the bar and poured himself another whiskey. "I've been so rude," he said. "Would anyone else like one?"

"Yes please," replied John wanting something to staunch his nerves. The others declined Phillip's offer. Phillip poured the amber coloured liquid into two antique crystal tumblers and wandered back to the table. He passed John his drink.

John took a small nip of the thirty year old whiskey. It warmed him throughout and gave him a sense of resilience. It bemused John that the whiskey was made in a time when things were a little simpler. John placed the drink down and looked over at Jenny with concern. He had a feeling that she must have been deeply affected by what Phillip had said earlier in some personal way. She had been fairly withdrawn during most of Phillip's confession, and John was sure there was something that Jenny wasn't telling him. Jenny continued to stare out the window refusing to address the rest of the group.

James was slightly on edge, fidgeting which seemingly annoyed Karen. He kept on wanting to speak up, but kept himself quiet. John felt that it must have been on Karen's request as she squeezed James' hand rather firmly several times and John was sure he heard a kick under the table at some stage. Ahmed on the other hand was still laying back on the lounge, deep in thought and remaining fairly quiet.

John turned back to Phillip and decided to lead from where they left off. "So what happened after The Guest left?" asked John.

Phillip looked up at John with a slight look of despondency. "We spoke briefly amongst ourselves," replied Phillip, "and came to the conclusion that we had no choice, but to follow *Them's* plans. Our hands had been rather forced. We also felt that if what he said was true, which Francois reiterated it was, then we must try for global stability rather than to lead efforts to prevent the effects of climate change. We made plans on what we would do next. We needed to work together to get the operation into action. We also vowed to keep it all secret, because if anyone found out, it would be the downfall of us all. It seemed a mammoth task, but we knew it was possible… certainly with strings being pulled at both ends."

"And that was Operation Warmth?" asked John.

"Yes," replied Phillip. "That is what it became known as amongst our group."

John couldn't believe his ears. This was betrayal. This was treason. His heart pounded in anger as the confessions of what had happened started to flow out of Phillip's mouth.

"So we came up with the idea that we would tell our own country's delegates that secretly each of the other countries were planning to pull back on their climate initiatives. We knew that it would put a dampener on each of our own country's plans. Our head ministers would then do the same, pull back, so as not to be seen as the frontrunner to their voters. It is seen as to be brave but foolish to be a leader, and no government wants that."

John could not hold himself back any longer. "But how could you destroy all the efforts that we had worked so hard for, for so long? You could have brought the new information to us. We could have fought for harder measures, better anti-greenhouse schemes and especially now with even better evidence. The world would act. We would have got you protection! It was never too late!"

"Yes it was, John," replied Phillip. "Don't you understand? We were well past the point of return. We were too late. We needed to prepare for the future. The world couldn't be saved. Wasn't it one of your ex-prime ministers who said *'Only the impotent are pure'*?"

"Yes. He was referring to internal politics and wrangling of the party," responded John, quite surly. "Make your point."

"You should listen to him. He had a point. If we were pure... If we all stood flat footed, not willing to compromise, not willing to see the true picture, we would have got nowhere. You know that, I know that. To try in vain to combat global warming whilst doing nothing to prepare for the years ahead, we would have faced a much worse disaster and world disorder than what we did – social unrest, global upheaval, climate wars. These were real and scary prospects. We weren't going to stand back. We needed to act!!"

John dropped his shoulders in a stark realisation. Phillip had hit a nerve.

"You've mentioned them before. What do you mean by 'climate wars'?" asked Ahmed slightly confused.

John was very familiar with the concept. He thought he'd better explain. "It was something that everyone in government feared," said John, "that is, those who actually believed in the reality of climate change. The fear amongst us, amongst many of our countries, was that with the rising oceans, it would displace people living in the low lying lands."

"Not only that," added Phillip, "we knew it was going to have major effects on fresh water supplies, farming, cropping, liveable land, reefs…"

"Not to mention the great changes in local weather patterns creating in many places catastrophic droughts and floods," continued John.

Ahmed still looked confused and somewhat dubious.

"You see, back then," said John, "we knew that a mere one metre ocean rise would displace roughly a hundred and forty million people, give or take several mill'… and that's no small figure. When you affect people's lives and livelihoods, their neighbours, their families, it creates a lot of political and social pressure eventually leading to instability, and this would happen in many, many countries. I mean, how on earth do you look after all those people?"

"And when people don't trust their governments any more…" said Phillip.

"…it makes them turn to other sources of guidance," added John, "mainly to help them search for the source of their pain. There would be huge pressures!"

"Governments were concerned that people would turn to religion," said Phillip, "especially the extremist side. They had learnt that after the 9/11 terrorist attacks, fundamentalism had strengthened in every global faith, and that was from an event that occurred in only one country."

"But..." protested Karen.

"Yes, I know! There were other factors that then spilled out to the rest of the world, mainly being Iraq, Afghanistan, and Syria, but those events were still small compared to what the effects of the ocean rise would have been. This was beyond a scale that we have ever encountered in history. As John said, a one metre rise was going to displace a hundred and forty million. We knew that an eight metre rise was going to happen. This was going to displace six hundred million. That is one out of every twenty people worldwide was going to have to evacuate. In the first world, its bad, but in the third world, this was catastrophic."

"That's an understatement," muttered Karen under her breath.

John thought of the ramifications at the time. It made him shudder.

Phillip took a sip of his whisky. "Our small group in that room had the knowledge. We knew that six hundred million were going to be made homeless in a relatively short period of time. Forget the religious aspects for a moment, though that is part of it. We knew that civil and border conflicts were going to happen. We knew that the world order was on the brink of collapse with just the sheer upscale of refugees. So we realised ... We needed to prioritise. We needed to face the fact that changing our actions was not going to prevent ocean rises. Our efforts needed to focus on ensuring the new world order instead. How to explain it to everyone that would allow the world to remain at peace."

"So what you're saying is that you guys and *Delugion* saved us?" asked Ahmed.

"In a way, yes!!" said Phillip calmly.

Ahmed was amazed. He shook his head in disbelief. "But you could have forewarned all of those nations that were devastated by floods and tsunamis – Indonesia, Sri Lanka, the Maldives... Millions of lives could have been saved," he said.

"Well, we knew that these events in general were coming," replied Phillip, "but not exactly when. We, at the meeting, thought it would be gradual, and nations could save their own people. Maybe *Them...*" Phillip paused in thought. "Maybe *Them* had deeper more accurate knowledge. I don't know... but we certainly didn't have that level of knowledge. Our own scientists never even predicted anything even close to that highly accurate model that we saw at that meeting. In any case, many millions more would have died in worldwide conflict if we didn't go ahead with the plan."

"And the destruction and depletion of all those religions by *Delugion's* consumption – Islam, Judaism... even fucking atheism?" asked Ahmed.

"Necessary victims, I guess," replied Phillip. "We didn't take the decision lightly."

"That's bullshit," muttered Ahmed under his breath.

"Ahmed, enough!!" interrupted Jenny. She glared at Ahmed as she returned back from the window and took her seat again. Her demeanour had hardened and she looked more in a business frame of mind. "Okay, Phillip. So what happened afterwards?"

Phillip looked slightly taken aback by the firmness of Jenny's control of the room. He took a deep breath and, not wanting to be ruffled by Jenny's presence, continued with a slight jab. "Well, *my dear*, our plan worked like a charm. The next morning I went to Wayne first thing. I told him how we discovered that the other countries were getting cold feet and that they had decided to pull back on their efforts in tackling global warming. I told him if our country was to keep going as we were, we would be seen as a clear frontrunner, a pioneer, but we may be left out in the cold. It was incredible, the effect. Wayne went white as a feather. The British elections were coming up and he didn't want our party to be seen as a 'pioneer', especially without anyone or any other country to follow him.

"So, Wayne didn't push as hard in the later Copenhagen meetings, and was a little more lax than he had originally planned to be. And the final outcome, was the Copenhagen Accord that came to fruition. That 'Accord', as you know, frankly meant nothing. Publicly Wayne was very disappointed, but privately, Wayne was thankful that his government didn't make itself out to be a patsy to the British general public."

Phillip studied his whiskey glass slowly before taking another sip.

"The others from the white room meeting had similar experiences, except for the antipodeans, the Australians, who were a little more obstinate, but I understand that Frank did try quite hard to quell down his government's actions. In fact, there had to be a little *outside* interference from what I understand.

"John, wasn't it only later in the following year, that your prime minister was ousted by members of his own party for being, I believe, a little too belligerent?"

"Yes," replied John.

"Well, there might have been a bit of pushing from vested interests, from what I hear," said Phillip.

"Hmmm," said John dubiously. "It was a bit of a sudden change, but I find it hard to believe that *Them* ousted our Prime Minister. The change was hardly surprising given the level of discontent from within the party."

"And who do you think sewed that discontent? Let's just say various disgruntled Australian business individuals known to *Them* may have been encouraged to make their feelings known to your political party. And from what I understand, it was quite easy to get the ball rolling."

John glared at Phillip, uneasy at the inference.

"So, we managed to keep global efforts in controlling climate change restricted as time went on," said Phillip. "It was fairly easy. The Rio Summit was a flop, Doha Climate Change Conference was a nice white elephant, and the rest followed suit."

"Over the next few years, stages one and two were well on their way. We saw the rise of Clive, and were asked to help fund him during his ascent. We were very creative in how we did it. The various members of our meeting in conjunction with *Them* helped create false charities and we got our governments to fund these organisations. These charities would then siphon money to the DF. *Them* made sure the trail was quite complex, by creating a web of interlinked organisations. That way the funding could never be traced back. Our UK government never questioned anything, and the general public had no idea.

"Over the years, the global financial crisis made its impact. Thankfully it had slowed any political will or public impetus to make any massive improvements in combating climate change. The GFC really was quite opportune for *Them*, especially with its timing, but I won't go into my own personal theories on how that might have been created. But because of the crisis, Governments were lobbied by big business to focus more on saving the economy and taking advantage of growing markets such as India and China, than looking at the environment.

"So basically, the green movements worldwide stagnated. We were successful."

Phillip took another swig of whiskey. The rain continued to pound incessantly in the dark reaches of the outside world.

"How many people are in *Them*? How many are involved?" asked Karen.

"In our government, it's still just myself and will only be myself," replied Phillip. "As I mentioned earlier, the first rule of keeping secrets in government, is to not tell anyone in government your secret. And the UK is no different. There are also the others that were at the meeting. As for the rest of the organisation, *Them*? I have no idea."

"And you're definite there is no one else in the government?

"Absolutely. I would know."

Karen seemed dissatisfied with Phillip's answer.

"So what else happened?" asked John.

"From then on, it was quite simple. Yes, all of our governments changed at some point, and we even lost power. That's the nature of politics. *Them* contacted us in their various ways and they assured us that they had everything under control and told us just to sit back for a few years, and we would be duly rewarded.

"Reward!!!" Phillip laughed at the word, "Our lives have been tied to this set of events without our choice. I couldn't really call it a reward.

"Well, before the great global changes occurred, all of our parties were conveniently reinstated into power, and we were made head ministers for climate change for our various countries. Our so-called reward! And then, stage three started.

"The floods, earthquakes, ocean rises and so on matched exactly to what the model had predicted. It was uncanny and deeply disturbing. As people perished, I began to hate myself more and more for what I had joined and for what I now stood for. I had to remind myself constantly it was for the greater good..."

Phillip pondered the thought, "...for the greater good. Interesting how we need to convince ourselves what we do is right when we do something so wrong, but I digress. The religion of *Delugion* grew in power, and they supported our governments as was predicted. Nevertheless, occasionally blips occurred that had to be ironed out."

"What do you mean, blips?" asked James.

"Well the blips varied. They we're often scientists coming close to solving what happened climate-wise, people trying to infiltrate *Them*, reporters questioning too hard, and so on. From what I understand, John's dear wife was thought to be a possible leak and was killed, and they must have thought that you John now was their mole too. I guess this time they really wanted to make sure that you were definitely the leak, especially since they frankly stuffed up in their certainty with Rebecca's role. They probably wanted to find out who else knew. They would be especially concerned as we are soon going into stage four. Sadly, Frank must have been seen as too much of a liability at that point and they killed him. Tragic really!!"

"Hang on," said James rising out of his chair. "Let's just go back a moment. You said that scientists coming close to solving what happened?"

Karen gently grabbed his arm.

"Yes. The biggest example here was when some scientists in East Anglia did research that was going to show the true reason for global warming – mankind. This would've discredited *Delugion* completely. We had been monitoring the research progress and were concerned about the outcome. So I let *Them* know as it could have derailed our plans. It would have destroyed all of our work. *Them* said that they would take care of things."

Phillip chuckled to himself. "The poor buggers didn't know what hit them. Their research was discredited, their lives were laid out to bare, and they eventually disappeared after the ongoing embarrassment."

"That was us!!" said James. He was shaking with anger. Phillip looked shocked. James launched across the table and swung a right hook at Phillip's jaw. The punch wasn't very well controlled and only clipped Phillip's cheek bone, enough to knock him backwards on his chair. James stumbled and landed on top of Phillip cracking his eyebrow on top of the chair. Blood started pouring down James' face. He regained control and went to strike Phillip again.

Phillip, who was now lying on the floor, pushed him back.

"For fuck's sake, get him off!!" yelled Phillip.

Karen and Ahmed dragged James back and restrained him as he tried to lunge at Phillip again. Karen started yelling at James to get some control. Jenny rushed over ordering James to settle and for Karen to calm down.

As the commotion ensued, John helped Phillip out of his chair and stood him up. The others were still arguing. As he pulled Phillip to his feet, Phillip whispered in John's ear, "I don't know what you've got yourself into my friend, but a word of advice. Be careful of that Jenny. She isn't quite so innocent or nice. She was the one who bombed the Mining convention."

"Why should I trust you?" asked John.

"Because I have no reason to lie to you anymore."

"You sure she did it?" John whispered back.

"Absolutely. It wasn't us or *Them* who did it. *Them* actually wanted information from us as to who could have done it. They wanted revenge. Some of their own were apparently killed."

Jenny turned around and apologised to Phillip for James' actions. Karen was putting pressure on James' eyebrow whilst Ahmed continued to hold onto his shoulder in restraint.

"Sorry, you probably didn't realise, but it was James and Karen's work that you seemingly discredited," explained Jenny.

"Why are you fucking apologising to him?" growled James.

"Shut it!" retorted Jenny.

"No, no, Jenny. Please, let me apologise," replied Phillip. He looked completely remorseful. "Your work, James and Karen, was truly amazing and I am very proud that Britain would have led the scientific world with it. Unfortunately, my hands were tied. We had to do what we did... I guess... what I got them to do, otherwise *Them* would have tried to kill you."

"They did try and kill us. They tried to kill us in a fucking accident with a lorry," yelled James. "The driver fucked up and got himself killed instead. I saw the proof on the driver. I know that he was after us."

Phillip looked shocked. "Then I'm deeply sorry. I never wanted any deaths to happen on my watch. I know that there is nothing I can do to make things right, but I will help in whatever way I can. In any case, let me get some ice for your eyebrow. I will definitely need some for my cheek."

James looked like a petulant child, forced to shake someone's hand. With Karen glaring, he eventually agreed and wandered towards the kitchen with Phillip. He kept the pressure on his eyebrow.

"Nice hook," said Phillip as they wandered out.

"Thanks. I don't fight much," replied James. "I always thought I'd be alright. I should've tried out for kick-boxing. It always looks like a good laugh."

They disappeared through the wooden archway

"He's never hit anyone before at all," said Karen once they were out of earshot. "I could've laid a better shot. With his coordination, he's lucky he didn't knock himself out."

They all laughed. The tension in the room was starting to settle. Ahmed picked up the fallen chair, and set it right. Jenny and Karen quietly chatted to each other about the night's conversation. John went to sit back down, when the lights suddenly went out with a flash of lightning.

CHAPTER 13

THE LARGE STONE construct of the room was engulfed in darkness as the power failed to return. Besides the sound of clattering raindrops, silence extended throughout the vast emptiness. The occasional lightning flash lit up the surrounds, giving a brief glimpse of what once was.

"Shit! Just our luck! A blackout," said John.

"Karen? Ahmed?" asked Jenny with a sense of urgency.

"Yeah. I'm checking on it. Hold on," replied Karen in a heavy whisper. "Shit. The neighbour's lights are still on."

"Get him hidden," said Ahmed.

There were three muffled cracks. Jenny grabbed John's hand and whisked him away through a door into a small room off the side of the grand dining room.

The room they entered was dark and covered in tiles that were cool to the touch. There were several cupboards that jutted out and John could feel the smooth edge of what he made out was a sink.

Must be the bathroom, thought John.

Jenny closed the door partially, and kept her eye out on the events unfolding.

"What's happening?" whispered John.

"I don't know, but I don't like it," replied Jenny.

"Jooohhnnnnnyyyy!!! Jooohhhhnnnnyyyy!!!" a deep Scottish voice sounded in the distance. A cold shiver travelled down John's spine. "Come out, come out, wherever you are."

John's heart started to race. He recognised the voice. It was the same person that had shot Frank and had abducted him onto the plane.

"We were so disappointed that you left us, Johnny boy." The voice was starting to come closer. "Obviously our uncomfortable seats and shite in-flight service didn't suit your likes. It's not nice to walk out on your hosts. Very uncouth."

John was sweating. He looked around the room he was in and even though his eyes were starting to adjust to the darkness, he couldn't see much. Lightning briefly lit up the room.

John's heart wrenched. He realised he was in a dead end. The bathroom he was in consisted of a shower, a toilet, a sink and mirror, and a small window just large enough to put a fist through. There was no way out except into the arms of his prior captors. He was trapped. There was nothing he could do.

"Jooohhhnnnnnyyyy!!!!" the Scottish voice continued, "You cannot escape us, my friend. We know your every thought, your every move."

"They're bluffing," whispered Jenny. She pulled out a gun and rested it in her hands at the ready.

"You see Johnny boy, we're smarter than you. Mind you, a lobotomised monkey that had to take self-help classes in peeling bananas would be smarter than you. We have eyes and ears everywhere. When you used your phone at the shopping centre, now that was a stroke of genius. What were you thinking? *Oh dear, I'm on the run. I better check my message bank. That won't alert the people after me.* Idiot!"

Jenny turned and looked at John with a sense of incomprehension and betrayal. John felt his throat clench up.

"You know? I thought your best message was the one from, who was it? Yes... Now I remember... Scarlet, that harlot secretary of yours... very pretty... very caring, especially when she said *Be Strong, Be Safe.* Very moving Johnny. I almost shed a tear. I'd be very surprised if you haven't shagged her by the way she talked to you on the phone. You know you are very silly to stay on the phone Johnny boy. Let me see, you'd been on the phone for what... five minutes and yet you still kept on listening. Then after our brief conversation, you luckily, if not by chance, managed to evade us."

The taunting paused for a moment. Silence continued to pervade the house, only interrupted by the slight creak of a floorboard.

"You know, you almost lost us there, at Taunton. But then you showed us your complete stupidity once again. It didn't take us long to work out which little vehicle was yours. You see, if you're trying to conceal yourself whilst being observed by satellite, it's not very smart to leave from the side of the van and then when you return, to get into the driver's seat, and especially when there's no one else coming in or out of the van. And who's bright idea was to use an open air car park."

Jenny looked at John with a slight sense of guilt. She had realised her error and had hoped that her mistake wouldn't have been so apparent.

Oh fuck!! How do we escape that? thought John. John felt sick with all the revelations the gunman was making. His breathing started to quicken.

"What did you think we would believe? *Oh I can't get out of the driver's seat. It's too obvious. No… Instead I will leave through the back door. That will throw them off.* I'm sorry but are you that dopey that they confused you with one of Snow White's dwarves. No, my mistake, you were too thick for the part. A fucking koala which had been hit by a car and could no longer climb trees would have been smarter than you, and I'm giving you credit."

The voice was getting closer.

"After that, following the van was rather like following ants to the nest… quite tedious, but really not that hard. The question is… how many ants are there? We've already squashed two. And just to let you know, you really shouldn't have murdered the British Secretary of State. Shot in the throat, and then the chest…. a very similar M.O. to your other murder.

The voice was now in the next room.

"Johnny boy, the way you shot your victims, you're not a great aim. It did seem to be quite a slow distressing death. And you're really turning into quite the serial hit man now. As for your other friend… his death was a little quicker. It's a pity that part of his head is now missing."

There was a brief muffled female cry. Some shots fired.

"Go after her…" the Scottish voice ordered with a heavy whisper. John heard one set of footsteps running off. The Scottish man was achieving his aim, flushing them out one by one. The Scottish voice was now closer, not too far from the door.

"Come on Johnny Boy. You are making this harder than it should be."

The footsteps were coming closer… *hang on… only one set…*

Jenny charged through the door and fired her gun three times. Several shots fired in another room, then silence. John peeked around the corner and saw the tall masked figure of Ahmed hiding in one corner and Jenny hiding in the other corner of the room. They both had their guns aimed at the grand table that they had just been sitting at. There was a brief period of silence.

Suddenly, several shots fired at both windows from under the table causing the glass to shatter and fall away. Rain continued to thunder even louder from outside. It started to splash onto the window sill spilling into the room. Shots rang out from under the table towards Ahmed and Jenny. They both took cover behind the stone pylons and a tall figure raced out from under the table continuing to fire shots. The tall figure backed off towards the demolished windows and jumped out into the darkness of the night.

Ahmed fired twice in the direction, but to no avail. He kept his gun aimed clearly at the broken window frames and signalled for John and Jenny to come through. He repeated his fire as they ran past into the corridor leading to the kitchen where James and Phillip had been.

The kitchen was slightly lighter due to the one street light glaring in the distance. It gently lit up the room through the rain streaked glass walls. The back door remained slightly ajar. Towards one side of the room near the kitchen bench lay three bodies. Karen was leaning over one figure kicking it several times and punching it. "Fuck you, you fucking bastard!!!" she screamed. "Why? Why?" She pulled out her gun and shot the figure twice in the chest. The figure froze and then slumped for one final moment. Jenny tried to pull Karen away. John came over to give a hand.

"No! Fuck off you arsehole," screamed Karen as she pushed John away. "Stand back! Get away from me! This was all your fucking fault! Your fucking stupidity gave our fucking position away."

John stood back. He let Karen get past and looked over to Jenny with an element of helplessness. He never wanted this. He felt a deep sense of guilt and shame. Jenny walked over and gently held Karen.

"Karen. Think about it," said Jenny. "This is exactly what *Them* wanted us to think happened. They've lied about so much. It's all a ruse. They're trying to split us up, trying to get us to turn on John and abandon him."

Karen paused and looked suspiciously at John.

"You reckon?" sniffed Karen.

"Absolutely," replied Jenny.

"Yeah, for sure Karen," said Ahmed affirming Jenny's view.

Karen nodded sadly. She walked over and knelt next to James' body. She gently caressed his hair and started to cry a deep and painful cry. Karen looked pitiful and broken as she came to terms with what had just happened.

Jenny, realising that they couldn't stay, pulled aside Ahmed to discuss their plans.

John felt helpless and sick. Both Phillip and James lay dead on the floor, along with one of the gunmen that had been after him. John felt responsible, but out of his league. It was a situation he never wanted to experience.

"Oh my James. My one, my beautiful, my love," sobbed Karen. "I'm so sorry. I wish I could have protected you. Don't go... don't go...." She kissed him gently on the lips and burst again into tears.

The rain was starting to ease and soon only the sound of water cascading down the pipes echoed from the garden outside. The plants' leaves gently rustled as a slight breeze whipped through them. The door out to the garden bumped gently with the wind startling John for a brief moment.

"You're sure there was only two," asked Jenny.

"Absolutely," replied Ahmed. "I reckon that's why he was so vocal. ...trying to bluff and intimidate us. Either that or he's extremely arrogant."

"Well..."

"I don't think he knew how many of us there were. I don't think he'll show his head again, at least not in the near future."

"Okay," said Jenny. "Regardless, we still don't know where he is right now, and I'm not going to risk any more of our lives."

Jenny turned and looked over to Karen. Karen was still clinging to James' limp body.

"Karen, it's time to go," said Jenny softly.

Karen gave James one last longing hug, kissed him on the lips and reluctantly left him behind. She walked over to Jenny, who gave her a gentle hug.

The four carefully walked through the open door of the glass covered room into the vast realm outside. They passed through the small garden and headed towards the van. Ahmed and Jenny kept their guns out at the ready, watching and monitoring every movement, every rustle of every leaf. The rain had now turned into a gentle drizzle which created a foggy haze to their surrounds. It blocked their general view of anything beyond a mere ten metres.

As they approached the tall stone arcades of the aqueduct, John was confronted by the sight of a large dark green four wheel drive parked right next to their van. John realised it was the same one from the shopping centre.

Karen quickly pulled down her night vision glasses. "I can't see anyone," she said with a sniffle.

"I can't imagine that they would have left anyone behind in their car," said Ahmed. "Still, let's not take any chances."

John watched as Karen and Ahmed slowly, but tactfully approached the four wheel drive with their guns poised. Jenny stayed with John to make sure he was protected. Karen and Ahmed were using the group's van as a cover whilst they checked for any signs of movement within the four wheel drive.

John looked back at the house. It looked eerily quiet through the mist, devoid of all that had occurred earlier. He wondered where the gunman was.

Karen and Ahmed signalled for them to come up. They were satisfied that no one was in the car. They quickly opened it up and searched through the vehicle whilst Jenny and John made their way towards them. It was all clear. John and Jenny soon caught up with the other two in between the two vehicles.

"Absolutely nothing," said Ahmed. "It was open. No one's in there. It's completely empty."

"How do we know it's theirs?" asked John.

"We don't," said Ahmed. "But it's a bloody big coincidence. My feeling is we take it and dump it. It should slow down their response somewhat and buy us some more time to get away. The darkness and cloud cover should also give us good protection from satellite tracking. It will make things a lot harder for them."

"Okay, fair plan," said Jenny. "Karen, can you get it started?"

"Yes," replied Karen. She wiped her face with her glove and then pulled a small flat metal rod device from a satchel. The object looked like an overly endowed screw driver. Behind the brass metal shaft, it had a thick plastic handle with various wheels and buttons. As Karen got into the driver's seat, she pressed one button and an amber colour LED lit up on the handle. She drove it into the car's ignition key slot and twisted the wheels on the handle until it lined up into a certain defined pattern. After a few seconds, the amber light turned green. Karen pressed a button and turned the device to start the car. It hummed to life.

"Karen, I'll get Ahmed to drive the four wheel drive," said Jenny.

"But..." protested Karen.

"But nothing!" replied Jenny with a stern facade. "Look, you've just lost James. I am finding it hard enough myself and can only barely imagine what you're going through."

Karen sat back in the driver's seat and nodded with a reluctant sadness. She got out of the car and let Ahmed take the wheel.

The faint wail of sirens sounded in the distance.

"Okay. We've got to go now," said Jenny. "Ahmed, we'll stick to the main plan, and do our usual vehicle swap."

"Yep. See you soon," said Ahmed.

"Your usual vehicle swap?" asked John.

"Get in. I'll explain later," replied Jenny.

John felt the evening's events were not quite over.

CHAPTER 14

JENNY, KAREN AND John loaded themselves into the van as Ahmed took off alone in the dark green four wheel drive down the empty street. Jenny took the van's driver's seat with John by her side. Karen crawled into the back and rested her head glumly into her hands.

Jenny started the van and drove carefully away. There was no sign yet of the police.

John was still in slight shock over the night's events, but there was one thing that puzzled him... the gunman. The gunman had not approached them during the whole time they had made their escape from the house. They had been left alone. It disturbed him despite what Ahmed had said.

"Why didn't the Scotsman come after us?" asked John. "He had ample opportunity."

"*Them* don't want to leave any evidence of themselves anywhere," replied Jenny. "Whenever *Them* are involved in altercations, they either remove or create a plausible case for the evidence left behind. It's how they have survived so long without being noticed. They need to divert any interest and remove any connections to themselves or any of their members."

"So what are you saying?"

"*Them*, I guess more specifically the Scotsman right now, is dealing with the three bodies and all the incidentals. If it wasn't for the fact that we killed one of his men and we had a big gunfight against him, he would more than likely just leave it all and allow us to take the blame. Who's to say that the gun that shot and killed James and Phillip wasn't from us?"

Karen looked up only briefly at the mention of James. She rested her head against the rain streaked van window and started sobbing quietly. Jenny looked back at her with a sense of guilt. She continued in a softer tone. "The real problem for *Them* is that we killed one of their men. The Scotsman now has to explain why his man was in the building and who that man was. Even if he took him away, the blood and DNA evidence would be too hard to explain anyway.

"It appears that invisibility for *Them* is still more important than capturing someone like yourself, which is good for us. Ultimately, I guess, it is self preservation for them."

"So what will they do?" asked John.

"Who knows?" replied Jenny. "I've seen some disgusting things happen to hide certain inconvenient events. Thankfully, it looks like one of Phillip's neighbours must have called the police. So the Scotsman's got a very short time to sort things out. One thing for sure, you can be guaranteed that the true set of events will never see the light of day."

John contemplated the scenario. *That's awful*, he thought. He looked back at Karen. He felt sorry for her by what she had gone through and especially now with the thought of what they might do to James' body. Tears were streaming down her face. She looked completely dishevelled. She had ripped her mask and goggles off which lay strewn across the seat, and she was tucked up in the foetal position. She looked a shell of her former confident self.

"So, what now?" asked John.

"Well, they've probably got a tracker on this van now," replied Jenny.

"What?? And we're still driving this thing?" said John incredulously. "Why the hell didn't we all go into the other vehicle?"

"Well, that's probably got one too."

"So what are we going to do?" asked John.

"Hold on," said Jenny. She slowed down the vehicle as she spotted Ahmed on a corner. He was all alone having abandoned his vehicle. She briefly stopped as he quickly jumped into the back.

"Thanks Jen," said Ahmed. He shifted Karen's gear off the seat, and gave Karen a comforting squeeze on the shoulder. Karen gave Ahmed a fleeting appreciative smile.

"All sorted," he said. "Left the four-wheeler in an underground car park. It should be hard for them to track and find, even with the newer tracking beacons."

"Good," replied Jenny.

"You know that they've probably got this van tracked too?" said Ahmed.

"Yeah. We were just discussing it," replied Jenny. "So, did you call Kat?"

"Yeah. I've got that all sorted. Kat's waiting in her vehicle around the corner up further. Drop me off at the third set of traffic lights ahead. Apparently it's clear of any cameras. And for that matter, so is the fifth, ninth and twelfth set. We'll meet up at each one."

"Okay. No problem."

Jenny continued driving along the main road as the third set of traffic lights quickly loomed. She briefly stopped as Ahmed Jumped out of the van and ran off down the side street.

"Kat?" asked John, curious in the turn of events.

"Yeah. A friend of ours," replied Jenny. "Thankfully, she's letting us use her place to crash and she's also lending us her car to get us out. We're dumping the van... I'm sorry Karen. I know it was James' favourite. You understand?"

Karen nodded her head and quietly burst into tears. Jenny briefly closed her eyes in shame. Everything that had been James was being removed from Karen's grasp.

Jenny spoke softer. "We need to dump this van real soon, otherwise we'll be in the shit again. Once we're in the safe house, we can relax."

"Why don't we just steal a car now with Karen's gadget?" asked John.

"We don't want anyone to report a stolen car. They'll know it's us. Numberplate recognition software will track us, there's also RFID trackers and there's the risk of the immobiliser cutting the car out. Better we use a car that we have permission to use, that no one else knows we have. Okay we're coming up to the fifth set. We'll have to move fast at the lights. Just do what I tell you."

Jenny gave them orders as the fifth set of traffic lights loomed. Jenny slowed the van to a crawl, signalling as if to pretend she was looking for a park. Two angry motorists fired their horns as they drove past. They looked into the driver's window, and shook their heads in a confirmed anger, determined that they were right on the presumption of the driver's ethnicity, sex or age. Jenny turned off the indicator as she stopped the van at the red traffic lights.

Almost immediately a white utility truck pulled up next to them. The driver briefly sounded the horn. Jenny looked across and saw Kat and Ahmed inside. Ahmed had the wheel.

"Okay it's a truck," she said in surprise. "It will do. Alright guys!! Start unloading."

Karen and John jumped out and threw several bags from the back of the van into the rear of the truck. The bags were bulky and heavy. They could only take one at a time and it took them a few trips to get them into the back.

"Cars coming!!" yelled Jenny. "Get in!"

Karen and John both jumped into the back seats and slid the door closed. Three cars came up from behind as the lights turned green. Jenny started driving off.

Karen stared out at the passing cars, hoping in vain to identify the Scotsman to exact some revenge. She fidgeted at her holster. Ahmed meanwhile drove the utility truck down a side street and disappeared out of sight. Karen sat back down disappointed that the cars had random strangers inside.

"Two more lights," mumbled Jenny to herself. "I better not go too fast."

She slowly accelerated the van with a jerk to give the impression it was having engine trouble. The other vehicles impatiently overtook the van and sped off into the distance.

"So why all this effort?" asked John.

"We can't let *Them* know where we changed vehicles," said Jenny, "otherwise it will be too easy to track who was around from Kat's immobiliser, if she's still got one. It's best for *Them* to think we dumped the car and got into a nearby one. They won't suspect we changed cars halfway. As long as we don't stop too long at one place, we'll be fine, otherwise it could give away our position too."

At the sixth set of traffic, the white utility appeared from the side street and joined up in tandem alongside the van.

"Okay guys. Last effort!" said Jenny. "I'll see you at the twelfth set."

"See you then," said Karen.

The two vehicles stopped at the lights. Karen and John quickly jumped out and started putting in the last items. Karen grabbed her mask and goggles and anything that might help easily identify their presence in the van from the front and middle seats. The lights turned green. They closed the doors and ran to the utility.

"Quick, get in!" yelled Ahmed. "There're more cars coming. We don't want any suspicion raised about us. The last thing we need is some arsehole ringing the terrorist hotline about people dressed in black moving bags and jumping from one car to another at night. It's not like it's suspicious or anything!"

"Alright Ahmed, settle down!" said Kat. "They're in. You don't have to be a dickhead!"

"I'm sorry. I just want to be safe. That's all," said Ahmed. "We've had enough shit today. I don't think I could put up with any more."

It appeared to John that there was more between Kat and Ahmed than just being friends. Ahmed once again turned the truck down a side street whilst Jenny veered off in the opposite direction.

"We're just going to do a little tour whilst Jenny drops off the van," said Ahmed. "We'll head up to the last meeting point in exactly five minutes and pick her up there. So far, so good. Oh... umm... Karen, John.... this is Kat. She's an old mate of mine, lives in the area."

"That's nice Ahmed," said Kat. "...*lives in the area*. God, you're an arse sometimes. My name's Katrina, but please do call me Kat."

"Nice to meet you," said John.

"Me too," said Karen.

"Nice to meet you both," replied Kat. "Probably would have been better in nicer circumstances, but you can't always have it that way. Ahmed told me what happened to your partner, Karen. I'm so very sorry."

"Thank you," replied Karen meekly.

The truck wandered through the rain soaked streets of the outskirts of the small town of Cricklade as the radio emanated songs from yesteryear. Small causeways were flooded in ankle deep water and were slowly draining away. The side streets were fairly empty as everyone had put themselves away in their cosy homes for the night to get out of the heavy spring storm. After only a few minutes, Ahmed turned the truck back to where they were to meet and approached the intersection. Several cars passed by as he waited at the lights.

"Where's Jenny?" said Ahmed impatiently. "She should be here by now."

"We'll have to wait," said Karen.

"We can't risk it," replied Ahmed.

They all looked around the intersection. It was empty. There were no people, there was no life, just various offices and shops lit up for the night.

"Where the fuck are you, Jenny?" Ahmed rapped his fingers on the steering wheel.

"Are you sure you're at the right traffic lights?" asked Karen.

"Absolutely! She should have been here by now. Something's gone wrong."

"But..."

"No buts. We're putting ourselves in danger right now just by being here. We need to stick to the plan. I hate to say it, but either Jenny's dead, captured or been heavily delayed for some god unknown reason. She wouldn't want us to wait and risk ourselves."

"But..." said Karen.

"Karen, I don't like it any better either," said Ahmed. "We've got to go right now."

The lights turned green. Ahmed drove through.

"Can we go back and check again in a moment?" pleaded Karen.

"No," responded Ahmed. "Jenny told me before. She was adamant. We must get you all to safety no matter what, even if she failed to turn up."

"I'm sure she'll be alright," said Katrina trying to comfort Karen. "She's been in worse before."

Karen brought her knees up to her chest. She bit her lip and looked out of the truck in despair. John reached out to touch her on the shoulder, to give her some comfort. She hit his hand away refusing to even look at him.

It was going to be a long night.

CHAPTER 15

John was in a room. He recognised it, but he couldn't quite work out where he was. It was a bedroom. He heard someone sobbing in the corner of the room. She was talking on the phone. It was Scarlet. Of course, he was in Scarlet's bedroom. A window smashed downstairs. He ran over to the bedroom window and looked out. Someone below was trying to wrench the door open. He couldn't quite see them. He turned to Scarlet and yelled for her to run. She didn't hear him. "Be strong, be safe" she said into the phone. She hung up the phone and looked around. She had a look of fear and panic in her face. He went to grab her. She ran past not seeing him. She climbed out of the window with a small knapsack on her back. Someone tried to jam open the bedroom door. Scarlet stood on the edge of the roof. John was now standing next to her. He looked back inside. Someone kept thumping on the bedroom door trying to break it down. He looked back at Scarlet. She was looking at the branch of a tree about six feet away. "No!!" yelled John. She didn't hear him. "Don't be an idiot!" She took three steps back and then made a running leap. Knocking....

There was knocking at the door. John sat up on the couch. It was still dark. He looked at his watch. It was just after 1:30am. Katrina came running down the stairs in her dressing gown and looked through the peephole. She quickly opened the door.

Jenny walked in wet and shivering.

"You okay?" asked Katrina. She walked over to the hallway cupboard and grabbed a towel.

"Where the fuck was Ahmed?" asked Jenny in a mild fury. "He was supposed to fucking pick me up."

Katrina handed Jenny the towel and she started to dry herself.

"We went to the set of lights," Katrina replied as they made their way into the kitchen, "where we were supposed to meet up with you, but you weren't there. Ahmed said that your instructions were that if you weren't there by the time we got there, we were to leave and get everyone to safety."

"Yes. That's right, but I was there. I got there in less than five minutes as we had always planned, at the third set of lights from where we dropped John and Karen off."

"The third set?"

"Yes."

"The third set?" Katrina repeated.

"Why?" Jenny paused. "That fucking bastard!! I'll kill that prick. He got it wrong, didn't he?"

"Um… Yeah. I told him on the phone that the fifth set was safe from where we saw you last, and that's where we were."

"Bloody men!!! They're fucking useless."

Katrina tried to diffuse the situation. "Did you want a cup of tea?" she asked. "You must be freezing."

"That would be great. Thank you," replied Jenny trying to calm herself.

John got up from the couch and wandered into the kitchen. Katrina looked relieved that it wasn't Ahmed. Jenny was sitting by the table drying off her hair, and Katrina had put on the kettle. It was slowly firing up creating a familiar faint whistle. Jenny looked tired and frustrated.

"You poor bugger," said John. "You must be exhausted."

"Yes. Fairly tired," said Jenny curtly.

"Did you want a cup John?" asked Katrina.

"Yeah, that would be great," he replied. "Um.... Sorry... I overheard what happened. I didn't mean to eavesdrop. I've had trouble sleeping and when you're only a corridor away...."

"Oh, don't worry about that. That's okay," replied Katrina. "It's not like we're having a secret women's meeting."

"So what happened to you?" asked John.

"Ahmed, the genius he is, fucked up the rendezvous point. Didn't he?!!" said Jenny. "So when you guys didn't turn up, I thought something must have happened. I risked it and decided to wait another five... ten minutes and still no one came. So I thought I should make my way to Kat's. I didn't want to use my mobile as I had it off, and thought they would track any phone signals in the area from where I dropped the van off. I've had to chuck it just in case. Thank God I've got a spare one."

"Well, then why didn't you catch a cab?" asked John. Katrina handed around the cups of tea.

"I couldn't. Similar problem. All British cabs, Uber drivers and hire cars have GPS trackers on them so the car companies will know where they are at any given time. Apparently it's for their own safety. It's easily hacked from what I've been told. I didn't want to risk giving our position away, or for that matter putting Kat at risk. Any cab in the area would be tracked by *Them* as a precaution. The only safe option really was to walk down here."

Jenny sipped at her tea.

"We've learnt from the past, often the hard way. Anyway, I've calmed down now. Enough about me. How's Karen going?"

"She's still in a mess," replied Katrina. "With James being killed, and you going missing, it's really quite understandable. I gave her something to help her rest properly. If you don't mind, it might be an idea for you to pop into her room later and let her know that you're alright. At least it'll put her mind at ease."

"Absolutely," replied Jenny. "Poor thing. Her and James had been through so much over the years. They were such a great couple. James was a really good guy and for him to go out in such a horrible way... I... I just feel so responsible."

"Jenny, he knew the risks of pursuing these matters," said Katrina. "We all know the dangers that many of us have faced. It's the risk that we all accept."

"I know," said Jenny wracked with guilt. "It doesn't make me feel any better though."

Jenny stared off into the distance, before bringing herself back to the reality of the world with a sip of tea. "How are you going John?" she said. "I know that Phillip was a friend of yours too. It can't be easy."

John thought back to the image of Phillip laying on the black slate floor, dark red blood spreading around the bullet torn neck. The sobs of Karen plaguing his mind as she lay over the corpse of James, hugging him... not letting go....

"Coping... just," said John. "I guess I'm feeling... a bit numb at the moment." John paused. The violence of the night troubled him. "Why did Karen shoot him? I know she was upset, but why shoot him in such a cold way?"

"To be honest, I don't blame her," said Jenny. "These guys have destroyed her love, they have destroyed her life. Wouldn't you do the same if you were in the same position?"

John thought back to the image imprinted in his mind of Rebecca lying prostrate in the morgue. Her fragile body laid out on the table ready for a perverse form of show and tell. He would have moved the world to save her.

"It's just... It's been a bit much really, the past few days. I'm sorry. Don't worry about me. I am coping. I'll be fine."

"You sure?!" said Jenny. She reached out and gave a comforting stroke of his hand. The warm soft touch eased his wandering thoughts.

"Yeah," replied John with an appreciative smile.

Katrina tried to redirect the conversation. "So, Ahmed told me everything that Phillip Cudsworth told you guys. It beggars belief. Do you think what the minister said was all true?"

"I think so," answered Jenny. "As far as I can see, he had no reason to lie, especially with John there."

"I agree," said John. "It all fitted. I think as far as he was concerned, we were his out. Or possibly, his last confessional."

"And he was in it from the start?"

"Yeah," said John. "It seems that both our governments were heavily influenced over the past twenty years. Quite scary really."

"And the *Delugionists*? Do you really think that they were created by *Them*?"

"I don't know," said Jenny. "I'm not entirely sure that they were created by *Them*. It is possible, but at the same time who could control *Delugion*? It's now such a well-entrenched religion. If there appeared to be any sinister hand in it, even just a tiny bit, surely we would know by now."

"For sure," said John. "We had one of our government security agencies check their background thoroughly when *Delugion* reached our shores. We've had our fair share of cults and religious nuts like everyone else, and to be honest, nothing unusual turned up about them. Well... besides the fact that they believe that God is back and likes to speak on TV and the radio."

Jenny cracked a smile as she finished off her tea.

"However, I'm not entirely sure about that so-called model," said John. "It just seems too good to be true."

Jenny stared at her mug in contemplation, and laughed briefly to herself. She placed her mug down. "Anyway guys, sorry to be rude, but I'm absolutely wrecked," she yawned. "I think I might head off to bed and get some sleep. Thank you for the tea Kat."

"You're welcome. I have some cushions and bedding set up in the study. I hope it's comfortable enough for you."

"That will be fine. I really do appreciate it. Thank you for helping us Kat, you're a life saver. We owe you one."

Jenny made her way out of the kitchen. Katrina followed.

"Sleep well John," said Jenny.

"You too. G'night," said John. "I'll see you in the morning."

Jenny and Kat wandered off towards Karen's room. John went back to the couch. Despite all of the day's events, they were still no closer to clearing up matters. John rested his head against the pillow, pulling up his sheets and thought about Rebecca.... Frank.... The mess... It was such a mess that they were in... How could they ever sort things out?

"You Bastards!!"

John sat up. The scream came from the next room. John ran into the lounge room to see what the commotion was.

Karen had the television on and was bawling her eyes out. The British Prime Minister was on screen giving a speech for the morning news.

The people of the United Kingdom are united in grief, said the Prime Minister, *over the heinous act that has been committed upon one of our dear members of parliament, who now is no longer with us.*

This morning I have the saddest of news that the Right Honourable Phillip Cudsworth MP, a member of our cabinet, a dear friend has been murdered in his Cirencester home along with his bodyguard. Phillip Cudsworth was a highly valued member of parliament and we will deeply miss him. I know that I will miss his insightful knowledge and camaraderie. Today, the United Kingdom has lost a faithful servant, a wife has lost her beloved husband and two children have lost their dearest father. I will truly miss you Phillip. May your soul rest in peace.

There was commotion from the press gallery as various questions fired off. During the speech, a text bar had been continuously rolling at the base of the screen. Two sentences stood out that caught John's eye: 'MP murdered: suspects on the run'; 'Muslim extremist terrorist found dead in MP's house.' When the last of the lines rolled past the screen, Karen growled at the television screen in an exasperated frustration. She stood and paced around the room in anger. Jenny,

Katrina and Ahmed came running into the lounge to see what had happened.

I'm sorry, said the Prime Minister as he welled up with tears, *I cannot answer your questions right now. This tragedy personally has been a great shock and has caused immense grief to myself, my family and the British cabinet. I ask that, at this time, you will let us grieve and I will answer any questions in due course. I will hand over today's proceedings to Chief Inspector Anthony Green who will answer any further questions.*

The Chief Inspector stepped up to the podium.

I would like to start by saying that last night's events present a truly tragic situation. I am happy to answer any questions, but you'll have to understand that our investigations are still ongoing, so there are some matters which I cannot and will not discuss.

The reporters started interjecting.

Chief Inspector! Is it true that the Pakistani Muslim eco-terrorist James Thomas was found dead in the minister's house?

Yes he was. Next please?

"He was not fucking Muslim for crying out loud," pleaded Karen to the television. "He is a second generation British born Anglican. His grandparents left Pakistan when they feared for their safety being Christians. For fuck's sake, he fucking celebrates Christmas...."

"We know Karen, we know," replied Ahmed. He gave her a hug as she burst into tears.

Chief Inspector! Another reporter spoke up. *You said that a bodyguard was found dead in the house. Did the minister know that his life was in danger? Is that why he had a bodyguard?*

We are looking into that matter, replied the Chief Inspector. *The body guard is not one of our own. Currently we are trying to determine from*

*which agency the bodyguard came from, so we can at least get in contact
with his family. Hold on a moment.*

There was a brief pause as the chief inspector was handed a note.
He read the material.

*We have identified the bodyguard as coming from a small London
agency and it appears that he has no immediate family.*

The press yelled out over each other. The Chief Inspector pointed
towards the side of the screen.

A voice yelled out. *Chief Inspector! There have been reports that the
minister was tortured? Is this true and if so, what were the reasons for
the attack?*

*I decline to give immediate details of the investigations, but yes there
does appear to be a torture element.*

"Torture?" asked John. "We didn't torture him!"

"They're probably referring to the bruising on Phillip's face,"
replied Jenny. "You know, from James' punch."

"You can't call that torture!"

"I know, but they'll try and make it more dramatic if they can, and
God only knows, with the amount of bullets that were fired, it won't
be hard."

Chief Inspector, Chief Inspector!!

A new line was scrolling at the bottom of the screen: "England
mourns: Minister tortured before being murdered"; "Minister feared
for life before assassination"

Yes, you! replied the Chief Inspector.

Are you looking for any other suspects? spoke an anonymous voice from the television screen.

Currently we are on the lookout for any known acquaintances of James Thomas – Karen Blackstone, Caroline Chiswick, Ahmed Johnson, David Marshall and Jenny Fitzgerald. If seen, please call the police on the number that we have provided to your TV stations, but do not... I repeat, do not approach any of these people as they should be considered extremely dangerous.

I would also like to add on a separate note, there have been sightings in the southwest of a key suspect from an international incident... a mister Jonathon Frankston, who is accused of the recent killing of an Australian Member of Parliament. We are unsure if these killings are related and whether or not he has been in contact with any of our suspects. Nevertheless, he must be considered armed and dangerous and once again if sighted, please call the metropolitan police, and do not approach him.

John looked around the room. Everyone had gone silent and looked worried with the latest information coming out of the press conference.

Will the Government be ramping up security of the cabinet? Continued another from the press gallery.

Jenny turned off the television.

"What do we do?" asked John. "We can't go to the police or ASIO for that matter anymore. They'll all believe that we're working together to kill off government officials."

"Yes. You're right," said Jenny. "With Phillip dead, we lost our witness. It's going to be hard to prove all of our innocence."

"Yeah," said John. "We have nothing." Things were starting to look bleak.

Everyone looked at Jenny for guidance. She thought for a moment, then took a deep breath. She looked at John in earnestness. "We need the source, John," she said. "The one who can help us the most."

John thought about it. She was right. They needed to follow the path.

"Francois?" he asked.

"He's the one we need," said Jenny. "He'll know more than any of the other ministers at the White Room Meeting. He knows the links between the government and *Them*. He knows *The Guest*. He can expose them all and clear our names."

"But..."

"We have no choice John," said Ahmed. "It's no longer just about finding the truth."

"I know," replied John dejectedly. "I know! But I just don't know where he'll be."

"Well that's going to make things a lot more difficult," said Jenny. "Nevertheless, whatever will be, will be. Still, we've got to find him."

Jenny dragged one of their bags from the corner. She reached in and pulled out two tablet computers. Ahmed groaned. Karen looked glum. It looked like they would have to search the 'old fashioned' way – trawling internet sites, Facebook and Twitter.

"Just don't leave an obvious trail," said Jenny. "Don't use any of the key-words we know are risky. I've put in fresh chips in them to scramble their ID. Still, they can only be used once, so don't waste them."

CHAPTER 16

THE DAY HAD dragged on with a smattering of news reports about the previous night's events. The four had confined themselves indoors whilst Katrina had gone to work at her workshop despite it being a Saturday. She said it was necessary with the way the economy was going, and she couldn't close up without causing major discontent. In the meantime, the four had trawled through the internet looking at the fallout of the night's events, gradually realising the worsening position they were all now facing.

John was amazed at how the previous night's events had been manipulated in what seemed to be such a short time. News stories were everywhere telling of the horror of their supposed terrorist activities. There was no escaping it. Images of them appeared throughout various news sites with whatever frowning, gaping or puzzled expressions that could be publicly found.

They never use the glam shots, thought John. *Better to use the most distracted shot possible.* John roused on himself for belittling the seriousness of events. He was deeply concerned.

The group often had the television on in the background in case any updates or newsbreaks occurred indicating the latest situation. A deep expose was supposed to be coming up, and Ahmed was keeping an eye out for it. John continued to search for Francois's whereabouts.

"John, you're not going to find his exact itinerary," said Ahmed.

"I know," replied John, "but you never know for sure."

Karen was lying on the couch just staring into space trying to console her emotions. They hadn't got much out of her that day.

"Hey guys, it's on," said Ahmed drawing their attention to the wide screen television in the softly lit lounge room. They all gathered around, except for Jenny who was in the kitchen busy replying to messages and emails with her various contacts.

"Ahmed!! Do we really have to?" asked Karen looking drawn and tired from her grief.

"You don't have to stay and watch," said Ahmed sympathetically. "I'm only watching it because it will help us know what we need to look out for."

Karen nodded in acceptance and sat up on the couch. She reluctantly looking up at the screen. Karen knew he was right.

'This is a special extended edition of the six o'clock news on BBC1. You're with Candice Clark. Now to our main story. The United Kingdom is in shock after the right honourable Phillip Cudsworth MP and his bodyguard were gunned down last night in the minister's Cirencester summer home. It is believed that members of the fanatical environmental group tERROR are responsible. Adrienne Smith reporting.'

The screen flashed over to a rather petite woman standing on a cobbled street. John recognised the large stone aqueduct in the background. It certainly looked less mystifying in the light.

'Today the British public are mourning,' said the reporter who John now assumed must be Adrienne Smith, *'the untimely death of government minister, the right honourable Phillip Cudsworth MP. Minister Cudsworth was shot dead in his Cirencester home at around 8pm last night allegedly by members of the eco-terrorist group, tERROR.*

The front door opened and Katrina came in carrying several bags of shopping. "Hey guys!!" she said as she waddled past, annoyed that no one was coming to give her a hand.

"Not now!!" said Ahmed. "It's the special!"

"Wha'???"

"I'll explain later."

Katrina placed the bags down and sat next to Karen. The reporter framed on the large flat screen television continued,

'The assassination occurred here, in this sleepy little village in the heart of the Cottswolds. It appears that there was a torrid gun battle inside the minister's house between the gunman and security guard who was only recently hired to protect the minister. The security guard managed to take out one of the terrorists before sadly giving his life in the defence of the minister. The British secretary of state was subsequently tortured and murdered shortly after. Only his neighbours would bear witness to what were to be his last hours.'

'We're from next door,' said a rather dumpish woman at her front doorway. *'It was terrible. There were so many gunshots. And then those horrible, horrible people just walked out and drove away. I was terrified. I've heard that tERROR was involved. I've never liked those eco-groups, they are always so self-righteous and now with all these terrorist events happening everywhere, you never feel safe. I thank God every day that Delugion now steers us in the right direction, as opposed to those useless, worthless scientists. I can only hope that they catch those horrible people soon.'*

Ahmed groaned in annoyance.

"Unfortunately, it's what everyone out there is saying," said Katrina.

"Really?" said Ahmed.

"Really!!"

'And what do we know of these gunmen?' posed Adrienne Smith. 'Well according to police, it is believed that there were five gunmen. One has been definitively identified as James Thomas who died from injuries sustained during the brief battle. James Thomas' notoriety began with the East Anglia Angel-gate affair from which he was found accused of scientific fraud including charges of forgery and bribery, presumably in an attempt to discredit the teachings of Delugion. It is thought that his girlfriend and Angel-gate co-collaborator, Karen Blackstone, a former Sergeant Major of the Israeli Defence Force, was also part of the combat team that attacked the minister's house.

'As for the others, they are believed to be Ahmed Johnson, Jenny Fitzgerald and the Australian fugitive John Frankston. Jenny Fitzgerald, the leader of the London branch of tERROR, was made most infamous after the Paris bombing in 2015. Since then, she and Ahmed Johnson, a former Greenpeace activist, are responsible for countless eco-terror operations.

'The group are believed to have most recently helped get John Frankston into the country, who is wanted for the murder of Australian government minister Frank Tsoukalos which occurred only four days ago. It has been hypothesised that tERROR has an agenda to seek action on the environment ministers. Why these two countries? The reasons are yet unknown.

'Questions have been asked. Why was there so little protection for the secretary of state if he thought his life was in danger? How did such a lapse in security occur to allow an alleged but wanted murderer enter this country? Is this the end of a series of tragic events, or can we expect more?

'We put these questions to the British Home Secretary.'

A man in a blue tweed suit appeared on screen.

'Home Secretary, thank you for giving us the time to talk about the tragic set of events of the past twenty-four hours. We understand that you are extremely busy, especially in the light of the yesterday's events.'

'Thank you,' replied the Home Secretary. 'I would like to first start by saying that we are deeply saddened by the death of one of our most beloved ministers. Our hearts go out to his wife and children. The prime minister *and cabinet are inconsolable. Phillip was a personal friend of mine, and to lose him in such a horrid way, I am beyond words.'*

"So are we!!" said John.

'The country shares your grief,' said Adrienne. 'So, Home Secretary, was the government aware of the risks posed upon the minister? And if so, why did the government not provide their own increased security for the minister?'

'We are currently reviewing internal safety measures and procedures,' he replied. 'We had no intelligence on the danger that the minister was apparently in. We always have crackpots that make idle threats, but none have been directed towards the minister in recent weeks, or for that matter months.'

'But obviously the minister thought his life was in danger. His Australian counterpart, their climate minister, was murdered only three days earlier. Wasn't this warning enough to increase security around our own ministers?'

'The murder of Frank Tsoukolos was conducted by his own political advisor. At the time, it was considered to be most likely a personal matter, rather than an organised assassination. We had no reason to believe that Phillip Cudsworth's life was in danger.'

'So why then did Phillip Cudsworth hire a private body guard rather than use government protection?'

'This forms part of our investigations, so I cannot answer this question at the moment,' explained the Home Secretary. 'Nevertheless we have stepped up security arrangements for all members of His Majesty's Government.'

'Okay I'll move onto the next question. As mentioned earlier, fugitive John Frankston is believed to have been part of the group that raided the minister's house. So how did a known fugitive enter our country?'

'As we are talking, we are investigating this matter,' he replied. 'We currently do not know how he got in, but we are reviewing all security

footage of the past four days at Heathrow and Gatwick airports as well as footage from all ports and the Chunnel. We hope to be able to answer these questions in coming days.

'We will be reviewing all of our national border security procedures to ensure that events like this will never happen again. Currently we have increased security in all airports, ports and roads out of the country. They will be caught.'

'As you've mentioned,' stated the reporter, *'there's been the murder of the Australian minister Frank Tsoukolis, and now we have the murder of our own minister Phillip Cudsworth. Are they related and if so, do you believe this will be the end of the current tirade of tERROR?*

'We do believe that these murders are related as John Frankston was present at both. We do not know if these attacks will or will not continue. We are still investigating these matters, and will be increasing security arrangements throughout the country.'

'Thank you Home Secretary. We hope to catch up as more information comes to light.'

'Thank you Adrienne, we will keep you informed.'

The screen returned to the news desk.

'That was Adrienne Smith reporting. The metropolitan police are asking the public for any information that may help catch these alleged offenders. If sighted, please contact the number on your screen and once again, we advise that you do not approach the alleged offenders as they should be considered armed and dangerous.

'Now onto a lighter note. Tomorrow embarks the final leg of the world tour of the Grand Delugion, Clive, who will be arriving in the UK...'

Karen turned off the television. She brushed her face with her hands, mentally drawn out from all the commotion. Ahmed gave her a squeeze on her shoulder and kissed her on her head. The comfort was appreciated, and Ahmed's presence reassured her.

John could see that Karen felt lost. He felt sorry for her, especially as her whole world had crumbled around her. But ultimately, they were now all in the same boat. Whether they could control the direction they were heading was yet to be seen.

Jenny walked into the lounge room carrying a tray full of cups of tea. "Hey guys! Hi Kat!!" she said as she placed the tray down on an old wooden coffee table. "Here's something to help keep us going."

"Thanks," said John. He reached over from a blue faux suede recliner and grabbed his cup. The others did the same. Jenny sat down on another recliner and tool a sip of her tea.

"Did anything new come up?" she asked.

"Not really," replied Ahmed. "Just stuff that they've been covering all day – murder, mayhem, how we are the most evil bastards in the world and are to blame for everything, including the third Reich. You know, the usual stuff! However, they did have an interview with the Home Secretary, but he was pretty tight lipped."

"It's hardly surprising," said Jenny. "The Home Secretary wouldn't give away too much information, but it's good for us to know what our position is."

"What do you mean?" asked Ahmed. "We know what our position is. It's shit!"

"Well, yes, true I guess," she replied. "I wonder how much the home secretary truly knows?" She pondered the thought for a moment.

"So what do we do now?" asked John, bringing Jenny back to the picture.

"Well, as far as I see our situation, right now we are sitting ducks," said Jenny. "We'll need to move on soon, as we're putting Kat in too much risk by us just being here. Our faces are our worst enemy.

Everyone is looking for us, and the pricks at *Them* have managed to get us all linked together in this thing pretty convincingly. Right now, none of us have an out."

"So, any tips in camouflaging ourselves in public?" asked John.

"I got Kat to get us some hair dye. I know it's corny and clichéd, but if it means that someone won't be so quick as to identify us, so be it."

"Whatever we need to do," replied John.

"Has anyone worked out how we can get to Francois yet?" asked Jenny.

"Well the good news is," said Ahmed, "is that Francois will be in the country tomorrow ahead of Clive's big sermon on Sunday at the *Delugion Dictate*."

"And you're sure about this?"

"Yes. According to Delugion.com, he's going to be one of the international dignitaries meeting with Clive before the big sermon. Many of the gossip sites say he's a big fan of Clive's. And well, now *we* know pretty much why! In any case, this means we can avoid having to travel to France which makes our lives a lot easier, given the new border issues."

"Good," replied Jenny. "But how are we going to get him?"

"I haven't worked that out," replied Ahmed. John was lost for ideas too.

"Draw him out," replied Karen. It was the first time she had joined in the planning since James' death. "We need to draw him out. He'll be protected. There will be increased security around him, and you can bet that *Them* will be keeping an eye on him."

"But how are we going to draw him out?" asked John.

"Do you know where he stays?" asked Karen.

"No," replied John. "I wouldn't have the faintest clue."

"What about the French embassy?" asked Karen. "Will he be there at any stage?"

"Probably. I'm sure he'll be there sometime during the day to meet with the ambassador. It's normal protocol for most countries."

"Okay then," said Karen. "That's easy then. We can get him out."

CHAPTER 17

J OHN STARED INTO the bathroom mirror. It was hard to get used to his reflection. His now black hair accentuated his strong features somewhat, making the angles of his face seem harsher. He preferred his old sandy hair and definitely did not like his new style.

"Black suits you," said Jenny, as she popped her head around the corner. He quickly made sure his towel was tucked in around his waist.

"I'm really not a fan of it," sighed John. "I look like a bloody forty year old emo rocker. All I need now is some black mascara, and I'll be set. But I guess you do what you have to do."

Jenny laughed. He looked back at her. She was standing in the doorway dressed in a loose checked shirt. She had cut her hair shorter and was now framed with dark brown hair. It showed off the supple arch of her neck, bringing out the beauty of her delicate skin and face. She walked into the bathroom and sat on the bathtub's edge. John was pleased to have her company.

"You look beautiful," said John. "I certainly preferred you as a redhead, but you pass amazingly well as a sexy brunette."

"Thank you," replied Jenny with a furtive smile. "It's one of the looks I've often resorted to in the past. Mind you, I've never had it critiqued, so it's good to know."

"So I take it you've tried several looks?"

"Yeah, red's my natural, but I've gone blonde, brunette… never got to try blue rinse though."

"Maybe… in a few decades????"

"When hell freezes over!!"

They both laughed.

"So, you reckon Karen's plan will work?" asked John.

"It is probably our best chance to get to the French minister. If we don't get to him now, he'll head back to France, and it will be a long time before we can sneak our way out of the country. Internal security's a bit strong after last night's actions."

"That's for sure. I can't believe this shit we're in!"

"Well John, you shouldn't go around murdering all those people."

John paused in thought. "It's hard to laugh at, isn't it?" he said.

"Yes. *Them* can destroy everything you stand for with the greatest of ease."

"Have you heard from Scarlet?" asked John.

"No, not since she let us know about your abduction," replied Jenny. "I'm starting to get worried. She's already been reported in the Aussie media as going missing under so-called 'mysterious circumstances'. They're questioning if she had something to do with Frank's murder, or whether she too has been murdered by you."

John raised his eyebrows in surprise.

"To be honest," she said, "given the current situation, we expected that, but still we should have heard from her by now."

"So what are you going to do?"

"Nothing we can really do. I've sent out a few feelers down there in Oz and we've just got to hope for the best. I am worried about her." Jenny looked somewhat apprehensive. "So what's this about you getting contacted by ASIO?"

John suddenly remembered the gunman's taunting.

Jenny continued, "John. You should have really told us, you know, about you using your phone."

"I know. I'm sorry," apologised John. "The whole affair back there was probably my fuck up."

"Look. We both stuffed up. They still could have got to you even with a quick phone power up. Yes, staying on the phone made it easier for them to locate us, but the van door situation was, let's just say, more than unfortunate. But what happened with ASIO?"

John felt more confident in trusting Jenny. He described the phone messages he received, including the one from his sister and ASIO.

"Interesting," said Jenny. "Don't worry about your sister. She'll be fine. *Them* will leave her alone. I just don't know if we can trust ASIO yet. We're not too sure if *Them* has infiltrated the secret services of one or even several countries including yours. We have our suspicions. We just can't work out how *Them* could have so much power over the internet and people's information. Some in tERROR think that they must have access to special government computers and databases. But I guess, really, who knows?"

John started to relax. He thought he might pry a little.

"One thing that I've never worked out is what's in it for you?"

"What do you mean?" Jenny looked a little uncomfortable.

"Well I understand Karen and James were seeking revenge for the destruction of their life's work. Ahmed, well he's just an ex-Green Peace fun nutter, but you? You're smart, beautiful, resourceful, practical... You could have achieved so much more in the right way, but you chose not to. Why did you entrench yourself in all of this eco-terrorist shit?"

Jenny became slightly agitated. "Revenge for *Them* setting me up with the Paris bombing."

"Well... Yea... No... No... There's more than that. No way that you would have started all this just for the Paris bombing. The Paris bombing happened after you joined *tERROR*. You knew what *tERROR* was about. *tERROR* has been known for their anarchic activities for the past two decades and I'm sorry, but you don't seem to be the anarchist type."

"I did it for the greater good. To help the environment," she said a little nervously.

"No! I still don't buy it. No one and no thing is truly selfless. Everyone has an ulterior motive even for selfless actions whether it is to make yourself appear better in another's eye, including God if you believe in him, or whether it's for revenge. We know what is mine. So what is yours? What made you join *tERROR*?"

Jenny stared at John, studying his face in a brief fury.

"Fuck you!" she said and stormed out.

He knew he shouldn't have pushed the point. Still, he was surprised at her reaction. *Oh mate!* John looked back at his strange reflection in the mirror. *Just take it easy John. Just take it easy. Definitely a sore point!*

CHAPTER 18

*I*t *was dark* outside. *Francois was pacing up and down on the thick shagpile in the room. He looked nervously at the hunched figure reclined on the settee. The man's back was only visible to John, but John still thought he recognised him. The man sat quietly clenching the end of his wooden cane with his scarred hand.*

"What if they don't go for it?" asked Francois with a slight jilt in his voice.

"They will. I promise you. This will be a situation they cannot resist, or should I say will not resist."

"You can't..."

"We will, and that's only if we have to. It's important the work we are doing, and there was always going to be consequences. You knew it from the start."

"Okay. But let me speak to them first."

"As you deem necessary?"

John woke with a sore head, slightly confused as to where he was. He slowly regained his bearings and walked into the kitchen to grab some water. The alien green glow of the digital clock glared in the dark. 3.30am. *I've got to stop having these dreams.*

The morning had been busy. Katrina had managed to organise, from her various contacts, two vehicles for them to use. The vehicles had rocked up early that morning, from which Karen and Ahmed started fitting them out for the day's activities.

After a cup of tea, John and Jenny made their way to the garage. Karen was inside the front of one, removing certain objects and setting up various attachments on its dash. Ahmed was busy underneath the other doing what seemed to be the final touches. Jenny explained to John that with what they were doing to the vehicles, it would be nearly impossible to identify the vehicles' true owners if a trace was made.

"False plates?" asked John.

"Well... Yes! Basically that's what we've done. Geez you know how to ruin a moment," replied Jenny. "In any case, Ahmed and Karen are also deactivating the cars' immobilisers, RFID's, Wi-Fi, Bluetooth, GPS's and Sat Nav's just in case. The amount of technology in cars these days is truly mind boggling."

John was impressed. "And what's in those two metal boxes?"

Beside each of the two vehicles lay a small dark scuffed metallic box, both of which had seen better times. The thick metal of the cases carried heavy hinges and catches which gave the impression that something sensitive or dangerous was contained within. Jenny grabbed one and opened it. John was surprised to see four small plastic discs with suction cups nested in foam.

"Here we have several RFID devices with different electronic signatures to allow us through various check points like tollways and other stuff. We have different ones in there so that we can get in and out of the city undetected."

"But why the heavy duty boxes?"

"To block any scanners from identifying them by accident when they're not needed. Basically, these devices have small antennae that reflect signals at certain check points to identify the vehicle and as we have a few in there, mainly to be safe, the boxes are lead lined. That way there's no chance that any detectors will mistakenly pick them up."

"I don't get it," said John. "Why don't we just remove all devices and go in with none?"

"We need to try and make the cars seem as normal as possible in the street. We cannot risk arousing suspicion of our activities, and that includes making sure we have the right vehicle signals getting picked up at the right time. So, if we want to change our identity, we change the signal that we're sending. That way, with a change of number plate and a change of signal, to a computer network in effect, it's a completely different car."

"Now I get you."

"John, no one looks for cars anymore. Yes, they can use image detection, but so many vehicles look alike, it's hard for them to tell one from another. So, now they mostly use electronic signatures – numbers and codes. That's all they need, numbers and codes. But if we went in a vehicle with no numbers or codes... Now, that would stand out."

John was impressed. Their method would make it very hard for them to be detected by government authorities and for that matter anyone else who could hack into the government's systems. By having an effective digital camouflage, they would be able to easily slip themselves in and out of Greater London undetected.

As the pair continued to work under the two cars, John helped Jenny load in various items. Soon the two vehicles were packed with all of the boxes that they had arrived with the other night. Ahmed finally came out from under the car, which set John into a fit of laughter.

"What?" said Ahmed.

"A wig?" replied John.

"Well, I do have short hair, and it was the only way I could change my appearance properly. It's not as easy for me as for you guys."

"But dreadlocks?"

"It's different. Doesn't it work?"

"Ahmed..." said Jenny.

"What?" replied Ahmed slightly offended.

"John's right," she said, trying hard not to burst into laughter. "You do look a bit strange, a six foot tall fair skinned dreadlocked male. We're trying to blend in Ahmed, not make everyone piss themselves laughing."

Karen slipped out of the car. "You idiot," she said with a wry smile. She picked up another wig from inside Ahmed's toolbox and threw it at him. "Put this one back on."

"Karen, you always ruin my fun," replied Ahmed with a laugh. "I had these guys going for it. You've got to admit though, it would've been a great headline—*Mysterious tall Rastafarian abducts French minister.*"

They all laughed until it dawned on them on what they were about to do.

"Hopefully it won't get to that," replied Jenny somewhat sombrely. She set back to work.

Karen looked to Ahmed for direction, realising the fun was now over. Ahmed shrugged and gave Karen an encouraging hug. "Don't worry," he said. "You'll be right."

The four continued to prepare themselves for the day's events. Jenny made sure that things were set up right in each of the vehicles and that nothing was forgotten. Ahmed made sure everything was secure. Karen checked that everyone had the arsenal they needed, and that included John.

John felt uneasy holding a gun. He didn't like the idea that he might have to use one, especially in their attempt to woo Francois over to their side, but after the other night, he understood the necessity. The black pistol was heavier than John imagined.

"You know how to use one of these?" asked Karen.

"Sort of," replied John. "I've shot with a rifle before, but that was when I was a kid. Nothing really since, and definitely not with one of these."

"Here I'll show you," said Karen and took him through the proper technique of safety, firing and loading. "We don't have time to go and practice somewhere, but if you do need to use it, remember safety off and just fire several times in the person's direction. As you're a beginner, ideally aim for the chest, not the head. It's a bigger target. Even if they are wearing vests, it will still knock the wind out of them, and if you need to, you can go in close for a head shot."

John looked a little nervous.

"Hopefully it won't have to come to that," said Karen. "But don't forget what they did to James and Phillip. They won't hesitate with you."

John appreciated Karen's direction and knew how hard it must be for her given the previous days.

Katrina popped in occasionally to see if they needed a hand. Jenny was grateful for her offers but would reply that Katrina had done more than they could have ever asked for, and that they were fine and should keep out of her hair. Jenny explained to John that she said that mainly so there would be as little linkages to Katrina if the vehicles were ever found.

John found out that Katrina was a fully qualified mechanic, and quite a good one at that according to them all. So, for her not being allowed to help was quite a frustration for Katrina. Instead, to compensate, Katrina decided to help in her own way and brought in tea. She kept up a constant supply.

After they had finished their fifth cup of tea for the morning, they said their farewells and set off into the Sunday traffic. Karen and Ahmed took one car and John and Jenny headed off in the other. They headed out of the back streets of Swindon onto the freeway towards London. Karen and Ahmed quickly disappeared as they moved off to their destination.

"Okay," said Jenny. "Whilst the others do their work, we need to head off to an internet café and send that message to Francois. One of my friends knows of a fairly safe one in Reading which doesn't require you to show any ID. It's not too far away. It should only take us about half to three quarters of an hour to get there."

"What? Do internet cafés require ID now?"

"Yes. It's bloody annoying. The British government in the late 2010's tried to crack down on internet security after a crackdown on ISIS would-be Jihadists and a few domestic incidents. They now make people show their ID at any internet café before being able to use a computer. The ID then gets logged with the date and the computer's IP. The idea was that if government intelligence tracks suspicious correspondence to an internet café's IP address, they then could work out who was in that café using that specific computer. The problem was that as always the government was way behind the times, mainly because terror groups started using smart phones instead."

"So why don't you use a phone then?"

"Because *Them* or the government will potentially identify the phone and then use it to track us down. Once you use a phone for suspect activities, it's flagged, and unless you throw the phone away, they can track you down. And I really don't want to change phones and nowadays, you can't change their chips either."

"You could turn it off once you've used it."

"Yeah, but as soon as you turn it back on, they'll track you almost immediately. Don't you remember something similar happening to you?"

"Oh yeah," said John somewhat embarrassed.

"What's more of a concern to me is that they'll follow the phone's tracking history and get to people we know. I cannot and will not risk that. It would be a real nightmare. We could get a brand new phone, but we don't have time, and stealing one would put some other poor soul's life at risk. Regardless, even though the ridiculous legislation passed, it hasn't lead to any major arrests that we know of. It's a pain in the arse, but we know ways around it."

"Like your friend's cafe."

"Exactly!"

Over the next hour they drove through the heavy weekend traffic which built up as they got closer and closer to London. Eventually they arrived at the small cafe on the outskirts of Reading city. Jenny pulled up on the other side of the road just past the cafe. John could see in, but they were far enough away to not draw attention to their car.

"Wait here. I'll be only one moment," said Jenny.

"No worries," replied John.

Jenny jumped out of the car and quickly walked across the road towards the cafe. John peered out the car window.

The café was moderately sized, nestled between a hairdresser and an antique toy shop. It was nicely set up with various wooden round tables hosting a variety of brightly lit screens. They also had several tables and couches for patrons to relax and recline and enjoy a coffee or small meal. Behind the bar, a barista was busy making coffees for several patrons, whilst a waiter was frantically plating up some cakes and pastries. The café was fairly busy with people typing away at their various computers. The front window allowed everyone to look out and conveniently, for John, to look in.

John was amazed that people still used these cafés in this day and age. *Must be tourists and foreign workers*, he thought. *Even so!!* The patrons appeared to be a mixture of nationalities. It was common for foreigners to hook up in internet cafés to avoid exorbitant data charges on their own mobile devices.

Jenny walked in through the front door arriving at the front counter. She started talking to the cashier. The cashier responded shaking her head. Jenny suddenly got heated and started yelling. The barista looked up at the commotion. The woman behind the front counter seemed shocked at the outburst and then appeared to apologise. Jenny looked apologetic and ashamed at her outburst, but it seemed to have achieved its goal. She fumbled in her bag for her money and handed it over to the woman. The woman behind the counter pointed her to a table and typed something into the computer.

Jenny thanked her and walked over to a computer near the window. She sat down and started typing away. John watched the receptionist, waiter and barista, concerned that they might have recognised Jenny and call the police. John's fears were allayed. The young receptionist pulled an emery board from her bag and started filing her nails, whilst the barista continued to make more coffees. The waiter seemed unphased.

After a few minutes, Jenny left the computer and wandered back to the front counter. She appeared to thank the young woman and left the building. She ran back to the car.

"Done!!" said Jenny, as she got back into the driver's seat.

"He'll get the flowers?" asked John.

"Sometime in the next three hours. Hopefully he'll be at the embassy today, otherwise we're screwed."

"He'll have to be, especially after the international implications of Phillip's death. Their government will want to make sure he's safe, and he's probably a bit nervous that he might be next, especially with the way the media's portraying it."

Jenny started the car and pulled out onto the street. If things were going to plan, they had to move quickly.

Hopefully Karen's plan will work, thought John. *Oh God! I hope it works, otherwise we are screwed.*

CHAPTER 19

FRANCOIS MAURY, THE French Minister of Ecology, was sitting in an office of France's embassy staring blankly at the computer screen. The chain of the week's events had startled even him, especially with the rapidity and ruthlessness of it all. He grabbed the coffee next to the keyboard, which had by now turned cold, and took a large sip. The cold milky liquid congealed in the back of his throat as he swallowed it. Francois grimaced.

The computer screen glared back at him with a multitude of emails that he had to respond to. He dreaded having to read through them all. It was the middle of the parliamentary sittings in France, and he had only just managed to get away to England to be able to meet with Clive. The French ministry was very supportive for Francois to meet with the Grand Delugion, but in doing so, it meant he would have to spend the rest of the weekend in the embassy.

He sighed with the tasks ahead and opened the next email. It was some French government directive about personal security. He quickly scanned it...

...In light of recent events, all ministers must take personal measures to increase the security of their family and....

Blah blah blah, he thought. He put down the coffee. He couldn't stomach any more. *Bloody English coffee.*

There was a knock at the door. The ambassadorial secretary let himself in.

"Monsieur Maury."

"Yes?" said Francois.

"There are some flowers here for you. They've gone through security and it all appears okay."

"Do you know who it's from?"

"Some environmental energy group. I get confused by them all. You will probably know them."

"Thank you Sebastian. That will be all."

"Yes, Monsieur Maury."

Francois waited for Sebastian to leave the room.

Flowers? Who would send me flowers?

It was a large bunch of orchid blooms interspersed with white lilies and fern fronds. He never expected to receive flowers and was surprised that someone would have had the forethought to have sent them to the French embassy.

Francois looked at the card. It was handwritten with only a shop stamp down the bottom. There was nothing familiar about the writing. *The florist must have written the message*, he thought.

Francois read the message.

Dearest Francois,

We are deeply sorry for the loss of your colleague in arms, Minister Cudsworth. Them and many of us feel your pain, and we wish that there was more we could do for you. We hope to see you in the future to meet once again.
Yours sincerely,

Paul & The Staff of the Coalition of the Environment
and Sustainable Energy
Level 2, Findler Building,
New London, SW1X 8SH.

He looked on the back of the card. Nothing. He looked back at the note.

The idiots, he thought, *No....*

He read it again.

No..... Very clever. Very very clever, the pricks.

Francois grabbed his coat and left the office.

"Monsieur Maury!" called the secretary.

"Not now, Sebastian! I need to go to get some air."

"Do you want me to call you a vehicle?"

"No! I'd rather walk."

"But it's not safe monsieur! Not after what happened to Minister Phillip Cudson."

"I'll be fine Sebastian. I'll be fine," reassured Francois.

Francois started to doubt his own words as he left the office. No he wasn't fine, not in the least.

PART 3
DELUGION

JOHN STARED OUT of the tinted window of the gun metal grey sedan. Karen's plan was coming to effect. It was, in John's opinion, a very clever idea to use flowers to send a message. It certainly didn't leave an obvious trail. The only issue was, what message would Francois understand without arousing other's suspicions?

John looked down the street. Most of the parking spots were taken up by a barrage of pastel coloured vehicles, but the street was now quiet. John was concerned. Francois was still nowhere to be seen.

John surveyed the large building across the street. This was their meeting point in the heart of Knightsbridge, St Paul's Church. The Victorian architecture of the church was quite beautiful with its grand antique stained glass windows, large clock tower and gothic styled weathered grey brick walls. John was pleased to see that sections of London still retained their old architecture.

The church appeared to be quite packed, being a Sunday morning, with people streaming in earlier to hear the morning services. Like other religions, Catholicism had embraced *Delugion* at its forefront, and church services were now very popular amongst its followers. It was quite common to see even the smallest of churches packed to the brim with its congregation. As far as the Vatican could see, the modern time was a golden age for religion with a massive swelling of devoted followers, even attempting to merge with other religious roots to remain relevant for all. With all the opulence of the Vatican, the other religious bases saw this as a great worth.

So, for Jenny to arrange their rendezvous with Francois at the church, it was the perfect cover. Francois was supposedly now a devout *Delugionist*, and proffered this information in many public domains, and the church was local to the French embassy. It would not be unusual for him to head to this church on a Sunday.

"He's not here yet," said John. "You're sure he'll understand the message?"

"He will," replied Karen emphatically.

They had picked up Karen in London after her and Ahmed had finished their side of the morning's affairs. Ahmed wasn't needed at the moment, so he was busy arranging for the arrival of their party.

"Even Francois will know that the postcode of New London does not start with SW," Karen said. "If he works out the postcode, which he will, he will find us."

John looked slightly confused. That part he still didn't quite get.

"Look, the UK postcode system is quite unique," explained Karen. "Each post code is made up of a combination of roughly seven numbers and letters, and this code basically represents either an office space, house or a group of buildings. In effect, the British postcode system acts like GPS coordinates and these can be used to find locations quite easily. New London is in the South East District, so would start with SE. Francois knows that the Embassy's postcode starts with SW, and so does this place. With the strange message we sent him, he'd be inclined to look for hidden text or messages. He would be aware of any little nuance, like an altered postcode. And once he works it out, all he needs to do is follow the code."

"How do we know he won't just go to New London?"

"Even he wouldn't be that stupid," said Jenny. "He must realise that we now know what happened. He'll be looking for the hidden message, and will want to act fast. What's more is that *Them* will eventually find out about our message, and that will put him in danger. He will need to find us if he wants to stay safe. *Them* will soon be after him too."

"And speak of the devil," said Jenny.

The familiar figure of Francois appeared in the distance. He was walking briskly up the street dressed in a black pinstripe suit. He looked quite formal for someone going to church on a Sunday morning. Francois appeared vaguely annoyed, but was in a determined rush. He quickly approached, turned up the church's pathway and entered the building.

"See?" said Karen with a sense of triumph.

"Okay," replied John somewhat impressed.

"Karen, you stay here and look after the car," said Jenny. "John and I will go and get Francois."

"Okay," replied Karen. "Just be careful."

"Always," replied Jenny with a reassuring smile.

Jenny and John both left the vehicle and walked briskly up the pathway into the church. Pipe organ music was emanating from the main chamber as they slipped in. John was taken slightly aback by the large expanse inside the building. The windows were lit up with a multitude of colours, dispersing the sunlight into the vast wooden beamed ceiling. Each heavy beam was stunningly held up by a beautifully carved angel looking down upon the congregation. The majority of the church's pews were packed tightly by the church's devoted.

The congregation was in song. John didn't recognise the tune as it was a modern-aged hymn singing the praises of Jesus and Clive. The room had the appearance of a normal Sunday service, except for one man standing alone silent in his pinstripe suit in the back pew. Francois looked completely out of place in the church, overdressed, alone and slightly concerned that no one had been there to meet him. John and Jenny approached and stood beside him.

"Hello Francois," said John.

"Hello John," replied Francois with a slight air of annoyance. Francois and John knew each other well from the multitude of intergovernmental think-tanks and discussions that made up their governments' interplay. It was often John's job to help facilitate Frank's involvement. The music continued to rise and fall in melodic chains as the congregation sang along to the hymn.

"You're not surprised to see us?" asked John.

"No. I needed you," he replied, "but I had no idea how to get hold of you. I believe my life is in great danger. I am thankful you contacted me, though I do not think your message or this place is safe enough. I think we better leave, no?"

"No. We will wait," replied Jenny. "We'll go when the congregation leaves as cover."

"But that may be too late..." said Francois with a look of panic. "They will start to look for me soon. I said I was only going for a quick walk."

"Nonetheless, we need the cover," she replied firmly. Jenny's pocket flashed with life. She quickly looked at it. A sense of dread entered her face.

"What is it?" asked John.

"Ahmed sent a message," she replied. "Not good news. Francois is right. He's in more danger than we anticipated. Apparently Friejda Stodden, and Henry Kroezon, the other ministers from the white room meeting have been killed too. It's apparently all over the news."

"Oh, putain!!" cursed Francois under his breath. He looked even more nervous.

John felt his unease. "Okay," he said. "What do we do? *Them* seem to have cleared out the rest of the group. They'll be after Francois for sure. He's the only one left now."

"Exactly," sighed Jenny. Jenny paused in thought as the congregation sang the chorus. "Francois. We have to get you to safety. Do you have your mobile on you?"

"Yes," replied Francois.

"Is it on?"

"Yes."

"Fuck. Okay. We can't use our car. They'll know that Francois is here. If we use it, they'll follow us on satellite like they did back in Taunton. We'll have to do something different. The subway!"

"Why don't we just turn Francois' phone off?" asked John

"No," replied Jenny. "They'll expect that. Instead, let's give them a trail to follow. To be safe, I'll get Karen to leave without us now. At least she'll be able to get away whilst Francois is in here."

Jenny quickly sent a message from her phone. Francois in the meantime grabbed his own phone from out of his pocket and started to read it. John looked on. There were already three missed calls from the embassy. He definitely had been missed.

The singing stopped and the pastor spoke into the microphone. *In the name of the Father, the Son, the Holy Spirit and the Grand Delugion, I bid you all well. Spread the news of God's word, and peace be with you all.* The service was finished.

"Time we go," said Jenny.

The congregation all stood and slowly massed towards the exit of the building. Everyone was bunching up as they approached the church's doors, slowing the group to a relentless crawl.

John looked through the crowd. The church's parishioners were all dressed very casually in sleeveless shirts, pants and dresses. "Francois, take off your jacket," said John. "You look far too formal amongst this crowd. You need to blend in better, especially outside."

"Good thinking," said Jenny. "Try to look inconspicuous. The less people remember our presence, the better." Jenny gave John a quick smile.

The three of them waited for a large part of the congregation to move forwards. They stood and joined the throng.

"Okay, where's the nearest train station?" asked Jenny.

"We've got a choice between Knightsbridge and Hyde Park Corner, I believe?" replied Francois. "I've used them both once or twice before when I used to take my children on the train. They're not far from here."

"Any issues with any of them?" asked Jenny.

"Well, we have to go past the embassy to get to Knightsbridge."

"That's no good," she replied.

"I agree. The embassy probably has someone out looking for me. I already have three missed calls from them."

"Okay Hyde Park Corner it is!" said Jenny.

"How far is it from here?" asked John.

"Just under half a mile," replied Francois.

Jenny was looking at the map on her phone.

"It shouldn't take us long," he said.

"Francois, I need your phone," said Jenny.

"But..."

"Just give it to me. I'll explain later."

"Okay," replied Francois. He passed his phone over to her.

The three continued to slowly make their way to the grand doors as the rest of the congregation slowly exited. Jenny studied each person as they shuffled their way out. When she saw one man, roughly the same age as Francois close by, start to head in the embassy's direction, she gently slipped Francois' phone into his pocket.

"There," whispered Jenny. "That'll give them someone to follow."

John was shocked. "But what if they kidnap him or worse?" asked John under his breath.

"Don't worry, once they realise that Francois is not there, they'll leave him alone," she reassured.

John didn't like it at all. It made him a little nervous at the risks Jenny was willing to take. Out in the open air of the street, John suddenly felt exposed. He looked up and down the road and saw people getting into their various cars, whilst others walked in either direction to the railway stations. A group they were with started to walk in the direction of Hyde Park Corner station. They followed close by. John looked back to see if Karen was still about. Thankfully her vehicle was now gone from the parking space.

John, Jenny and Francois moved from the bitumen road down to the cobbled small back streets and lanes of Knightsbridge. They remained anonymous amongst the small group of parishioners. Leaving the vicinity of the church, they passed several small cottages and buildings. They were only a few hundred metres away from the station when the sound of sirens started to wail in the direction of the embassy.

"The embassy must have called in the police," said Francois, slightly worried. "They'll have people out looking for me as well."

"Well, more reason to keep moving and get to our rendezvous quickly," urged Jenny.

They soon emerged from the small back streets into a large open section of parks and thoroughfares. Across the road, a bronzed Angel of Peace stood atop of four charging horses staring down at them from a great height on top of a massive stone arch, as if only to mock them from above. The grassy parklands were packed with the weekend's inhabitants trying to absorb every last sun ray in a vain attempt to maintain their health and looks. People materialised from the underground station in great groups and dispersed into the green fields like dandelion seeds in a strong breeze. There was no escaping it. They would soon be exposed to all. It made John feel uneasy.

The group they were with split off in various directions leaving the three stranded on the corner.

John, Jenny and Francois quickly crossed the main road and raced towards the subway's entrance. It felt like an eternity. John's heart raced with fear that they would be found. As they reached the entrance, a sense of relief waved across John's mind. They had made it. They quickly raced down the darkened stairwell into the safe deep confines of Hyde Park Corner Station, where only the presence of unaware commuters threatened their resolve.

"You guys stay here," said Jenny. "I'll get the tickets."

Jenny walked over to the electronic booths and started to punch in the details. John and Francois waited near a lightly tiled pillar.

"This is absolutely insane," said Francois. "Why are we going by train?"

"Look, if it wasn't for what we've been through, I would've thought that this was insane too," replied John.

Francois looked dubious.

"Francois, it's necessary," said John. "With the measures that *Them* have taken recently in trying to catch us, it would've been suicide if we took the car. I wouldn't be surprised if your mobile hasn't already been tracked down by now. They would've followed any cars leaving the church, and because it's a clear day, they could've tracked us by satellite."

John had a slight laugh at the words coming out of his own mouth.

"God. If you'd asked me about this a week ago, that someone would be this determined to chase after us, I would have told you to piss off. It's scary how things can change so quickly."

Francois looked frustrated. "She's insane, you know?!" he said.

"Who? Jenny?"

"Absolutely," he replied. "The number of people she killed in that bombing, is unforgiveable."

"She didn't do it."

"Are you so sure?" said Francois. "Is this what she told you or what you know? Anyway, enough now. She's coming back. We'll speak about this later."

Jenny came back carrying three paper tickets.

"Thank god for tourism," said Jenny. "If it was completely up to the British government, we'd all have to use registered cards."

They each took their ticket and entered through the turnstiles. They made their way through the brightly lit corridors of the station past posters of the latest West End show and several with various religious messages purporting the word of Clive. The three descended down an expansively long escalator to the depths of the station. It seemed as if it would take a week to reach the bottom, so they quickly ran down the moving staircase and made their way onto the ornate tiled platform.

Only a few people were standing there on the platform, scanning their phones whilst waiting for the train. John recognised some of them from the church. It amazed John that people were so hooked to their mobile devices, that the telcos had installed transceivers in all stations and tunnels to ensure a smooth continuous service.

You can't have a dropped call, thought John.

Suddenly, a slender cylindrical train penetrated the silence.

"This is us," said Jenny in a low voice. "We'll make our way to the rendezvous. Just try not to draw too much attention. People still may recognise us."

They entered the rear cabin and took a seat. Two women from the platform entered the same cabin chatting away. They were heavily engrossed in their own conversation and paid little attention to John and the others. The conductor's whistle blew and the train slowly drew away from the confines of the platform.

John breathed a sigh of relief. They were underground and safe. For the next several minutes at least, he didn't need to worry about events above ground. John looked at his companions. Francois was deep in his own thoughts, and Jenny was busy sending a text message. It started to worry him with the safety of her phone.

Well if she's been doing it so far..., he thought.

John looked around the carriage as the train whittled through the darkened tunnels. There were no others in the carriage besides the two women who had come aboard with them. John recognised them from the congregation at St Pauls. They were quite animated in their conversation, excited about their day's plans. One looked down at her phone and her expression hardened.

"Oh my God!" said the woman staring at her phone.

"Don't say that," said the second woman. "You shouldn't blaspheme. Didn't you hear what Father Eccleston said about blasphemy?"

"Oh shut up, Sarah!" said the first woman. "This is serious. Apparently someone was shot just now. From our congregation!!"

John gave Jenny a quick elbow in the ribs. She looked up.

"Is it serious?" asked Sarah.

"Oh, God!" said the first woman again, reading further on her phone. "Yes, it was! Apparently he was killed on the way to Knightsbridge Station, just after he left St Paul's."

"Oh dear!" said Sarah. "Anyone we know?"

"Don't know! They don't say, except that he was male and in his fifties. They say he was shot shortly after leaving the service, and that friends and family with him are in shock over the senseless killing. Then, more to come."

"Geez!!"

"Yeah!! It makes you think, doesn't it?"

"What?" said Sarah. "That it could have been any one of us who got shot?"

"No," said the first woman. "Basically Clive is so right! We must always place our faith in God. We never truly know when our time will come."

John shook his head in disbelief and annoyance in what had happened. Jenny stood up and grabbed her gear off the seat.

"This is our stop John," said Jenny. "Francois, we need to go onto another train."

"You said nothing would happen!!" whispered John angrily. He stood up and they moved to the exit. Francois remained silent as he followed.

"I never said that nothing would happen," replied Jenny. "What I hoped was that the worst case scenario would be that they would kidnap him and realise that he was the wrong man. Nothing more."

"And now he's dead!"

"Alright, I fucked up! Okay!?!" retorted Jenny clearly upset. She stared at John. The train grinded to a halt. "What would you prefer? That they come after us?"

"Sorry," replied John.

The doors to the platform opened and they exited onto the platform. John looked up. They were at a place called Green Park. He and Francois followed after Jenny to the next platform where they boarded once again the rear carriage of the waiting train. The carriage, this time, was completely empty to their relief. Just as the train doors were closing, a well dressed man in his mid-thirties jumped onto the train.

"How long till we get there?" asked Francois. "I'm not comfortable being this out in the open, especially after what just happened in Knightsbridge."

"Not far," replied Jenny.

They stood there momentarily in silence. The man who had boarded the train was staring at them, studying them. It made John feel uneasy.

"Hey, are you guys famous or something?" asked the man. "I recognise you from somewhere."

"No. You must be mistaken," replied John. As soon as the words came out of his mouth, he realised it was a mistake. The man turned pale.

"I know you."

The man started fumbling for his phone. John panicked and swung a punch connecting with the man's upper cheek. It was hard enough and took the man by surprise. It knocked him unconscious, and he crumpled to the ground.

"Shit!!" said John, as he rubbed his sore hand.

"No. That's fair enough," replied Jenny. "We can't have him recognise us. Francois, can you help John move this guy."

Francois looked startled at what just happened, but nodded and agreed. Jenny leant over and picked up the phone that had fallen out of the man's hands. Both Francois and John gently placed the man in a carriage seat. They tried to make it look like he was just resting.

"Guys, hurry!! We need to get off here," said Jenny. "It's our last changeover."

John and Francois quickly caught up with Jenny as the train slowly pulled into the station. It was a lot busier with the platform full of people. John looked at the wall. Victoria Station was emblazoned along its length. Even he knew where they now were. This worried him. They were arriving at the second busiest station in London.

"There are too many people here," said Francois. "It is madness for us to get off at this station."

"We have no choice," replied Jenny. "If people come on this carriage and the man wakes up, and we're here, we're in major trouble. No. We have to get off here."

Francois looked nervous, but understood he had no choice. He knew it had to be done.

As the train pulled in, several people were already lined up to enter their cabin. The doors opened and the three jumped out pushing their way through the crowd. Jenny casually dumped the phone into the nearest bin. They quickly raced away from the train and made their way through the various stairways and thoroughfares. The multitude of people in the crowded station were too busy trying to get to their various destinations to even notice who they were. They eventually found their way onto the final platform and they waited patiently. John, Jenny and Francois stood back from the gathering mob. Soon a silver train pulled in, grinding to a halt. The public announcement system blared ...*all stops to Ealing Broadway. First stop Sloane Square, then South Kensington, Gloucester Road...*

"This is us," said Jenny quietly. "Just to be safe, split up! No standing! No talking! Just sit away from everyone else. We get off in seven stations at Stamford Brook. That's seven stations! We'll meet out the front of the station once we get there."

They boarded the train separately and took various seats. John sat in the back corner where he felt he was relatively hidden. The train filled up and soon was bustling. John found a newspaper that someone had left on the seat next to him.

Don't see these as much these days, he thought.

He opened the paper and used it to shield himself. To his astonishment, there on page three was himself staring back with the words *Australian Assassin – Public Enemy Number One* plastered above. His heart sank. Things weren't getting better. It was going to be near impossible to get his life back.

Might as well read what they're saying about me, he thought with a sense of resignation.

The train lurched as it started to head towards their waiting party.

CHAPTER 21

T HE TRAIN ARRIVED at Stamford Brooke Station and the trio individually made their way to the front entrance. The trip had been uneventful for which John was thankful. They regrouped outside and started off towards the rendezvous point.

"So far, so good," said Jenny as she scanned the map on her phone for directions. "We'll make our way to our room. Ahmed and Karen should be waiting there."

They rounded a few corners and soon came upon a large twentieth century red bricked building. John stared up at its expanse. The building was bulky with a great multitude of uniform glassed windows lining its rough bare walls. It was nothing spectacular. In fact, it looked more like a hospital than a hotel in John's mind.

As they neared, John could see it was quite busy with people bustling in and out. Most of the people seemed young, maybe in their late teens, early twenties. The reason was soon answered. Emblazoned on the front entrance of the building in bright yellow letters were the words *The Wander Inn & Hostel.*

"A hostel?" said John incredulously.

"The security's low. The record system's lax. No one's going to pay attention to who's coming and who's going. It's perfect," replied Jenny.

"You sure?"

"Absolutely. We've often used these places, never the same one of course, but they've been very handy, especially when trying to keep a low profile."

"Okay. If you say so," said John.

"Actually we used one nearby when we rescued you off the plane. It worked perfectly well."

They moved through the front doors of the building into the hostel's reception. The brightly lit room was quite colourful and compact mainly taken up by a small wooden counter covered in a barrage of posters, and two snack food machines full of various long life food for the needy and desperate. Three small screens lay upon the wall advertising hostel services and garish tours of London.

Around the room, several doorways led off to dimly lit hallways and stairwells. Above them bore signs in heavy bold indicating the kitchen, the bar and guest rooms.

The reception was full of activity with a number of people in matching deep blue shirts checking in at the front counter, whilst others bustled through, heading either towards the bar or kitchen. The young receptionist looked stressed, busy admitting the blue shirted people.

As the front doors closed behind the three, a few from the blue shirted group turned to see who had come in. Initially they didn't care, but then one of them smiled a smile that concerned John. It was a smile of recognition. Panic started to set in.

"Hey guys," said the smiling young man to his friends. "It's Francois!!"

John was shocked. *How the hell do they know Francois? ...and of all places, here!!*

"Who?" asked the girl next to him.

John looked to Jenny. Her face portrayed concern, stress and confusion all at once. Obviously she hadn't considered people recognising Francois either.

"You know! Francois!! Francois Maury!?!" stated the young man. "The French MP. The one who is a close confidant of Clive!!!!"

"Really?!" asked the girl.

"Yeah! Really!! You're Francois aren't you?" questioned the young man. "I bet you've come to see Clive again, haven't you?"

"Oui," replied Francois answering both questions at once. Francois gave Jenny a quick wink. He had the situation under control. "What about you? Are you here to see the *Grand Delugion*?"

John looked at the young man and his female companion. The dark blue shirts that they wore had the symbol of a cross superimposed upon a drop of water rolling into waves. It dawned on John who these people were. They were *Young Delugionists*.

"Yeah! Absolutely. We're here with a bunch of other YD's for tonight's *Delugion Dictate*. It should be awesome. Actually, the whole hostel is pretty much filled with YD's. It's pretty crazy."

"Really? Fantastique! What are your names?" asked Francois.

"I'm Kevin McLeod, this is Jemima Hensworth and the other two *rude* friends of mine are Eric Caffides and Amy Smith."

The two at the front counter briefly turned and feigned a smile.

"I will make sure that I tell the *Grand Delugion*," said Francois, "that I met with you and tell him about how excited you are to see him tonight. I am sure he will be thrilled with your enthusiasm."

"Oh, like wow! Thank you!!" said Jemima excitedly. "That is so awesome."

The other two quickly turned now realising Francois' significance.

"Yeah. That'll be so cool," agreed Kevin sharing in the excitement. "So, why are you here? I thought you'd be staying in some grand hotel or something."

Francois thought for a moment and replied, "Doesn't Clive say that we should share shelter with those less fortunate than us so we can truly understand and help those in need?"

"But in a hostel?"

"Well, we must start somewhere!"

"That's true." Kevin looked somewhat perplexed.

"Kevin, stop bothering him," said Jemima. "I'm sure he has more important things to do. He has people with him. We can't keep them all waiting."

The security door to the stairwell opened. To John's relief, it was Ahmed.

"Hey you guys! You're already here," he said. "Good to see you. I've got our room and keys. Everything's sorted. Come on up."

Kevin looked devastated that his new friend was now about to leave him. Jemima grabbed his hand and directed his attention back to the waiting receptionist. He reluctantly surrendered.

The sense of Francois' celebrity amazed John, especially as Francois only spoke to Clive on the odd occasion. It seemed that almost anyone associated with Clive became a B-list religious celebrity. *What next?* thought John. *They'll beatify Clive's house cleaner?*

"We'll see you guys later," said Francois to the young Delugionists as they headed towards Ahmed.

"Absolutely," replied Kevin. He looked happy at the thought that they might meet again.

The receptionist looked up with panic, now realising John and the others were not checking in. Ahmed quickly intervened before any questions were asked.

"Don't worry, they're with me," said Ahmed. "I booked them in when I arrived."

The receptionist nodded and continued typing away. She appeared quite flustered, but glad that she didn't have to admit more people. The group started to head off.

Kevin, realising that he might not see Francois again, quickly turned back. "Hey, Monsieur Maury?" he said.

"Oui?" replied Francois.

"If you feel like it, you could come down and join us later for a lager before the dictate. There are a tonne of YD's staying here. It would be really cool for you to meet some of them. Maybe a selfie or two?"

Jemima elbowed Kevin heavily in the ribs. "Leave him alone," she whispered under her breath.

"No. It's really cool he's here," he whispered back. "I wanted to ask." He rubbed his ribs whilst feigning a smile to Francois as if Jemima hadn't said anything.

"Maybe later," replied Francois with a grin. "I will definitely think about it, but no selfies. I will hopefully see you later. Au revoir."

"And guys," said Jenny, "nothing in social media. The minister needs to remain focused on tonight's meeting with the Grand Delugion, and not have people hassling him."

"Absolutely," said Kevin.

"Wouldn't dream of it," added Jemima giving Kevin a knowing glare.

John gave a quiet laugh. He knew very well the stare Jemima was giving her partner. Rebecca often had done the same to him.

Francois turned back to their group and they made their way through to the stairwell. As they walked past the glass front doors, John looked out and saw dozen's more blue shirted people coming down the hostel's pathway. It appeared to John that they had picked *'Young Delugion* Central'. *Strangely appropriate*, he thought.

Ahmed opened the security door with his electronic key, and the four made their way up the stairs to an upper level of the building. They walked down a fairly bleak corridor lined with pale lime green linoleum. Occasionally dotted along the wall were placards welcoming *Delugionists*, wishing them to enjoy their stay. The air of the hallway tasted stale and musty which John perceived was from a lack of ventilation.

I hope the room is a bit fresher, he thought.

It took them a while as they traversed the expanse of the wing, eventually ending up at a room on the far corner of the building. Ahmed swiped his card and let them in.

Their room was quite spacious, but frugal with four basic beds, a few plastic chairs and a small wooden table. The walls were painted beige and were offset by several large windows. Around the openings of each window hung tattered grey curtains that looked as if they hadn't been changed or even cleaned since last century. Conveniently, and much to John's relief, the room's position was well selected. It looked out over the car park and front walkway allowing them to see who was coming and who was going. The room wasn't luxurious, but it offered everything they needed.

Ahmed looked out and studied groups of blue shirted people coming in and out of the building. He didn't appear to recognise anyone. Suddenly, the sound of water flushing emanated from a side door. Karen emerged from the en suite bathroom.

"Nice spot," said Jenny.

"Yeah. I thought so too," said Karen as she rejoined the group.

"It's all in the preparation. We can see everything from here." Ahmed soaked in the praise. "You guys alright? No problems?"

Jenny started to explain to Ahmed and Karen about what had happened during their journey. She told them about their leaving the church, the phone planting and how it had gone wrong, and about the man that John knocked out on the train.

"That's awful! Poor man! Is he dead?" asked Karen referring to the shooting.

"I believe so," replied Jenny looking somewhat stressed. "I feel terrible. I never wanted that to happen."

"I guess they're upping the ante now," said Karen in contemplation. "We won't be safe in the streets."

"Absolutely!"

"So, John, do you think the man on the train recognised you?" asked Ahmed.

"Yeah," replied John. "Not that I knew him or anything, but I reckon once he heard my accent, he put two and two together, and Bob's your uncle."

"Bob? What?"

"Oh. Sorry, an Australian term... *He worked it out.*"

"Oh... that's not good," said Ahmed.

"I agree," replied Jenny. "When John knocked him out, I hoped that we might have bought us a little extra time by dumping the guy's phone, but the train filled up as we left. I guess it will all depend on how long it takes for the guy to wake up. In any case, some people might've been concerned with his unconscious condition, and gone over to help..."

"And then the guy'll call security on someone's phone..." added Karen.

"And then they'll check the security cameras on the train," continued Jenny, "and it's only a matter of time before they work out where we went. And on top of all that, I don't completely trust those guys not to put something up on Facebook."

"Shit!!" swore Ahmed. "So now the train network's out for us. Great!! With all those fuck ups..." Ahmed bit his lip in annoyance. "We're starting to get strangled here guys."

"Ahmed, we had no fucking choice!" retorted Jenny. "It was either we got identified there and then, or do as John thankfully did, knock him out. Because of that, John allowed us time to escape further."

"You could have been more careful!!" snapped Ahmed.

"How?!!"

"I don't know. Hidden your faces better?!"

"Like we didn't try to do that already? It's not like we wanted to go by bloody train anyway. We were lucky to get here at any rate."

"You could have killed him instead," said Ahmed sombrely.

Jenny glared back.

"You know it's true," said Ahmed. "It would've worked out better."

"Guys…" interrupted John nervously. "We're getting side tracked."

Ahmed and Jenny both looked annoyed, but realised that arguing about the situation was futile. They each sat down on the edge of the metal framed beds. Francois, in the meantime, had found himself a seat in the corner of the room and was sitting quietly watching.

Ahmed was bothered over the situation. He looked over at Francois.

"Why did he come so easily?" asked Ahmed.

"What do you mean?" said John.

"Francois came along too easily. According to you guys, you didn't have to argue or convince him heavily. He came along willingly."

"The other ministers all got killed," replied John. "He needed to get to safety."

"No. The word got out that they were killed once you were in the church, not before. He wouldn't have had any idea of that."

Karen pulled out a gun and stood, pointing it at Francois. Jenny looked troubled that she had not checked Francois out further. Francois slowly raised his hands, mildly amused, but not surprised at the change of events.

"Why are you here?" asked Ahmed.

"I was wondering when you would ask me that," he said. "It shows that you aren't as stupid as you have been made out to be."

"So answer the damn fucking question," said Ahmed.

"Okay! Okay! I was scared. With Phillip and Frank murdered, I knew it was only a matter of time before *Them* came after me. I knew it wasn't you John who had murdered them. You had no reason to kill both Phillip and Frank. The only thing that made sense was that *Them* had done it. It's what they do. And as you can see, with the rest of our group now killed and the misdirected botched kill on me, I was right to be paranoid. Now I am the only one left.

"You need me and basically, I needed you. I had no idea how to safely get in contact with your group. I was sure that my every move was being watched by *Them*. It's what they do. They can get easy access to all forms of tracking... phone signals, Bluetooth, RFID, Wi-Fi. I hoped you would contact me but would not be so stupid as to make it easy. Whoever came up with the idea of sending flowers was very clever. Thank god it was sent in time. But they *will* eventually work it out."

"So tell us!! Really! Why then do we need you?" asked Jenny.

"You came to me!!"

"I know, I know!! But why didn't you go to the authorities instead if you were so worried?" asked Jenny.

"There's nowhere safe! *Them* would intercept me speedily. They have a small group of, how do you say, trained mercenaries. These people would have intercepted me before I could have got to any authorities, and those who I spoke to would have had their lives put at risk. You were the ones who also had nothing left to lose. That's why I needed you."

"Great. So you put our lives at risk?" said John. John quickly realised the stupidity of his comment.

"Isn't that what is already happening?" Francois looked confused. "John, I am a dead man walking. I knew it way before Freija and Henry were killed. I had to get out."

"But what we want to know is are you going to be any help to us?" said Jenny. "John thinks you might be, but we know you helped create this bullshit. So, why shouldn't we abandon you?"

"Because I know *Them*. I know how they work, how they act."

"So tell us something we don't know!"

"I then can assume you already know a lot from Phillip most likely. You know about the white room meeting?"

"Yes."

"And you know about the guest?"

"Yes. Are you going to tell us anything new?"

"I don't know. What don't you know?"

"Okay then!!" said Karen. "How do they have such easy access to manipulate all of that data? Facebook, YouTube, phone records…"

Francois laughed. "This is nothing for them. Not only do they have easy access, it is quick. I will explain this to you later, as it will make more sense then."

"You still haven't told us why we should trust you," said Ahmed. "How do we know that you're not working for *Them* right now? For all we know, you could've been the one in control at that White Room meeting and had that lackey doing your work. As you said, you are the only one left. That is very convenient"

Francois looked annoyed at the inference. "You can trust me because of everything I am about to tell you. I know how we can get us out of this situation. I know the way around *Them's* internet filters. I know their secrets. I know how to help us, how to save us. But most of all I cannot do it without your help. I want this finished once and for all. I am sick of it. I want to expose them. But most of all I don't think you realise how much you need my help. For without my help, you will not succeed."

CHAPTER 22

FRANCOIS HAD EVERYONE'S attention. If what he said was true, then John and everyone could get their old lives back.

"To fully understand," Francois said, "we need to go back to the beginning, when I first met *Them*."

Everyone looked on waiting to hear on what he had to say.

"Go on," said Jenny breaking the brief silence. Jenny motioned to Karen that everything was fine. Karen sat down uneasily. She rested her gun on her lap. She wasn't convinced that this wasn't a ploy.

"It all started back in 2008," said Francois. "I had already been in parliament for four years, originally on the back benches, but then due to my science background and my supposed charisma, I got pushed up the political ranks. I was made the Minister delegate for Ecology, Sustainability, Development and Energy. Minister delegate basically means I was the back up to the real minister of the time, but I still had a few things that I was in charge of.

"I was put in charge of transport, sea and fishing – pretty boring portfolios, but ultimately a necessary government department. It meant that as part of my job, I had to meet with a variety of important and not-so-important people. I would often meet with oil companies, lobby groups... and I got to know a few of the big mining magnates quite well. I even became good friends with a few of them. It was an interesting time, and I hoped that this was the start of my big rise in politics. I was ultimately happy.

"But things change. They always do. One of the mining operators who I knew, Jean-Paul Fortiér, came up to me one time and said that he needed my help."

Francois took a deep breath as he contemplated the moment. "He said he needed my help in understanding something very important. He wanted to know the true political implications of some sensitive material that he had been involved with. He believed it would be extremely impactful on an international government level, and thought that my involvement would be of great benefit to everyone. My involvement is something I have now come to regret."

"Jean-Paul Fortiér?" asked Jenny, recognising the name.

"Oui."

"He died in the Paris bombing," said Jenny.

"Yes he did," replied Francois angrily. He glared at Jenny.

"Go on," said John in an attempt to return the conversation's direction.

Francois reluctantly returned his gaze back to the group. "I agreed to help," he said, "as I thought that it was in the best interest of our government. We always want to look into every aspect that might help improve the way we do things, especially if it helps our country and ultimately helps our party stay in power. And every political party knows mining magnates have a lot of power and a lot of money.

"Initially I said I will get our ministry staff to look into the thing he needed help with. You see I was quite busy with ministerial activities, and had little spare time. He said that this thing was... how do you say it? ...strictly confidential. So I agreed to personally have a look at it sometime. He said that it wasn't immediately urgent, but he would arrange for a special meeting.

"I didn't hear from him for a while, and thought not of it. These affairs are often brought up in politics and amount to nothing. We don't mind, it's just the way it is. Anyway, Jean-Paul called up later that year and said he had finally organised a private function for us to discuss these affairs. By then, to be honest, I had lost interest and wasn't too keen to attend, but Jean-Paul insisted, so I agreed to come.

"The function was at this private residence in Paris. It was quite a grand house, but you wouldn't know it coming from the street. From the road, it looked like a simple townhouse flat, but inside it was different. Jean-Paul greeted me at the door and took me through to this large dining room. It was a beautiful place with ornate French oak tables, antique crystal chandeliers... stunning... but I digress.

"It appeared that everyone was already there waiting for when I arrived. There were about a dozen people there at this function, many of whom I recognised, some that I did not. Jean-Paul introduced me to them all. A few were some of his international mining counterparts, and the others, I came to only know by name. Whether it was their real name or not? I do not know. But what I do know, is that I could not find any public record of them anywhere. It was as if they were invisible people.

"The function was quite uncomfortable with all of its opulence and overt callousness. The meals were exquisite with perfectly cooked wild game and fresh exotic foods topped off by some fine wine from their best cellars of their personal chateau's wineries.

"Jean-Paul's friends really were quite fanatical and forceful, spouting callous extremist right wing views, but, even so, eventually I got to appreciate their charm. I mean ultimately that's why they're so successful. They could make the devil seem like a sweet angel with the right words.

"What they were saying was quite challenging, but I had heard it all before. They were all going on about how governments were out to ruin their profits with all this garbage about combatting climate change and global warming. Back then, of course, the green movements were gaining good momentum in getting governments to commit to climate change mitigation. So I tried to allay their fears.

"I explained to them that it is true, yes, that climate science was strong, but not to worry. Even though we were putting in efforts in combating global warming, our government was trying to do things to keep the economies going strong including keeping mining active. I told them we needed to do something to correct the wrongs we had done in the past as we could no longer ignore it. The public wouldn't accept it. I promised them that mining would always have government backing.

"They appreciated the fact that we were still trying to help them, but said our actions nevertheless hurt their business. And if their business hurts, so does the government's. One of them, who seemed to be the leader of the group, nodded to Jean-Paul in confirmation. I don't know for sure, but I felt as if she was saying that I was the one, because after that moment, they truly let me into their circle.

"The tone of the room changed. Suddenly everyone was truly serious. They said they had a big game changer, something that would blow everything I knew apart. I was curious, and asked them what it was. They said it was hard to explain, but it be best that it come from the babe's mouth. One of them got up and went off to a separate room and brought out this young man carrying a tablet computer. He was... How do you say? ...quite geeky looking, but also quite strong and fit in physique."

"Who was he?" asked Karen.

"I had no idea. Someone who I hadn't met before," replied Francois. "I asked them to introduce me to this young gentleman and they said his name was Karl, and that was all I needed to know. This took me a bit aback. It seemed ridiculous to hide this young man's true identity. I mean, what was the point?

"I later learnt that the less I knew, the better for my safety. In actual fact, the reality was, the less I knew, the better I could live with myself.

"Well, they told me that this man, Karl, was a researcher from the Creative Institute of America. They said he was a very bright young thing and was now one of the institution's leading academics."

John grimaced. The Creative Institute, as the name implied, was a creationist run organisation in America where their main aim was to prove that The Bible was scientific fact, word for word. They repeatedly tried to so-call scientifically prove the power of prayer, creative design, biblical floods... the list went on. The institute even had created theme parks where Adam and Eve were in the Garden of Eden living next to a vegetarian styled T-Rex. They truly were the laughing stock of the scientific world.

In politics, John often had to read their climate change denial propaganda as many climate sceptics and religious zealots would present their material to him to try and sway his party's views. So for anyone to use the Creative Institute as a go to scientific institute, it would automatically make anyone question the legitimacy of the science.

Francois noted John's reaction. "I know. I laughed," he said. "It's absurd. Yes, they do research, but it is mainly garbage that is disregarded by most, if not all of the scientific community. I found it very hard to take them serious when they said they were taking the word of someone from that institute, but they urged for me to listen.

"It turned out that these mining people had been funding the Creative Institute in multiple research projects on the proof that global warming was not real. As you probably know, this institute is one of the biggest denial researchers in this area, and in a way it made sense that my dinner colleagues would be one of their biggest benefactors.

"However over the years, their investments had not been fruitful. The Creative Institute had failed in delivering what they needed. They had ultimately come up with nothing substantial or credible. In fact, the Institute and *Them* had to eventually resort to creating climate denial propaganda. The group mainly used this to try and sway public divide.

"But the Institute and *Them* still had one project left. They had one project that they thought might work, and this was Karl's work. Karl was a computer modeller and a brilliant one in that. It was amazing. What Karl had done was revolutionary, but not well known. Karl had studied at MIT, one of the US's top universities and had studied climate science and computing. He had finished with honours in both, and then completed his PhD in computational modelling. Originally he was on the sceptics side and truly believed that global warming was all hokum. He saw gaps in the science. He saw flaws. He thought that the data that the climate models had been modelled on, was flawed due to inaccurate modelling and believed the then current models did not account for variables such as retained heat from urban sprawl. We of course now know that when these factors were corrected for, the data still held true that the global temperatures were rising. In any case, this was not known at the time. So, he was determined to show that through his own revolutionary modelling, global warming wasn't real.

"Karl was a technical wizard, a genius. He had special insight, special techniques. The only thing stopping him was money and that is where the Creative Institute came onto the scene. They saw promise in Karl and had this immense financial backing from their benefactors, in particular from my dinner colleagues, and they helped fund the research that he wanted to do. The only proviso was that his research was to be kept quiet for such a time until they wanted to use it. The last thing the C.I. and *Them* wanted was research coming out that proved global warming real. This is what often resulted whenever any of their people looked at climate factors.

"Ultimately once again, that is what happened... except to a phenomenal level. Karl had created a climate model beyond any other model that had been created before. It was the Mount Everest of models compared to measly hills. It was immensely powerful. It was amazing that one model could do this. But ultimately, it was the way that he was able to create this that was genius. It was hoped that this model would show that the other models were flawed, and that emissions by mankind would result in nothing. This was not to be. This model was amazing."

"What was so special about this model?" asked Ahmed.

"He used a new technique in creating his model. He used a thing called evolutionary modelling. It was brilliant. They started using evo models in drug development about twenty-five... thirty years ago... at the start of this century, but the amazing thing that Karl tried, was to use evo in climate modelling.

"Look the concept of evolutionary modelling is simple and complex at the same time. If you think about it in simple terms, what you have is two climate models. The computer tests each model and sees which one is the most accurate. The accurate model survives, the other is killed, then the computer mutates the successful model slightly and compares it to the original. If it is better, it survives and the other is discarded and it keeps going. A sort of survival of the fittest. Now multiply this a hundred fold. No... even a thousand fold... a million fold, and you start to see where this could lead. As they kept throwing more climate data at it, the model became more and more accurate in predicting events.

"Then Karl explained that he thought it would be more robust if he started allowing break-offs from the model on occasions, like a different species, to evolve. And it worked. He started to get hundreds of different models. Some survived well. Others died relatively rapidly. Some survived for longer and then were superseded by better, stronger models. He was able to start to predict things... different things. Some were better at predicting temperature, whilst others were better at predicting wind patterns. Some could predict mountain rainfall, whilst others could predict heatwaves. Some worked well with each other. Others didn't. Then, he decided to allow some models to interact and incorporate smaller sub-models within them, like organelles in a cell, the mitochondria of models.

"It was truly amazing to see. Karl showed me the model development on his tablet. It was like watching evolution occur in climate modelling and not only did it see one model evolve, there were dozens and soon hundreds that would interact and act like its own ecosystem. As more and more data points were piled in, such as tide, sun spots, ocean current patterns, earth tremors, wind patterns, global mining, volcanic eruptions, the data they were able to pull was enormous and amazingly accurate. Soon not only could he predict the effects of global warming, but he was able to predict earthquakes, cyclones, floods, any major weather pattern with surprising accuracy. The more data that went in, the more the models evolved to predict what would happen.

"Occasionally, Karl explained, the model had to have a major mutation. If a major event, like a nuclear explosion or release of radiation occurred, such as thanks to the North Koreans or the disaster in Fukushima, this then had to be incorporated and the model mutated, adapting to this new change. Of course some of the smaller, weaker models got wiped out with each of these explosions, but then others mutated in to fill their place.

"This became Gaia in a way. It was the program of Earth... how it functions, how it operates. Karl could predict what would happen around the world in the next day, the next month, the next year or even century. Of course, North Korea got really annoying as the model had to keep on recalibrating, more so on a short term rather than long term scale, but the model easily adapted, and as the computing power improved over the years, the quicker the model was able to adapt."

"That's amazing," said Karen.

"Absolutely," replied Francois. "This was beyond what they had envisaged. The mining companies who funded this, realised the potential of this model, but they also realised the danger it put them all in. It completely confirmed man's role in climate change and primarily the role of fossil fuels."

Everyone sat quietly. John thought that the story was almost unbelievable, if it weren't for the facts of their current status quo. "So, Karl had apparently proved not only that evolution works, but man-made climate change was real. That wouldn't have gone down too well," said John.

"I understand the irony, but it was true," said Francois. "Karl also realised this and saw what impact this could have on humanity. In his judgement, he also realised the impact on world governments, and for that matter, his financiers. So in his wisdom, he told his backers. The group were shocked, but ready for this. They decided that they had to do something with this new information.

"It was true! They now knew it! Climate change was real, and their businesses were responsible! They realised that this could be the downfall of the world order as it stood, especially if this information were to get out. Currently this model was safe in their hands."

"So why didn't they get rid of Karl and his model?" asked Ahmed.

"Their biggest concern was what would happen if someone else came up with something similar. They couldn't risk it. Karl was their hope. They knew what was going to happen worldwide. They knew they would be blamed. Karl could help them time their efforts.

"Not only that, with Karl by their side, and his computer genius, they recognised the potential use of evo modelling in other things. If Karl was able to predict global climate and environmental changes with great accuracy through evo modelling, then they could use evo for other things, like developing ways to infiltrate computers and servers by bypassing their secure software.

"It was actually quite easy according to Karl. He managed to get the computer to develop ways through evolutionary methods to crack even the most complex of codes. And soon they were not only able to break into any secure system, but to do it in the most efficient and effective manner. Karl had created software that self-programmed itself into being able to amalgamate information from across platforms and social media sites on common themes and threads, almost immediately as they came up, and even alter them as necessary. Through Karl, *Them* were able to monitor the media, control social responses and infiltrate organisations."

"So why then did they come to you?" asked John.

"You know the answer," replied Francois. "As I said, climate change had been shown to them to be real. They knew it was going to happen, and when it did, they knew it would only be a matter of time before people would be coming baying for blood. And now they even knew the date of when this would happen.

"The only two things they really couldn't control were governments and the people. They certainly could influence government through financial backing and lobbying, but it was not going to be nearly effective enough as having someone in power that you could control and trust. That is why they came to me.

"They needed someone who they trusted and who could help them along the way. Jean-Pierre chose me as I was a fellow countryman of whom he knew well. They needed help from someone who had good connections and understood government, and who was not from their inner sanctum."

The four all remained quiet as the information sank in. The growing cacophony of people outside echoed around the room as people moved in and out of the building's entranceway.

"I understood the implications," Francois continued. "I understood the fallout that would occur. I knew what was required and I agreed that we couldn't stand by. So I told them. I told them that we will need more people involved. We would need them from different governments around the world, and mainly from the more key democratic states where opinions could and need to be moulded.

"They of course agreed. They believed that the US should be left alone as they already had good control of them through religion and oil, which I might add, was one of the big reasons why the US hadn't already signed the Kyoto protocol. But the other key areas that they believed needed to be controlled were Africa, Europe, the UK, and Southeast Asia.

"Central Asia, mainly India and China, they knew they had no hope of influencing any of the governments there, so they let them be."

"Why is that?" asked Karen.

"These countries were in the midst of major development," replied Phillip. "So in actual fact, these countries at that time would not have dreamt of reining back their carbon outputs without causing social unrest, which frankly suited my dinner colleagues.

"I then asked them what about the people of the world? They would not stand idly by! My colleagues told me that they had discussed various ways to control them. They felt it would be hard, but they believed they had a way. They felt the only way they could achieve this, would be through religion.

"This surprised me. It was an interesting concept, but had a lot of merit. How else were they going to explain to people what laid ahead without laying the blame at their companies? How else? By blaming someone else! So, they told me of their idea of creating a cult where they could use the information they already had foreseen to make a leader seem such a big religious and prophetic figure, that he would be considered a messiah, and then this person would lead the masses.

"The whole concept sent shivers down my spine. I now realised that this information they were telling me was putting me on a one-way street. They were more than serious. There was no way that I would be able to refuse to help these people without my life being forfeited. They had already told me far too much for me to be let go free. I no longer had a choice, but to help them. And I made my decision there and then that I would.

"I asked them what they had done so far. They told me that they had been busy. They were monitoring several cults. Occasionally they were slipping the various religious leaders information, of course on a mutual understanding, and then watched to see if these religious leaders would use this information to lift their status in an effective way. I personally thought it was too risky and told them so. They agreed. They said they unfortunately already had to assassinate two groups. They told me to not to worry, as it was alright. They made it look like group suicide.

"This frankly scared me. They said it with such absolute calm, as if it was only a minor bump in the road. They obviously weren't afraid at showing their hand to me of what they were willing to do.

"So, I thought about this religious idea further. The idea of using existing cults was ridiculous. I couldn't let them put more souls in danger, no matter how deranged these people were. No cult could ever be controlled. The leaders of these groups are insane and unstable, or at least have major agendas or egos to control people. I will admit most of these leaders are charismatic, but many are also psychotic. No! It was a bad idea to use cults. Then I had an idea, one that would change things."

"And what was that?" asked Ahmed.

"Create a new religion! Start one from scratch!"

CHAPTER 23

J OHN WAS AMAZED. Everything was now starting to fit into place.

"I had this friend in Nanaimo, Canada," said Francois, "who I thought would be perfect for the job. You know him as Clive. Well, Clive and I go a long way back.

"We got to know each other quite well when he did a student exchange at our home back in his teens. I had kept in contact with him over the years. We'd often chat and he'd tell me what he'd been up to and what latest thing he'd been investigating. He had a thirst for knowledge. He was a very intelligent young man, but he found religion the most fascinating.

"Clive was actually an atheist in heart, yet he keenly wanted to learn about all religions. What their teachings were, their reasons and their ways. He had even gone to the extent of joining a local Christian church to study the religious practices from a personal cultural perspective. He of course went with the pretence that he was a convert that had only just discovered God.

"Clive, over the years, studied the religions of quite a few different faiths and we used to discuss them over the phone quite often. It was usually about the latest religious revelations he had heard and how absurd they had been. It was always interesting, and we used to have quite a few laughs and quite good debates. Clive was quite persuasive with his views.

"This sort of person... this character, was what, in my belief, we needed. Someone level headed, well educated, someone who could formulate an argument, someone who had a moral compass and was not self-centred. This, in my opinion, was far more reasonable than using a cult. I thought Clive would revel at the idea. The others at the dinner respected my opinion, and decided to strongly consider the idea. Jean-Pierre by that point looked pretty pleased with himself that he had brought me along.

"And that's what they did. They told me not to have contact with Clive for a while, as they wanted to have as little linkages between them, myself and Clive. They said they would erase any context of my and Clive's previous interactions. So, after that dinner, I gave Clive one last call as I knew it would be a long time before we would meet again. I owed it to him. We had a great chat about life, the universe and everything. Eventually I pondered the idea before him, of course only in a hypothetical sense, but when he said he would be fascinated whether it could be done, I was relieved. So then, I told him of the offer.

"He was shocked initially, but then he thought more about it. And to my amazement, he agreed. He thought it was important that it should be done, especially with the environmental challenges ahead. And thankfully he did, because I found out later that *Them* had tapped all of my phones. If he rejected the offer, Clive would've been no longer."

"So that's how they came across Clive?" stated John.

"Oui," replied Francois. "*Them* later made preparations for that white room meeting to happen later that year so that they could coerce your political representatives. As the meeting got closer, *Them* monitored the model's predictions closely. They wanted to make sure the weather and global events were right, so that the model continued to be confirmed. They allowed me to observe this, so that I too continued to believe and trust them. And it did just that.

"And then the major event of Copenhagen occurred. The most important part of the whole conference was not in the big halls or amongst the big players, but it was in a small meeting room in a hotel with junior ministers from five countries. This meeting made sure the course of action we desired definitely happened. I was the one who organised the venue for our quick meeting so as to seem real. I let *Them* know. That's when I met *The Guest*."

"Did he have a name?" asked Jenny.

"It was never actually directly said, but I did eventually overhear it in a conversion at a later stage, when someone was talking to him. I believe his name was Guillerme, or at least something along those lines. I'm not sure what he was exactly, but he preferred to be called *the arranger* of the group.

"He made me nervous. He had a control of things that sent a shiver down your spine. Even though he appeared harmless, he had a confidence, a strange confidence, one that you knew he could make things to happen at a moment's notice. No, worse than that, even before you knew the moment occurred. I never liked him, and have tried to have as little to do with him as possible."

Francois stood and wandered to the window. He stared out at the bleak view of the occasional tree and tall buildings. "So the meeting occurred, and *The Guest* and I got all the various ministers involved in the operation. You said you know about this?!"

"Yeah," replied John. "Phillip told us all about that before he got killed, the poor bugger."

"Very well," said Francois saddened by the thought. "He will be missed."

He turned away from the window and headed back to the back to his seat. "After that meeting, it was time for the cult, the new religion to begin. And so started *The Church of Delugion*.

"Clive was given the predictions of the global events and social upheavals. He was told that he must announce them to various religious leaders in his area, and that should be all that he needed to do.

"It was pretty clever of *Them* getting the other religions involved. By doing that, *Them* managed to have all of the major religions following Clive from the start. It managed to keep everyone on side. The last thing a religious order wants, is to join onto something as a catch-up. They wouldn't want to be seen as being outsiders coming in on late. It might make them look bad.

"Clive did well. He did it gradually and he did it carefully. He cleverly got the head of his then church to organise a meeting of the local religious heads, and that's where he announced the early prophecies to them all. As usual, *Them* didn't quite trust what would happen within that meeting, so they made sure they had a trusted person there to watch it all and guide things if necessary."

"Maria Rodriguez?" asked Ahmed.

"Oui," replied Francois.

Maria from the Holy Entourage! It made perfect sense to John. She had always seemed to be the odd one out of the Holy Entourage. For a supposed cleaner of a church, she had always had a very vocal presence, and held a lot of sway in the Church of *Delugion*, even sometimes countering Clive's views. For a cleaner to supposedly be at the meeting, never felt like a neat fit for the narrative, but now there was obviously good reason for her being there.

Her presence seemed very logical. How else were they going to infiltrate that meeting and join onto the learned, unless they had a plant? Pretending to be Clive's friend would have caused too much scrutiny to fall on the taker's part, whereas being a mere cleaner was far more anonymous and non-reverential. Heavy public scrutiny on Maria's part would have seemed like picking on the poor and unfortunate.

"Apparently they made sure that the regular cleaner was sick," said Francois. "Maria was able to temp in and clean the hall at the time where they met. Of course, she is now part of this new mythology, but that is another story for another time."

Ahmed started tapping his leg. John could see Ahmed's frustration in not exploring Maria's history further. Ahmed bit his lip as Francois continued.

"So," said Francois, "Clive fed the group those early prophecies that ultimately became true. It was to be a mixture of climate and social predictions."

"So why not use just weather events for the stories?" asked Karen.

"Because of the risk that eventually someone would work out our model independently," said Francois, "and prove that these prophecies could have been computer generated and not be the word of God. Also having the prophecies only linked to natural events is too convenient in people's eyes. We needed more. We needed other world events, manmade and natural for proof of 'God's word'."

Francois paused as he collected his thoughts. Everyone remained quiet.

"The first one, which you may have heard of," continued Francois, "the Chilean Earthquake of 2010, was an easy prediction. It happened exactly as the model said. Actually, it was the first quake that the model predicted with strong accuracy."

"So that was the first one?" asked Jenny. She seemed slightly incredulous. Everyone looked at her strangely, but Francois ignored her disbelief.

"Oui," replied Francois.

"So why didn't they go for the 2010 Haitian Earthquake instead?" asked Jenny, not quite satisfied with his reply. "The one shortly after the Chilean quake? It occurred around the same time. It was a lot more destructive, and it killed far more people."

"It was because *Them* didn't take in account things like the construction of buildings, the depth of the quake and so on," said Francois. "The strategy at the time was to go for power... the strength of the shock. The Chilean earthquake was more than five hundred times more powerful than the Haitian one, but admittedly it was deeper and further away from the major population centre. Still in Chile, it killed over seven hundred people, and damaged over three hundred thousand buildings. If it were not for the strict building codes, it would have been far worse.

"Haiti? Haiti was different. Over two hundred thousand people died. And that's because buildings there were constructed like a deck of cards. So when the quake hit, even though it was a much smaller quake, thousands of buildings collapsed. That's why so many people were killed, not to mention sanitation problems and so on. Their quake was shallow and a lot smaller, but it happened in the right place, and with the right conditions. That's why there was far more death and destruction in Haiti than Chile.

"Nevertheless, it was a lesson. *Them* learnt from the Haiti event. They made sure that future predictions took into account likely destruction rather than just the size of the event."

It disturbed John the way that Francois talked of this massive disaster like it was an unfortunate mix-up. Francois seemed more upset that *Them* failed to predict its destructive nature, than the level of death and distress it caused. It disturbed him even further to think his close friend Frank was also part of all of this. It seemed too callous... too psychotic. *How could people sit by with such depravity!* John decided to probe further.

"And what about the other predictions?" asked John. "Why take out the Polish president?"

"Ahh, oui! The second prophecy... Well, president Lech Kaczyński had apparently pissed off some in the group by pushing for energy independence for Poland. Poland was sitting on the European Union's biggest reserve of shale gas. By moving to energy independence, they were going to cut off some of the big global suppliers to their country and for that matter start competing against big energy."

"But surely one country wouldn't be seen as a threat?" asked Karen.

"Well, let's face it, many did! For example, back in the early 2010's, Abu Dhabi, the capital of one of the big oil producing nations, they partially funded anti-fracking movies as they saw gas production as a threat to their economy. They weren't interested in ground water protection, just reducing competition. It was the same for *Them*.

"Going after Kaczyński was purely a competitive decision and, to a greater extent, it was revenge. They saw the perfect opportunity available. They knew where and when he would be flying. They had the opportunity. They had the means. It was to be a tragic accident. *Them* had decided that Kaczyński would be the perfect fall guy for a prophecy. I'm not sure exactly how it was done, but it almost failed."

"What happened?" asked Karen, somewhat intrigued.

"There were some traces of high power explosives found on the plane wreck," replied Francois. "And there was also a witness who heard two explosions before the plane went down. It would have been a disaster if the authorities had truly found out. But *Them* managed to adulterate the official documents and so the level of explosives were able to be explained as contaminants. And, *conveniently*, the witness was found hanged in his home a few months later. The papers reported suicide, but others were more suspicious. Let's just say his death was just very opportune timing.

"To *Them*'s amusement, most conspiracy theorists blamed the Russian government for causing the crash, saying that the Russians hated Kaczyński for standing up against Putin. It's very handy when there are conspiracy theories that are far removed from the truth. It took any discernible attention away from *Them*."

Francois stood and walked towards the window. He seemed more relaxed, as if a weight was finally lifting from his shoulders. John understood it must be truly freeing to be able to talk about all that actually happened, but still, he found it hard to excuse. It appeared the others felt the same. Francois rested against the white window sill and looked back.

"The next prophecy was the Deepwater Horizons explosion," said Francois. "The one that caused the massive oil leak in the Gulf of Mexico and devastated the coastline in the area. This, of course, was done by *Them* quite easily on one of the BP oil rigs. With a few bits of hi-tech explosives, and your own investigatory team that are personally selected, and it works quite well. It's easy to make it look like an accident.

"Even the next prophecy of the Australian prime ministerial downfall was quite easy according to Jean-Pierre. He told me all about it later. Apparently there had been deep tensions within your government at the time with their factions. Hence the reason they chose them. He told me that the rift within the government only needed a small push from the mining moguls and a few of their business friends, and the rest was easily taken care of. Of course, Frank gave a helping hand in these things."

John was annoyed at the now apparent manipulation that had occurred within his own country. Even more so, it deeply disturbed him how easily people could be controlled, governments influenced, and policies subverted for the whims of certain individuals. It scared him of what else could be done.

"However, the Middle East uprising was a different scenario," continued Francois as he made his way back to the edge of the bed. "*Them* helped things along of course through their control of oil and they also helped influence a few of the uprisings. Apparently it took a bit of work, especially as they needed to hack into some of the social networks to push more of the social discontent. Some of the people of *Them* took a small hit in a few of these countries' uprisings, but ultimately it worked out in their favour in the long run. It truly was quite amazing to see it all unfold."

This riled Karen. "But there were major civil wars! Hundreds of thousands of people died!! Not to mention the rises of ISIS," she anguished. "Innocent people!! Children!!! There were bombings, gas attacks! How could *Them* justify something that horrible?" She was clearly upset by Francois' plain candour and lack of emotion over that set of events.

"It was always going to happen," replied Francois sombrely. "All they did was accelerate these matters a little, to suit their cause. It wouldn't have been any different if it happened five or ten years later. The rise of ISIS at the time was unfortunate."

Karen appeared dissatisfied with Francois' response. She turned away in anger.

"In any case," said Francois, "it wasn't the Spring Uprisings that upset me, it was the last event that I personally found the most disturbing. I understood it was quite necessary, but it didn't make things any easier. For years after I did not sleep well. As you know, this was the prediction of the Japanese earthquake and tsunami, and, believe me, it was amazingly accurate. This was the one event that *Them* saw the model predict well over twelve months before. It stood out like nothing else.

"*Them* needed this event to show what they could predict, what Clive could foretell. As you may know, it was this event that cemented him into becoming a significant religious leader, a figure that now stands the length of time. The event of course came true to a horrific extent, and I have never forgiven myself for not doing more to help all those innocent people."

"And yet you could live with the hundreds of thousands of people that died in the Arab Spring and under ISIS?" retorted Karen.

"Karen!" scolded Jenny.

"Come on!" said Karen, "You can't forgive that."

"By having this set of accurate prophecies," explained Francois, "*Them* were able to gain control of enlightenment. They could stop wars. They could save people... many hundreds of thousands, potentially millions. They could now explain any event, any event they wanted to through a religious context and the world would listen."

Karen sat back quietly sulking.

"Go on," said Ahmed.

Francois continued, "As more prophecies were made and proven to be true, Clive's word became stronger, and more and more began to follow him. The only risk to the organisation was discovery, the discovery that Clive's prophecies could be explained in other ways. If

Clive's word was found to be fallible, it would be the end of *Delugion* and we would be in a worse situation than we what we started with. So it was important... No, it was necessary that any attempts to derail our work, was to be quashed.

"Many people had to be silenced. All of yourselves included. You John were obviously a mistake. But these are the measures that *Them* are willing to take."

Francois took a deep breath. "So this brings me back to why I am telling you all this. It was important, for *Them*, that they monitor and control all media. So once again through evo modelling, *Them* developed programs to remove, or at least allow themselves to edit any material that might possibly make it out to the public that implicated *Them* or threatened their work. Sometimes we had to use drastic measures that I know Ms Blackstone can attest to."

Karen looked up at Francois disgusted at his mention of her name.

"So how is this useful to us?" asked Jenny. "You haven't given us any information we can use. Obviously they will now censor any material that you are involved with too. They would have worked out that you're with us by now. So what is it that you can tell us that will help? And still, why should we trust or believe you?"

"Think of it," said Francois. "Yes. All of our material is being watched and controlled. It would be suicide if we tried to contact anyone about what we know. But who is the one person in the world they wouldn't dare control, not even censor for even a moment?"

It suddenly dawned on all of them at once.

"Clive," whispered John.

"Oui!!" replied Francois.

CHAPTER 24

"S O CLIVE ISN'T censored at all?" asked Ahmed.

"Absolutely not," said Francois. "Too many people listen to and watch him. People would talk if they found out that any of his materials had been altered or removed. No. He is untouchable. He is helped by *Them*, but not controlled by *Them*."

"So what are you saying?" asked Karen.

"I'm saying that if we want to save ourselves and let the truth come out, then Clive is the one. He is the way. We need him to be able to send our message, to let the truth be known."

"But you said you thought it would be a disaster if the public knew about all of this," said Ahmed somewhat surprised.

"*Them* have now gone too far. They have removed… killed everyone from our group, and as you've probably realised, they would have got me too if it weren't for you. It's my belief now that they want to take total control of *Delugion*, and no group should have such control."

"That's rich coming from yourself," said Karen. "Didn't you and *Them* give Clive control?"

"Yes, but he is just a man with no great hidden agendas. I know him and trust him. *Them*, I do not, especially after what has befallen my colleagues in the past week. I am no longer safe. I no longer know what they'll do."

"But…"

"Enough everyone!" said Jenny.

The group fell quiet. Jenny pondered the situation for a moment. She stood up and walked to the large glass window overlooking the courtyard. Streams of people in blue shirts were leaving the building heading towards the busses that were parked outside.

"So we need to get to Clive," stated Jenny.

"Oui," replied Francois.

"And the sooner the better as far as I can see," said Jenny.

"I still don't know if we should trust Francois!" protested Karen.

"We have no reason not to," replied Jenny. "Francois almost lost his life trying to get here. He's put himself in danger just by being with us. There's no reason for him to lie. In any case, he is right. *Them* wouldn't dare touch Clive. If anyone found out that someone had interfered with their religious leader… No, more than that… their God, there would be hell to pay. Clive is our only hope."

Karen grumbled but conceded that Jenny had a point. Ahmed was still contemplating the whole situation.

"So how do we get to him?" asked Ahmed.

"The solution is right in front of us," replied Jenny looking down at the blue shirted people. "The Delugion Dictate is on tonight and there is a sea of people heading straight there from this building. We will just merge in with them. Francois, that group we saw earlier, do you think we can get some blue shirts off them?"

"I can try," he replied. "They might already be gone."

"Hopefully not. They were keen to catch up for a beer, so hopefully they're still around. Ahmed, before, when you let us know about the murders of the German and South African climate ministers, did they mention anything about Francois?"

"No," replied Ahmed. He quickly looked through the article again on his phone. "And there's still nothing further there."

"What about the shooting outside the embassy? Anything?"

"No... at least nothing about Francois. Still just a mysterious shooting... not much detail. I'm also just doing a search for Francois himself and there's nothing, except the usual happenings in France and with Delugion."

"Good," said Jenny. "That means no one will be overly suspicious of Francois' presence. Okay, Francois... You and Ahmed will go down to the group like they asked you to and see if you can get some shirts off them for all of us. Say something like that you wanted to see what it was like from the YD perspective, and needed some shirts for your friends too. I'm sure they'll wet their pants in excitement and give you the ones off their back."

"Okay," replied Francois with a wry smile. "I will try."

Ahmed looked slightly annoyed at doing the menial task, but willingly went along. They both left the room and headed off down the corridor.

"Karen," said Jenny. "Are you right to get whatever equipment you think we'll need from the cars. There's no way that we'll be able to drive up there to New London and find a park. The way I figure is that we'll only need enough weapons for three of us to carry. I'll explain my plan on the way, but we need to move soon. Will you need a hand?"

"No," replied Karen. "All good. I know exactly what to get."

"Good," said Jenny.

Karen headed out of the room and as the door closed, John could just see her enter through the stairwell fire door signposted to take her to the building's car park.

Jenny sighed. She flopped against the bed exhausted. "I can't believe it, John. I just can't believe it," she said. "After all those years... Finally!! Finally I can truly get my revenge!"

"Revenge?" asked John somewhat surprised.

"You know the Paris bombing?"

John nodded.

"I lied. It was me."

CHAPTER 25

"WHAT?!?" SAID JOHN.

"I did it," replied Jenny.

John was shocked. He felt a sense of betrayal. "What do you mean? You told me adamantly that you didn't do it! Why lie to me?"

"I've lied about it all my life, that whole affair," said Jenny, wiping a solo tear away from her face. "It's hard to face the truth when you've done something that awful. I guess I've ultimately lied to myself, so I can face myself on a day to day basis. You see, the people I killed, most were innocent."

John stared at Jenny uncertain of his trust and belief in her. After all of her promises, this was not what he expected.

"There was something there that Francois said just now that was either a lie, or he doesn't know the whole truth," she said.

"And you do?" asked John.

"No. But there are some other things that I do know. I know that they did predict events before the Chilean earthquake, actually quite big ones for that matter."

"And how do you know this?"

"Because I was there when it happened."

John was dismayed and confused. He didn't quite know how to take her at that moment.

"Do you know of my background?" asked Jenny.

"Not a lot," replied John. "Only that you were an industrial chemist who was skilled in bomb-making."

"Only half true. Yes I was an industrial chemist, but I was never into bomb-making except for one time really. Before tERROR, I actually used to work for a big mining group."

"Really?"

"Yes! Really!!"

"Which one?" asked John, somewhat surprised that an environmental activist was once a miner.

"Stratum Mining Corporation, but it's hardly relevant to be honest. And yes, I was an employee of a mining corporation that wanted to strip North Indonesia's land of trees, mine their hills and contribute majorly to the decline of the country's orang-utan population. I was someone I now hate. But I was young and naive and didn't think about the problems of the world I was contributing to at the time.

"Well, I was twenty four and had just finished university on a scholarship. I was one of the top few in my year, but as part of my scholarship, I had to work for SMC upon graduation for at least three years.

"It was fine. I was excited to be heading out to work in the real world and to work for a big mining company was a great opportunity. Even if I didn't have the scholarship, I would have leapt at the job.

"For my first job, they sent me to this small town in the northern parts of Sumatra, mainly to help analyse their mineral deposits. It was exciting, especially for a new graduate. For the first time in my life, here I was, able to use my new skills in this far off exotic location.

"The small team I worked with was fun and we had a great time. They helped me along with whatever I needed and guided me whenever I had any challenges. Our office was great. It was by the water and we had beautiful views over the Indian Ocean. I really couldn't have asked for more.

"Our group was made up of various scientists, geologists and engineers. The way things worked was the field team would go out and bring in various samples from their exploration sites and we would analyse them. We had a good bunch, and the work was interesting."

"So what's this got to do with *Them*'s predictions?" asked John.

"It was 2004, and the area we were in was Banda Aceh," replied Jenny somewhat sombrely.

"Oh," said John, realising the significance. The pieces were starting to fall together.

"The area we were in was fairly poor, and a lot of the people were in poverty. So, it was really nice to be able to give back to the community there, especially by employing some of the local people and supporting their economy through other means," she said. "Still, it wasn't easy. Aceh was a Muslim area, and Sharia law had only been introduced a few years earlier. So we had to abide by their laws like no drinking and women not showing too much skin in public, but to be honest, it wasn't heavily enforced at that time. We didn't have to wear head scarfs as such, but it made some places easier to travel if we did. We knew where to go, and how to dress properly in certain areas and we got to know the local people quite well. And in Aceh, that's where I fell in love."

"With a local?" asked John.

"No," replied Jenny with a smile. "Many a local did try to romance me, but I wasn't looking for anything at the time, and besides, back then, I had big plans for my life. I didn't want to be tied down. I wanted to go out and explore the world." Jenny laughed at the thought. "Life in a far off country was never going to be a permanent option for me. I guess I always wanted to be a free spirit."

Jenny sat closer to the edge of the bed. "We all worked hard there. It was mainly just analysing materials and processing the data to see if the sites were viable for mining. And then occasionally one of the area mangers would come down and spend some time in the area having meetings with various officials and checking over operations. There was a sense of routine.

"But late in 2004, after I had been working there for almost a year, this new guy comes down. He said that he was going to be with us for a few months as there were a few jobs that needed *overseeing* by those higher up in the organisation. Of course, we thought nothing of it, and he moved his gear in taking up one of our offices."

The sound of the crowd outside grew louder as more people moved out of the building. Jenny sat closer to John so as to not have to speak too loud.

"This guy... He was fun actually," said Jenny with a smile. "A little bit older than most of us, but quite good looking and quite relaxed. He would often smuggle in alcohol for us and we'd have some fun big nights. I got to know him quite well, or so I thought.

"His name..." Jenny took a big breath. "His name was Peter Luckton. Said he was born in Cambridge, studied geology and economics at Oxford and rose up the ranks of SMC quite quickly. The perfect profile! He carried it off well. He knew his stuff. He knew how to read people. And he knew exactly how to sweep me off my feet.

"Well, one day he invited me out on one of their flyovers to check on the company's test drilling sites. I was excited as I had never been to any of them before, and being stuck in the lab was getting pretty boring. So to go off to several of the sites, some of them very remote, was a real thrill.

"The day was pretty cool. We went to sites in the middle of the jungle, some near rivers, some at the base of mountains, and after we had inspected them all, we were flown up to the top of Mount Hulumasen, one of the largest mountains in Aceh. Peter had specially arranged it, so that the two of us would be left alone to watch the sunset. I was quite taken aback initially as I didn't realise his intentions. He apologised for his assumption, and said that he understood completely if I preferred to head back to town instead. At the time, I actually thought it was quite sweet and decided that it would be really nice to join him.

"So, he pulled out a carefully hidden picnic basket and sent the crew away for an hour. He had it all planned. It really was beautiful. We sat back on the mountainside at sunset, looking over the vast majestic scenery of the Aceh ranges, whilst enjoying fine food and chilled champagne... things that I had sorely missed from back home. It was stunning up there. And as the sun slowly melted into the horizon, he leant over and gently kissed me. I was cactus. I was immediately smitten."

Jenny held a slight remembered smile on her lips. It was quickly replaced with reproach.

"After we arrived back in Aceh, he told me he had to leave the next day. He said that the main reason he took me up was he wanted to let me know his feelings before he left and hoped that I felt the same. He was glad I did. He promised he would be back in a month or so, and really wanted to see me again. I was of course disappointed with him going, but I liked him. I made him promise he would keep in touch. And he did.

"Over the months, he told me about what was happening back in head office, and how he was telling his bosses about the wonderful work we were all doing. He was quite busy, but the times when he called, he told me how he missed me more than anything. I couldn't wait to see him again. He would ask what we were up to and I would tell him everything that was happening. He would often laugh when I told him about the latest antics with the locals.

"Then after two months apart, he told me that he was coming back mid-December and that he was going to spend Christmas with me. He said he couldn't wait. I was over the moon that he was coming, and counted the days. The weeks slowly whittled away, and then, as promised, he arrived.

"It was as if he had never left and we continued from where we left off. I took some time off and we spent the days together in the region going to the beaches and occasionally trekking in the mountains. We couldn't go far because he still had to do his work, and on top of that, it was the wet season. So there wasn't a great deal we could do without being inundated with heavy rains or risk being trapped by floods.

"We had a fun Christmas together, and that Christmas night, let's just say, was very special. While we lay in bed together in the early hours of the morning, Peter told me something that ultimately led to my life's change of direction."

"What was that?" asked John.

"What he told me scared me. He told me ultimately something that he shouldn't have... something that I should never have been told. He made me promise..." Jenny took a deep breath. "He made me promise that I would go away early the next morning, up to the mountains, and not come down till dark. I asked him why? I thought that maybe he had something planned for us up there, a surprise, something exciting."

Jenny looked away, not able to look John in the eye as her emotions and anger started to build up. "It amazes me even to this day that he didn't lie to me," she said. "He could have told me anything. He could have told me that he had a romantic day planned for us, and then not turn up. He could have told me that we were going to bungee jump off a tower in the sky... anything. I would've believed him and been none the wiser. I could have gone on with my life ignorant of what really happened. I could have been normal. Why?!?"

Jenny closed her eyes for a moment.

"But no! Of course not!!" said Jenny. "That would never happen to me. Lucky old me! That fucking arsehole decided for one stupid fucking moment that this naive idiot woman he had been leading along all the way, she needed to know the truth."

Jenny wiped the tears from her face with her sleeve. John remained silent.

"He told me that in a few hours there was going to be a massive submarine earthquake. It was going to be so big and so strong that a tsunami would rise out of the sea and devastate large amounts of Asia including the whole of Banda Aceh. He, for some stupid reason, decided that it was time to be honest. He told me that everyone in my team, including myself, was supposed to die in this event, but he now cared for me dearly and wanted me to live. If I went up to the mountains, I would be safe. That, he was sure of. I could then go on with my life.

"I thought he was just joking around in some stupid way. But he didn't laugh. He explained that he was here to observe what happened and make sure that nothing went awry. You see, they figured by our team suffering, it would take any suspicion away about SMC having pre-knowledge. It didn't make sense to me. He explained that if our team were to evacuate, it would seem to conspiracy theorists that it was very convenient, and *that* conspiracy could pose a problem in the future. He apparently had a helicopter for him to take him away the next day before it all happened, but he couldn't take me as they were not his instructions.

"Of course I didn't believe him, but he was adamant. I eventually agreed to his request to appease him. He said he would accompany me in the morning on our way out, and make sure I was safe.

"For the rest of that night, I couldn't sleep. How could I? I still didn't believe him, but what if what he said was true?" Jenny looked at John directly. "If what he said was true, and I did nothing, I don't know if I could live with myself."

"So, I waited. I waited until he was fast asleep and then quietly ventured out into the streets unnoticed. I didn't know what to do. I didn't know what to think of it all. If I called up my friends in town, they wouldn't believe me. I mean, I hardly believed it myself.

"So I walked to the beach, and sat and waited under a distant tree to see if it was actually true, to see if it was all real. If this earthquake was really going to happen, I wanted to be there to witness it all. I knew enough geophysics to safely assess what was likely to happen, and I knew that standing around poorly constructed buildings was not one of the safe options. You know, I was really dumb and naive when I look back on it.

"That morning's sunrise was strangely innocent. It was hardly marked by any clouds. People soon started to wander out onto the beach going about their daily routines. The odd foreigner occasionally jogged past on the water's edge. There was nothing unusual, nothing strange. Everything was normal. And that's when it happened.

"The ground shook like I had never experienced before. It was truly terrifying. People on the beach fell. The sound of walls and buildings collapsing created a deafening noise. The quake, it just seemed to last forever. And then everything fell silent.

"I ran back to the streets away from the beach. It was horrifying. There were people crying and screaming everywhere. People were trapped inside collapsed houses. Rubble had fallen on top of people in the street. People were calling out for help. Soon crowds of people piled into the streets from everywhere–buildings, their cars, bikes... They came out to free their injured friends and family, even strangers.

"But I knew that a lot worse was about to come. It terrified me. I needed to let people know. I needed somehow to get everyone, who was able, out. To run for high ground. And here I was, this white woman in a foreign country that knew only basic broken Indonesian. It was futile. I had little hope.

"I eventually found someone I knew, one of the street vendors. I told him that he must run to higher ground and so must all his family, and to spread the word. He thought I was mad and just panicking, and continued to help the trapped people. I yelled at him to listen, but he... he continued to ignore me. It was useless. People were just not listening.

"I tried to call my friends at work, to see if they were okay and make sure they were getting to safe grounds, but the networks were down. There was nothing I could do. All of a sudden the thought of everything that was happening just overwhelmed me. I broke down and I am afraid to say I just started crying. Everything just seemed hopeless. But I knew... I knew I needed to go. I broke myself out of my own despondency. I needed to get to safety.

"So I started to head down the road past various collapsed shops and buildings to where I thought it would be safe. And then I heard this crack and whistle by my ear. A searing wave of pain emanated down the side of my head. I rubbed by my ear and felt this wet patch on my head. When I looked at my hand, I realised it was blood. It was oozing from what seemed to be a long cut on the side of my head. I couldn't work out what had happened or where it came from, and then someone collapsed right in front of me. Blood started pooling in her shirt. She had been shot. Someone had killed her. The sight sent a shiver down my spine. Someone had just tried to shoot me. I turned around and saw Peter running towards me with a gun in his hand. The look of anger and betrayal in his eyes was evident. And then it dawned. He wasn't coming to help me. He was after me.

"So, I ran. I ran as fast as I could. I ran through the streets. I yelled for help, but people didn't care as so many were in desperate need themselves. It was as if I was all alone. The streets suddenly seemed empty, and yet they weren't. I ran through alley ways, weaving behind cars and around buildings. Occasionally another crack would ring out, which I could only assume was Peter taking another shot.

"And then this young boy, only about eight years old, came running from the direction of the sea. He was yelling something over and over again, but no one was listening. He was so young, so innocent. It suddenly was as if everything had become silent except for the young boy's voice."

"What was he saying?" asked John.

"Just three words in Indonesian over and over again. *Laut akan datang, laut akan datang.* The sea is coming, the sea is coming." Jenny paused, her eyes welling. "I looked at the ground. Water had started to ooze around my feet, and then I looked down the street past the many blocks of buildings towards the ocean. I saw this thing coming. It was like a mountain moving forwards. Water rolling wave upon wave, but it wasn't like normal water, the waves were pitch black. The tsunami was coming.

"I needed to find safety, and I needed to find it fast. The buildings all around were relatively flimsy. I knew that they wouldn't hold. But in front of me was this tall coconut palm that seemed to be well planted into the ground. I quickly undid my belt and wrapped it around the tree strapping myself in.

"I looked around. Amongst everyone running in the rising water, about a block away, I saw Peter slowly take aim at me. I was a sitting duck exposed out in the middle of the street strapped to a tree and there was nothing I could do. And then the waves hit hard.

"I quickly tried to scale the tree using the water to float me up. I wanted to get as high as possible. As the black water rushed by, the debris slashed at my legs. It was absolute agony. Regardless I was thankful and somewhat amazed that the tree was still. And then within a second everything went black.

"I was dunked deep under water, but it only lasted a short moment. The tree, I was attached to, had finally snapped and was swept up in the vast torrent of water. I thought I was going to drown. Suddenly I was flung out on top of a pile of floating debris with the palm tree still attached to my waist.

"The waters around me was surging violently. I held onto the tree for dear life as I was dragged on this floating debris pontoon down the Aceh streets. I knew I needed to get off, and soon without killing myself. I was scared. I had no idea whether this flotsam would hold my weight, but I had no choice.

"I released my belt and fell on top of the broken bits of wood and plaster. I managed to right myself somewhat and saw that I was now surrounded by other things such as floating cars, wood and any other materials the rushing waters were able to carry. By this time, I was floating just under the balconies of the second storeys of buildings. Many buildings scaringly had been washed away, but some were still standing.

"I started to float past this one large white solid building. People were standing out on the balcony watching and yelling. One man leant out on the balcony and called out for me in Indonesian to grab onto his hand. The pontoon which I was on was starting to rotate left and right depending on what hit it. It wasn't going to last. I scrambled out to the edge and was ready to grab onto the man's hand when the pontoon suddenly turned. I don't know how I did it, but I managed to leap in sheer desperation and I felt this iron grip grab hold of my hand. Another arm clenched onto my other hand and they both dragged me up, out of the torrent to safety.

"As I was being lifted, I looked around and saw my floating island in the distance disentangle and split apart in the foaming black water. If it wasn't for these guys, I know I would've died.

"I was hauled over the edge, and placed down on the balcony. All I could do was just sit and cry. The family made sure that I was okay and brought me out a cup of tea. It was sweet. They were so nice. I took comfort in it and just stared at the devastation that was happening all around. It just didn't seem real. I was so thankful to the family who had saved me and they eventually helped me inside.

"I looked at myself. My legs and arms were all cut up. I was a mess, but I really didn't care. I had only just managed to survive.

"I got up and looked out the window. This massive high rise of water was flowing past. It was unbelievable. And then it finally dawned the breadth of disaster that had befallen this country. There had to be tens of thousands dead, perhaps even more. It dawned on me that so many of those deaths could have been prevented. If a warning had been given out... Imagine!!!"

"Did Peter survive?" asked John.

"I don't think so. I would say no. So many died that day. I was extremely lucky to have survived myself. Almost a miracle I guess, but in reality just the small statistic of those that did. We were all lucky the building we were in managed to withstand the force of the water. It was well built.

"Soon the waters subsided. The whole of Banda Aceh had changed. So much had been washed away. It was never going to be the same.

"When it was safe, I walked the streets and tried to help where I could. I knew I had some serious wounds, but I didn't care. Eventually I managed to find one of my work colleagues. She was lying in her home, dead. She had been pinned down by the rubble from the earthquake and must have drowned when the tsunami came through. It was horrible. I couldn't find anyone else. I felt completely hopeless.

"I wandered the streets for hours upon end, trying to do anything to help, trying to find some meaning of everything. The more I looked, the more I realised that not many had survived. Occasionally we found one who had, beyond all odds, escaped certain death.

"Eventually I made my way back to the flat of the people who had rescued me. The people welcomed me back as their little miracle, almost as family. They helped me, tended to my wounds again and looked after me in whatever way they could. They had medicines and they ultimately helped stop my wounds getting too infected.

"After a few days, the Indonesian and foreign aid teams had finally made their way through to where we were and started the recovery process, basically removing the bodies and debris. The British government set up a tent embassy on the outskirts of town, where they had embassy staff to 'help any Brit in need'. I went over to their site, and when they asked my name, I hesitated. I just burst into tears. I knew that if I gave them my name, then whoever Peter had been working for would know that I was alive, and they would come after me, or at least that's what I thought would happen. But I had no choice. I just wanted to go home.

"So I gave them my name and just hoped that nothing horrible would happen. It was the only way I could get out of the country. I had to hope that Peter hadn't told anyone I knew of the prediction. I just hoped that he was too obsessed in chasing after me to call anyone.

"Soon I was taken by embassy staff into a private helicopter and flown out of Aceh. I never got to thank the family who had saved me and helped me in my dire time of need. They had lost so much more than me, yet they had been so sacrificing putting their own lives at risk, especially for a foreigner like myself. I owe them so much."

Jenny briefly paused, staring off into the distance. She took a deep breath and focussed back on John. The look of anguish was visible in her emerald green eyes.

"I spent the next three weeks in an Indonesian hospital. During that time, I got to think about the set of events and what had happened. I knew it wouldn't be the last disaster that SMC knew about and could have helped ameliorate. If they managed to predict this with that level of accuracy, then who knew what else they could predict.

"So from that moment on I vowed revenge. Enough was enough. They had sacrificed the innocent. They had sacrificed us. They had sacrificed my friends. They felt it was important that they took calculated hits with their own people, but what they didn't calculate was the lengths I would go to, to expose them all.

"It was only by chance that Peter had used me as a confessional. It wasn't about saving me. He didn't care about me. It was for his own conscience. He had felt that if he could save one person, allowed one person to live, then he was not a heartless killer, because he had compassion. It was okay to allow hundreds of thousands of people to die as long as he gave pity to one person, allow his compassion to save one person. It is the mind of the truly deluded!"

Jenny stood and looked out at the blue crowd in the hostel's courtyard. They had piled up and were now waiting at the doors of the rented busses.

"Mind you, he now doesn't seem to be the only deluded one."

Jenny turned back to John looking a little more resolute.

"I was flown back to the UK and SMC took care of all of my expenses. It took the authorities a while to find the rest of our team. A few of the guys could only be identified by dental records, some of them several months later. SMC flew each of their bodies back and made the funeral arrangements for them, one at a time. As distressing as it was, I made sure I attended each of their funerals. I relived that awful tragedy over and over and over... fully knowing that they needn't have died. It strengthened my resolve in seeking revenge.

"Over time I realised Peter mustn't have told SMC of his confession, or at least they didn't dare to act whilst so much government attention was on me. So I worked in the background over the months, trying to get information about the inner workings of SMC, and about Peter."

Jenny ventured back to the bedside. "I found no information in the company about him. He had no record whatsoever, nothing. It was as if he didn't even exist. I asked around to find out about the supervisors visiting our region in Aceh, and eventually found out that a contractor had been sent out to assist us with the test drilling, and his name according to the correspondence was not Peter, but John Jones. Peter? John? Probably just another pseudonym. He apparently worked for Allied Minerals Incorporated, AMI, a small contracting group that were supposedly specialists in mineral project management and operations. Their website claimed that they did temporary stand-ins for mining and mineral exploration groups when gaps were needed to be filled in for short periods of time. I suspected it was purely a front.

"I did some more research on AMI and made a few phone calls. Shortly afterwards, I was approached by my supervisor who said that I had been falling behind in my work. She said that she believed it was from the trauma of Aceh, and that I should go on indefinite leave and only once I passed a work psych exam, could I come back. I asked if this was her idea, or if she was pushed from above. She refused to say. I left and never went back.

"I was furious. I searched out to see if anyone had similar experiences, and came across a blog post from this environmentalist, Caroline Chiswick."

John recognised the name. "Wasn't she the one mentioned in the news report the other day?" he asked.

"Yes. I wasn't surprised that she was mentioned as we have worked closely together in the past. Anyway, back then, according to her blog, Carol was an environmental scientist who had worked for another big mining company, and when she made some enquiries on certain people including a contractor from AMI, she too had been swiftly fired. Apparently that chain of events raised her suspicions about some corrupt inner dealings and environmental mismanagement of her company. So she formed a small group of similar minded people to investigate and expose them all."

"I contacted her about my situation. She was excited. She told me all about her employment, her old company, and how they were badly destroying the environment. She told me how her job was to make out that it wasn't them causing the problems. And then she started to tell me about her recent investigations and the latest suspect activities that she had found out about her old company. She believed they were trying to conceal them at all costs from the public.

"Regardless, the stuff she told me was still far more minor compared to Aceh, but she was what I needed. Someone I could talk to who would listen and help act. I decided there and then that I wouldn't tell her about Peter and the pre-knowledge of Aceh tsunami as I didn't think anyone, including her, would believe me. What I told her instead was of my investigations of the inner workings of SMC and AMI, and how I got pushed out the back door.

"Carol wasn't surprised at all. She believed that there was something not quite right about them and that when we found out what, it would lead us to expose the whole truth. So we put our efforts together.

"The following years are another story, but in short, we got more organised. We found out many of the plans and workings of the companies we had been working for and then the plans of many more. There was a whole web of interactions, but nothing ever truly implicating about a grand conspiracy.

"What was obvious was the amount of destruction and damage that was happening from these companies and over the years as the science grew, what concerned us even more was their effects were not only local, but global too with their undeniable impacts on global climate. We went public. And with our considerable growing membership, we started to picket the companies and their projects. We made big attempts to derail many of the new projects, but none were too successful."

"Sorry," interrupted John. "One thing I don't understand, why didn't you just join one of the other environmental groups at the time? Why didn't you join Greenpeace, Friends of Earth, or even for that matter, the Earth Liberation Front? They would've welcomed you with open arms and you would have had greater input!"

"We wouldn't. Greenpeace and Friends of Earth were too weak, and let's face it, they still are. They're more about making people feel good about themselves and doing things nicely, rather than real climate activism. But the E L F, I'm sorry, they are just insane."

"But you guys are considered nutters too. Surely..."

"No John. You really don't understand. I've met some of them. They literally are insane."

"Really?!"

"Really!!"

"Sorry," said John. "So you said you guys were picketing projects?"

"Yes," replied Jenny. "In our own way. Our group, you could say, originally was like a hybrid, half way between Greenpeace and ELF. We would picket projects, and occasionally sabotage some in a more sophisticated way, mainly through our knowledge of the mining industry. We'd doctor samples, forge interfering paperwork, and so on. It really frustrated them. They eventually had no idea what was real and what wasn't.

"In the meantime, a few of us continued to search deeper mainly into the organisation AMI and ones that had dealings with them. As we dug deeper, it got grubbier and grubbier showing linkages to government and other industries. And then the name '*Them*' showed up. We started looking back and it became obvious. *Them* was everywhere.

"It was bizarre. As soon as we made this linkage, AMI suddenly disbanded and disappeared off the face of the earth. Even all the material we had found had somehow got altered, not even leaving a trace. They somehow must have found out about our investigations. Nonetheless, we had our lead – the group '*Them*'.

"We found ourselves over the next few years searching after this mysterious organisation that seemed to be strongly linked to many of the big players we had been hunting. It got murkier and harder to follow the longer we searched and hunted after them. The leads kept disappearing.

"In the meantime, our other activities had developed quite a big following and soon we had become internationally renowned. Many people across the world wanted to join us. So we went public. Other groups merged into ours. We even got good financial backing from the general public and several philanthropic individuals. So we tried to bring public attention to many of our theories, but our attempts failed in vain. Our internet posts and video materials got massively altered. So our attempts always seemed to be the ramblings of conspiracy theorists and tree huggers. Still, our following grew.

"People from all around the world were willing to try and help us get the evidence of what was really happening. It certainly brought out many mentally unstable people, but we were able to direct them to weaker, more harmless actions and causes. Some people, who were quite adept, like Scarlet, were used to help infiltrate organisations and meetings where we thought we could get the evidence we were after.

"But it was so slow and ineffectual. Many things happened that I believed *Them* knew about, the worst one being the Japan Tsunami in 2011. Every disaster that happened made me feel like we were getting further and further away from exposing them. So I decided to take things into my own hands.

"I waited for the right opportunity and one finally presented itself. That happened to be at the 2015 mining convention at *Le Palais des Congrès de Paris.*

"It was perfect. Close by. Easy Access. Low Security. I knew the venue well as I had been to conferences there before. I even knew where to get the bomb making materials easily. I knew how to carry it out. I knew the security wouldn't be too high. As an industrial chemist it wasn't hard at all.

"I chose to set it off below the auditorium. I knew that most of the people who I believed were involved would be there. It was a special session. Only those in control of those projects were attending that session. It couldn't have been any better planned. It was too perfect, too easy. I just thought..." Tears started welling up in Jenny's eyes. "I just thought that if I could stop them, then it would all come out. It would all come to an end.

"I was sick of hiding. I was sick of feeling impotent in what we were doing. I just wanted it to end once and for all. I just thought that if I stopped them, then they might be found out. And maybe millions more might be saved.

"And then it all happened. The bomb went off without a hitch.

"Oh god!! Why didn't it fail? Why couldn't it have stuffed up? For a moment, I couldn't believe it was real. I didn't want to, but it was… It was real. I realised what I had done and what I had become. I had killed all those people, about three hundred in total and most of them… most of them were innocent. I had become what I had despised. I was just as bad as them.

"I saw the news. I saw the aftermath. I saw the families crying for the victims. I saw their bodies being taken out in countless bags. I saw the mourning. I hated myself!! I hated myself for what I had done and what I had become. On more than one occasion I was on the verge of killing myself. I had the gun out. I had the rope ready. I had… I had…"

John came over and gently cuddled Jenny as she broke down in tears.

"I had to kill myself for what I had done, yet I was still the only one who truly knew what they had been able to foresee. What do I do? I was torn inside and out. I knew that if I killed myself, the world would never know. But how could I live after doing something that atrocious… that horrible? How could I??

"I did the only thing I could. I blocked it out. I denied it, even to myself. It was the only way... the only way... What else could I have done, John? What else could I have done?"

Jenny cried deeply and soulfully as he held onto her in his arms. Slowly and carefully John lifted her head staring deep into her sad emerald green eyes. He kissed her gently on the lips wanting to take her away from her pains and troubles. And for one small moment, everything was okay.

Then there was a knock on the door.

Chapter 26

Jenny quickly snapped out of the moment grabbing Karen's gun. It had been left on the bed. Jenny wiped away the tears from her face as she carefully walked across the green linoleum floor to the edge of the door. She made sure the brick wall gave her protection from the realms of the corridor. She motioned for John to get down.

"Who is it?" she asked.

"Jenny, it's me!" said Karen impatiently.

"Why don't you have your key?"

"Because Ahmed, the useless prick, only organised for one. Sorry I forgot to mention that when I left."

"How's your mother going?"

"She's fine. She's skiing in the Alps."

Jenny opened the door to Karen who was carrying two small black back packs.

"For fuck's sake, did you have to go for the secret message?" asked Karen as she traipsed in.

"Well…"

"Okay. I'm alright. I have our gear." She looked over at John. "And John, you can get up now."

John, slightly embarrassed that he was hiding behind the bed, stood up brushing off the dust he had acquired from the floor. Karen placed the bags on the bed.

Jenny kept quiet, appearing to be still contemplating her confession. She glanced over at John, seemingly confused. Calm was slowly returning to the room. Jenny gently touched her lips.

Suddenly Ahmed burst through the door with Francois in tow. Jenny was startled and raised her gun once again in the door's direction.

Karen looked at Jenny in concern. She obviously had worked out that Jenny was shaken about something. Ahmed oblivious to happenings in the room, was laughing in hysterics with Francois.

"Hey Jen, it's me!" he said, putting his hands up in a mock surrender. "It's okay! I'm sorry for bursting in like that, but look, what happened downstairs was too funny. We got a bit carried away. You okay?"

"Yes! All fine!" said Jenny, trying to compose herself without being too obvious. "What was so funny? What happened downstairs?"

"Well," said Ahmed, obviously itching to tell the story, "Francois and I went downstairs and had a beer with those guys, the ones from before, and let's just say, they are just a tad insane. The four of them are from this *Delugion* sect, now get this, known as *Apocalyptic Delugion* where they believe that the '*end is nigh*'."

"What, the world's going to end?" asked John.

"Yeah. They believe it and are convinced of it. And more than that, they're okay with it. They say it's just something that they believe, that

God will make it happen and that everyone who doesn't follow it, i.e. everyone else… is going to hell!!"

"Really?"

"Yeah! They're just sad that many of their friends are going to hell, but they accept it… just part of life!"

"Bizarre!" said John.

"Absolutely!!" said Ahmed.

"So are they prepared for it?" asked Karen.

"Yeah. They said it could happen any time. They even tried to convince us to make preparations. Apparently they have made bunkers, have a stash of tins, preserved good, water and various other survival gear to keep them alive until God comes to them and takes them away. You see, they reckon this is what the Great Deluge was. They believe that Clive is here to help people find God again before the rapture occurs and this will help save everyone who believes."

"And the atheists?" asked Karen.

"Hell!"

"Muslims and Jews? What's left of them?"

"Hell."

"What about newborns?"

"Karen, for crying out loud! I didn't ask them that!" said Ahmed.

"And they really believe it, don't they?" asked Karen with resignation.

"They do," replied Ahmed somewhat more sombrely.

"So now there are sects?" asked Jenny.

"Apparently!"

"Have you come across this before?" Jenny asked Francois.

"Oui," he replied. "It has started to appear in a few spots. It's only natural that religions split apart and sects start to form. And I believe Maria Rodriguez went with it and is feeding it. When I spoke to Clive, he said he was trying to rein them back in so that there wouldn't be any infighting. He was having words with Maria."

"Look, these people are completely normal," said Ahmed coming to their defence. "You saw them before. They just have a different interpretation on what has happened. They think that everyone's going to die sometime soon, but they're okay with it. It's just their own version of *Delugion*. Nothing to worry about."

"And what happens when they have kids?" asked Karen. "The kids will believe the same. I mean, what sort of life is that? We grew up with stories of Santa Claus, the tooth fairy… and they'll grow up with the story of the four horsemen of the apocalypse."

Karen's comment silenced them all. The burgeoning crowd outside burst into one of the hymns that John recognised from the church.

"Hopefully we'll get to expose it all soon enough," said Jenny, giving Karen a comforting rub on her shoulder.

"I know," said Karen. "It just makes me lose faith in humanity when I hear stories like that."

"We better move soon," said Ahmed. "The buses leave in less than ten minutes and they're our best option for getting to the dictate unnoticed. Francois has a rough plan which should work for when we're in the building. But we've got to get going."

"Did you manage to get the shirts?" asked Jenny.

"Yeah," replied Ahmed grabbing them out of a plastic bag. "The guys had spares. They were actually excited that Francois was going to wear one of their shirts. I offered them some cash for it, but they refused. They actually were really nice."

Ahmed passed the shirts around. They each put them on, and they soon appeared as if they were all part of some group of blue shirted groupies ready to go to a concert.

"You don't think we look too old?" asked John.

"No one will care," replied Jenny as she tied up her hair. "When you're in a sea of people who look similar, it's hard to spot anomalies. We'll fit in fine. Anyway guys, Ahmed's right. We better get moving. Karen, you take the backpack with the guns. Ahmed..." Jenny continued to explain the travel plan to the group as well as what to do when they arrived. Ahmed then explained what would happen once they were inside the building.

"Just remember, try not to draw any attention to yourselves. We'll split off into our two groups now. Everyone okay?"

They all nodded, and readied themselves to leave. John took a deep breath as they headed out the door. They made their way through the maze of corridors and joined the gathering crowd outside. This was it. This was going to be the one to sort it all. They were now on their way to the man, the man who was the centre of all that had passed, the man who was now the most powerful person in the world. He was the one who had moulded the people of the world to be a devout following, and now unknowingly he was going to be the one to help them reveal it all... that is, if he cooperated. So much was at stake, but they had little choice.

The hum of the crowd grew louder as they left the confines of *The Wander Inn*. Soon the five immersed themselves into the anonymous sea of blue people. Ahmed and Francois moved away as planned, thus ensuring that they all blended better.

The crowd moved slowly and methodically eventually winding its way into a dozen busses. They were on their way.

CHAPTER 27

THE BUS TRIP into London was annoyingly slow due to a combination of heavy traffic and altered travel routes. It frustrated John, but there was nothing he could do.

London was in full swing for the *Delugion Dictate*. The main thoroughfares had been cordoned off for a variety of special events and a multitude of open air performances happening throughout the great city. The final great culmination was to be *The Dictate* in the heart of New London at The Royal Diluvian Hall. The city was truly abuzz.

Despite the delays, everyone else on the bus was elated, often breaking into chants, songs and hymns of *Delugion*. Karen, Jenny and John had decided to sit towards the back of the bus to lower their profile, which to their relief seemed to work this time. They kept quiet throughout most of the journey, only sometimes pretending to sing along with the songs so as to not stand out. Even with their stammering through many of the songs, most people just ignored the trio as they were too excited about the coming evening.

Karen looked uncomfortable being surrounded by those of the *Young Delugion* movement. She regularly fidgeted with her backpack zip, restless to open it, yet knowing full well that if someone saw the contents, it would raise alarm.

The crowded bus broke into their next song.

...I'm only happy when it rains.

I'm only happy when its divinated...

Karen leaned over the seat between John and Jenny and whispered, "Why send Ahmed with Francois? If things get physical, you know that it's better I'm there. I have the training."

...and though I know some don't appreciate it.

I'm only happy when it rains...

"Karen, I know you're good," replied Jenny through gritted teeth. "But you know and I know that if we are trying to get through security with Francois without question, it is better for a man to go. *Delugion* hasn't solved the gender divide yet. You can't go. It would be too suspicious."

...You know I love it when the skies are mad,

and rains wipe out all those who have been bad.

I'm only happy when it rains.

Karen flopped back on her seat with frustration. The girl next to Karen briefly glared at her, but soon returned back to the song with her friends across the aisle.

Pour your Delugion down on me!

Pour your Delugion down on me!

As disturbing as the song was, the tune reminded John of one of the rock songs from his childhood. He thought the original wasn't religious, but he couldn't be sure. Regardless, it wasn't enough to distract him from the state of affairs.

John looked over to Jenny. He was concerned. There was a rift forming within his group. The control that Jenny had at the start was starting to falter. With her series of miscalculations resulting in deaths of not only James, but people in the general public, John could understand the other's loss of confidence. Ahmed had started to question her, Karen was arguing back, even Jenny looked less self-assured in herself.

John reached across and gently caressed Jenny's hand. She smiled back. The simple touch had helped ease her tension.

Soon the bus was making its way through the streets of Central London heading towards the large edifice that marked their destination. New London, as the area had been renamed, represented a small island opposite Westminster on the old grounds of St Thomas' Hospital. It had been semi-created when the Great Global Floods had lifted the level of the Thames by a few metres. The waters had flooded the roads and parks throughout London, but particularly those that surrounded St Thomas' Hospital and its associated buildings. It had only submerged these areas to a small extent, so most people could still wade across to the centre, but the waters had rendered a lot of the land unusable.

Nonetheless, cities move on and find solutions, and the church of *Delugion* gave a helping hand. Soon it was deemed, like in most major cities around the world, that a centre for the religious following was to be created to celebrate *The Great Global Flood* and the rise of *Delugion*. In the space of only a year, the historic buildings had been demolished, and the submerged roads surrounding had been excavated further. The land was lifted in the centre of the site to create a mounting island Mecca. By popular demand the island district and surrounding areas had been named New London, and it represented the change of British Culture to the masses.

There were statues, museums, art houses, and cultural centres to celebrate the modern age, but two buildings stood out, dwarfing the rest–the magnificent *British Cathedral of Delugion* and *The Royal*

Deluvian Hall. These two remarkable structures stood on top of the hill looking out over the great vista of London. They made Big Ben seem like a small plinth and Westminster Abbey merely a relic from the past.

To celebrate its glory, seven bridges had been erected around the island's base to allow access to all that *believe* with each bridge representing each year of *God's wrath.* Every one of the seven bridges had been designed to float so that the movement on the water would remind followers of what had befallen the earth and how close God's Great Deluge was. These bridges had been replicated at many *Delugion* sites around the world.

The buses began to pull up at the entranceway of each bridge, releasing the excited masses into the streets. John stared out the bus' window as the large crowds slowly flocked towards the great island. Just as their bus finally released its doors, the *Young Delugionists* broke into their next song.

...Raindrops keep falling on our heads...

Oh no!!! thought John. *Not this song too.*

...Exactly the way that Clive was told that God had said,

to help save me.

And now we're ne'er complaining about it never stopping raining.

Because we see, what the world is to be...

That was terrible, thought John. *Whoever wrote the lyrics should be shot!*

The three finally left the confines of the bus into the swarm of people outside. It was uncomfortable and everyone was closely packed. Karen and Jenny each carried their backpack over their shoulder. It didn't look too out of place as several other passengers had similar bags.

To John's surprise, there was very little security on the way to the island. He figured that they must be all at the main centre. Besides, it would be a very game person to disrupt the YD crowd. The crowd started to sing a *Delugion* rendition of what John worked out was Paul McCartney's *Let it Be.*

If God deems that the world tomorrow,

Is full of sin and treachery

Let him wipe the world clean

With the big blue sea....

"Couldn't they have come up with some original music?" sighed John.

"Well, they did for some," replied Karen. "But for most of their songs, you are right. The music is not original. They copied the tunes of mostly well-known songs to try and make their hymns contemporary and popular. It's something that sports clubs and teams have done with their chants and war cries for decades. It makes it easier for people to remember the lyrics and sing along. Far easier and more effective than writing original music."

John was surprised at Karen's knowledge of *Delugional* culture. He didn't hide it well.

"Oh come on!" protested Karen. "You don't think that with my Jewish background and time in the IDF that we didn't learn about this shit. My old country struggled enough to stop people going across to the '*Delugional*' side. Of course we learnt about it. We had to."

Jenny laughed at John's faux pas. "John! It seems that you still have a lot to learn about religious politics."

"Obviously," he replied.

Soon they were funnelled towards one of the floating bridges. John was impressed with its architecture and artwork. The entranceway was regal with an ornate sculpted stone archway marking its entrance. The archway consisted of flying angels pouring water down from above which then split apart creating a flowing opening. At the base of each side stood the figure of a man and a woman being doused by the angel's water, whilst at the same time standing safely on dry land.

John had seen these archways before. He was told by a colleague that they represented heaven cleansing the souls of its followers with *The Great Deluge*, whilst keeping them safe. John shook his head. In no way did it even attempt to portray the millions of people that had drowned from the floods and tsunamis. John quickly looked to see if there were any dead bodies sculpted into the base, but quickly refrained when he thought about the depravity.

As they walked across the low wooden walkway, John felt freer not being so heavily surrounded by the blue masses. He looked around and could see several of the other bridges transporting lines of blue people across the waterway. Some bridges were elevated, some were at the water's level creating a layered effect. The crowds all streamed towards the centre of the island where the magnificent structure of The Royal Deluvian Hall and Cathedral awaited.

John looked ahead. Upon the rise stood their destination, The Royal Deluvian Hall. It was modelled similar to the Royal Albert Hall but was even larger being able to fit over fifty thousand people. It pulled in strong elements of Roman architecture, particularly from the Pantheon with great marble spires and a massive concrete dome. As John got closer, he saw that it contained a lot of modern elements too with sculpted walls containing cascading waterfalls that flowed down the wall only to rise up at the bottom forming artificial waves. There were statues placed around the entrances representing images from the bible, especially Jesus and Clive himself. The building in John's opinion was undoubtedly *Delugional.*

John was relieved. Walking amongst the crowds, they had remained over the whole time unbothered. They had remained anonymous wearing their blue shirts. John figured the people attending were so focused on the event that they took little time to notice any strangers. Even the security guards seemed to not pay attention to their presence, more annoyed that they were wasting their time at such a sedate event.

The time when he and the others had been hunted by people from *Them* seemed a mile away to John. And soon he hoped, the tables would change. The secret behind it all would be revealed and *Them* would be the ones hunted.

Jenny signalled for John and Karen to follow her and the three walked off to one of the many green parks dotted around the island. They had to wait. It was now time for Francois and Ahmed to do their work.

CHAPTER 28

FRANCOIS WASN'T SURE that the plan was going to work. With Ahmed by his side, it would be a lot harder to get through security. He would have preferred to do it alone. Ahmed, however, seemed confident that everything would be fine. Francois started to tap his fingers impatiently on the bar. Ahmed gave him a reproachful glance.

Francois and Ahmed had made their way moments earlier inside the hallways of The Royal Deluvial Hall without any major hindrance. In fact, the entire trip, as Jenny had predicted, had been mostly uneventful. Ahmed had only been briefly held up through security because he was carrying four insulin syringes in his bag.

"What's this for?" asked the security guard earlier.

"Isn't it obvious? I'm bloody diabetic!" replied Ahmed feigning mild annoyance.

"Oh!" said the guard. As he was closing up Ahmed's bag, he looked up at Ahmed and Francois with some incredulity. "Aren't you two a bit old for this YD event?"

"Yes, but our kids are here," said Ahmed, "and we wanted to make sure they were safe. Of course, we're not allowed to be seen with them as it would apparently be too embarrassing. You know kids!?!"

The guard smiled. "How old are they?"

"Oh, mine? James is fifteen and Elizabeth's fourteen. And Frank over here, what is it? Your kid's fourteen too?"

Francois nodded.

"I don't blame you guys for coming," said the guard. "We had this one kid, one time… grabbed on the arse by this bloody weirdo. She was so upset about it all… It took her parents about four hours just to get through the crowds and everything. At the end of these things, it's all chaos. The island's architects made it bloody easy to get onto this island, but I tell you what, when it's all over, it takes bloody ages to get off."

Ahmed took note as he made his way through the rest of security. Since then, Francois and Ahmed had decided to kill a little time until it was safe to enact the plan. They were waiting in the refreshments area having what they told the bartender was a pre-Dictate lager. The bartender didn't care whether it was pre-Dictate, intra-Dictate, or post-Dictate, as long as they paid and he didn't have to talk to anyone.

They took their drinks and sat waiting in the corner of the lounge. The crowds continued streaming through the hall to their various allocated seating sections. Most people looked positively lost as they tried to work their way through the quagmire of various entrances to various sections and aisles. It entertained the two.

"You know he tries to come here about once a year now?" said Francois. "To 'support the cause'." Francois paused in thought. "I suppose if things go right tonight, it will all soon change."

"One can only hope," replied Ahmed.

"How did you get involved in all of this?" asked Francois.

"Nothing much really," said Ahmed. "Always believed in environmental causes, as well as religious and social freedoms."

"Yeah… But surely there's more to it?" said Francois. "You seem to be intelligent, resourceful, almost militaristic? No?"

"Actually, it's nothing too exciting," replied Ahmed. "Grew up in Barnstaple in Devon County. Parents were religious. I wasn't. Enjoyed my surfing, travelled the world and saw what damage we were causing the oceans. It got me kind of pissed off, so I joined some environmental action groups in the area. Things led onto other things and before you know it, I met with Carol Chiswick and then Jenny. They seemed to be onto something, and so I decided I would help out and the rest is history. Nothing too dramatic."

"But your weapons training? Your physical… err… compétence?

"Too much time playing on the X-box really and I enjoyed paintball in my youth. And let's just say, I've sought out the appropriate skills training over the years. I actually used to be quite weedy."

Francois smiled. The crowds were still thronging in the hallways.

"You said that you weren't religious, but I saw you had a quiet prayer at the hostel. What happened?"

"Clive happened!! When the Great Global Floods occurred, I saw the effect it had on people. People were confused and were unsure of their faith. Everyone started following him, abandoning their religions. There are not many that are Muslim, Hindu, or even Jewish anymore. Most are now *Delugional*. My parents died on holidays when the Hawaiian tsunami hit. So I thought I should honour their belief and learn to follow the teachings of Mohammad."

"So do you believe in Allah?"

"I do… to an extent. Being originally an atheist, it was hard and I mainly did it for cultural reasons, but over the years I guess it started to sink in, and I developed what you would call some faith. I didn't really abandon science or logic, but I did develop some belief in God and for me being a Muslim helped. But now, with the real story of Clive, it challenges you a bit. It makes you question whether people in power did this throughout the millennia, to control everyone. But, what about you? Do you believe in anything?"

"Not anymore."

Francois pondered his beer for a moment. The crowds in the hallway were starting to thin.

"You know that Jenny's insane?" stated Francois.

"She's not insane!"

"But she did do the bombing."

"I know that," admitted Ahmed. "She's refused to tell me over the years, but I know that. She obviously felt she had to do what she did. She's always had a good reason behind everything that she's done, even the more devastating ones. She wouldn't have taken it easy, and I believe those reasons have recently been revisited. I think that's why she's starting to make a few bad decisions. But she's never confided in me and I guess I've never pushed it either. I always felt she'd tell me in her own time."

"And you don't have a problem with that?"

"And you don't have a problem with allowing millions of people to die from global warming?"

"Touché!" said Francois taking another sip from his lager.

The chime sounded, and a voice emanated from the speakers. It was the final call for people to take their seats. Francois felt a cold sweat form on his body.

"It's time," said Ahmed.

Francois knew this was it. This was the inevitable moment that was always going to come. From the moment he got involved, he knew this would eventually happen.

They both stood up, sculling the last bits of their lagers. Ahmed picked up his backpack and shoved it on his shoulder. They left the bar and quickly walked through the thinning crowds towards a roped off section of the hallway.

As they had hoped, the security there was now lax with most of the security detail either being on stage, or situated amongst the hall's massive crowds. Francois had explained earlier that Clive never felt comfortable with a large security force. Regardless, the Vatican, along with the other religious groups managed to convince him to have some. As expected, only one person was manning the ropes. The person tensed as they approached.

"Bonjour," said Francois to the guard.

"Hello sir!" said the man. "How can I help you?"

"You may not know me, but I am Francois Maury, from the French Ministry," said Francois handing over his identification. "I am a close confidant of His Religious Excellency."

"Is he expecting you?"

"Non! Not yet! I was supposed to meet with him later tonight, but I thought it would be a nice surprise to come and meet him after his show."

"Just hold a moment, sir!" said the security guard. The guard pressed the button on an electronic device attached to his ear. "Hey guys! I have a Francois Maury here to see Clive after the show. He doesn't have any passes, but he says he is from the French Ministry. Anyone know if it's okay for him to come through?"

There was a moment's silence as they waited patiently. Ahmed was a bit uneasy as the guard stared at them both.

"They're just checking," said the guard. "It shouldn't be too long. Hold on!"

There was a brief silence as the guard listened. "Yes... Yes... Where? Yes. Okay! You sure? Okay!"

Ahmed was starting to look worried that things weren't going to plan. He slowly clenched his fist in preparation.

"Okay," said the guard. "They said it was all fine."

Ahmed relaxed.

"I just need to know if you are you okay to wait in his dressing room. It will be about an hour to an hour and a half till it's all finished."

"That will be fine," said Francois. "My colleague and I will happily wait there."

"Sorry! I can only let you through. They didn't say anything about your colleague."

"But I must have him there!! He is my assistant and he has organised all the important documentation we need for our meeting. I would be totally lost without him. He is very important. It is against all French government protocol to go without your assistant."

The guard looked dubious, but reluctantly agreed. "Okay! If he is your assistant, and it's part of protocol, then yes, I will make an exception and he can go in."

"Thank you!" said Francois with relief.

"Merci!" said Ahmed feigning a French accent. Francois gave Ahmed a reproachful look over his terrible accent.

"Just follow the curve of the hall," explained the guard, "and about halfway around, another guard will meet you and take you in. It's a fair way."

"Thank you once again and God Bless you," said Francois.

They took their leave as they were let through the barrier consisting of the one heavyset rope. They continued to follow the curve of the hallway passing many glass doors that led out into the surrounding parks. Francois saw Ahmed noting their security that obviously required an ID card.

I hope they've worked this out fully, thought Francois.

Ahmed reached into his bag grabbing something out of it that Francois couldn't completely discern. All of a sudden, there was a loud cheer that emanated from the auditorium followed by a muffled amplified voice.

They must be starting.

A second cheer arose. Ahmed and Francois continued walking around and eventually they met up with another security guard who led them to an inset blue door on the inner wall of the hallway. On the door were the words–*Authorised Personnel Only,* and in front of it stood a guard wearing a soft mauve beret with a blue puffed uniform– the outfit of the *Delugional Guard.*

Their companion briefly talked to the *Delugional Guard*, who nodded and proceeded to open the door for them. As soon as the *Delugional Guard*'s back was turned, Ahmed quickly moved in and jabbed what Francois realised was the insulin syringe quickly into the base of his neck. The blue suited guard quickly turned around in surprise. Ahmed gave him a rapid blow to the gut. The guard doubled over. He was about to reach for his gun when he started to sway and had trouble moving and breathing.

Ahmed turned his attention to the security guard that had accompanied them. Ahmed's gamble had paid off in his assumption of the guard's inexperience. The guard was completely surprised by the sudden turn of events, and was in a slight panic fumbling for his two way radio not even realising that it was attached to his ear. Ahmed quickly swung an uppercut and knocked the guard to the ground unconscious. Ahmed turned back to the *Delugional Guard* who was still trying to reach for his gun, but by this stage the guard had found trouble even pulling up his arms. Ahmed quickly removed *Delugional Guard*'s gun and handed it calmly to Francois. The *Delugional Guard* weakened further and collapsed to the ground.

"Quick!" said Ahmed. "Open the door. We've got to get them in before anyone notices."

Francois was amazed at the speed of events. He hastily unlocked the door with the key that had been left in the lock. Meanwhile, Ahmed had cable tied the security and *Delugional* guards' hands. Ahmed dragged both guards inside. He lay the *Delugional Guard* on the ground whilst propping the security guard against the wall. Ahmed quickly pulled out a plastic respirator from his backpack and placed it over the mouth and nose of the *Delugional Guard*. He started to squeeze the bag on a regular basis making the guard's chest rise and fall.

"What are you doing? What did you give him?" demanded Francois.

"I gave him a muscle paralyser," said Ahmed. "He'll be fine. He's still conscious but cannot currently breathe on his own. It'll wear off in a few minutes, but because of that, I've got to give him this too."

Ahmed pulled out another syringe. The security guard started to recover from his blow. He struggled with his binds and was about to yell out.

"Don't you dare call for help," said Ahmed looking at the security guard directly in the eye. "Otherwise I'll give you what I just gave him, and I only have one respirator bag, got it?"

The guard looked at Ahmed respirating the *Delugional* Guard. Realising the situation, he quickly nodded in agreement. Ahmed turned his attention back to the *Delugional Guard* who was staring up at Ahmed unable to blink or move.

"As you probably realise, I have given you a muscle paralysing agent."

Francois could see, that even paralysed, the guard's eyes showed distress.

"You will be fine. It will wear off," said Ahmed. "Now I am about to give you an anaesthetic which you will wake up later on, not remembering what has happened. I promise you, you will be fine. You will feel a slight nausea and then things will blur out." Ahmed turned his attention to the security guard. "The same will happen to you."

The guard looked terrified.

"I promise you, you will be fine."

Ahmed took the syringe's cap off with his teeth and injected the *Delugional Guard's* leg with the agent. He motioned for Francois to take over the squeezing of the bag, which he did. Ahmed wandered over to the Security Guard who was terrified silently crying.

"I'm sorry to do this," said Ahmed, "but you will be alright. I promise."

He injected the leg of the guard who winced.

"You have been brave, my friend."

The guards breathing slowed after a few minutes and soon his head dropped. Ahmed checked the guard's responses. There was no movement besides his breathing. Ahmed was satisfied that they were both asleep. He removed their keys and their communication devices he could find including their phones. Ahmed then cut the cable ties of the security guard and took his uniform. He quickly changed and then secured the guard once again.

"All good," said Ahmed to Francois. "Keep the respirations up till I get back."

"What if the other guy stops breathing?" asked Francois.

"He won't," replied Ahmed. He sent a text and left the room.

CHAPTER 29

FOR JOHN, IT seemed like that the wait would never end. John, Karen and Jenny had been hanging around the small parkland opposite The Royal Deluvian Hall for over an hour. The clouds were settling in and John was concerned that it would soon rain, but ultimately that was minor compared to what lay ahead.

Jenny sat waiting for the message from Ahmed for them to proceed. She seemed relatively calm, getting her previous control back.

Karen however was uneasy. She was anxious. She was worried that the plan was not working and that things had gone wrong. She still affirmed that it was better that she had gone with Francois. Jenny had more confidence and often had to reassure her.

"He'll be fine," she said as she rested against the stone statue of a frozen wave, one of many dotted around the parkland. "It's just going to take time."

Karen stormed off in frustration.

"It was never going to be quick and easy," said Jenny.

"I know," replied John.

Jenny stared at Karen who was now pacing around. "I just can't seem to settle her. I don't know what's got into Karen."

"She's been through a lot, Jenny," said John. "We've got to a point of no return and she's sacrificed a lot. It's not easy losing your partner."

"I know… but still!!" Jenny bit her lip.

"I've got a question for you though," said John with a wry smile.

"What!?!" quizzed Jenny with suspicion.

"Why tERROR?"

"What do you mean?"

"The Earth's Representatives for Revegetation, Order and Restoration. That's a terrible name. Why go with that?"

"Because we wanted a name that was a little scary and tERROR worked."

"But if you go by logic with your name," John said with a smile, "it should either be ERROR, or even better, TERF ROAR!"

Jenny laughed. "I know. Neither of those would have been good. Imagine! We've been attacked by TERF ROAR!!! Arrrghhhh!!!! Look, we wanted something scary. Names like CHAOS would have reminded people too much of the old tv show, Get Smart, HORROR was a little too gothic, and to be honest there weren't any other anagrams we liked. So we went with tERROR. That is terror with a small t, and don't you forget it!"

"So much scarier with a small t!!"

They both laughed.

There was a buzz from the phone in Jenny's hand. Jenny looked down and read the message.

"It's Ahmed. Everything is apparently going to plan. He's told us to meet him at the south entrance, but has said we've got to move now."

They both stood up, quickly brushing the grass off themselves. Karen took notice of their movements and hastily ran over. She still looked agitated.

"Karen!" said Jenny still concerned with Karen's demeanour. "I need to know you're alright. We've got a lot ahead of us, and I need you to have a level head. If not, stay back."

"I'm okay," said Karen biting her lip. She looked almost in tears.

"You sure!?!" said Jenny.

"Yes!" replied Karen nodding. She straightened herself up, immediately changing her manner. Suddenly she seemed much more calm and collected. "I'm ready."

"Glad you're back with us. It would have been a real shame to leave you behind. Let's go!"

They made their way out of the parkland towards the far end of the great hall. Initially John was concerned a security guard was manning one of the doors, but then the guard waved for them to come over. As they got closer, John was relieved to see it was Ahmed dressed in the building's security uniform. He had the glass door propped open.

"Come on guys!!" said Ahmed impatiently. "We can't wait around much longer. It won't be long till the whole thing's over."

"Okay Ahmed!" replied Jenny. "Just take us in."

"And whilst you guys dawdled over, I think the ocean rose another two metres!!" mumbled Ahmed.

"Alright Ahmed! Enough with the jokes!" said Jenny with a stern glare.

They were led through the glass doors into a wide corridor. John looked around. There was no one about the scant thoroughfare, but what he did notice were security cameras facing in various directions. Ahmed continued to lead them across the hall. Jenny and Karen, to John's amazement, looked totally unconcerned.

"Aren't you worried about those cameras?" asked John.

"Shhh!!" said Jenny in a harsh whisper. "Someone might hear you. When we're inside!"

Ahmed took them across to a blue door inset on the side wall and unlocked it. They all followed quickly. Once inside the dressing room, John was shocked to see two people collapsed on the floor. One was being ventilated by Francois, and the other was stripped down to his underwear fast asleep near the wall.

"Are they alright?" asked John.

"Yes," replied Jenny. "They've been given a horse tranquiliser, scaled down of course. They'll wake up fine. Ahmed knows a vet surgeon back home. It's always been handy."

Ahmed checked on the one being ventilated. He let Francois know that he could stop as it appeared that the guard was now able to breathe on his own. The two moved the man next to the half-naked guard and propped them both against the wall. Karen in the meantime unpacked the bags, making sure her array of equipment was ready.

John stared at the anaesthetised men. It made him feel uncomfortable seeing their limp bodies prostrate against the wall.

"Don't worry John," said Jenny sensing his concern. "Using drugs is far less traumatic than knocking them out physically. We've done it many times, and never an issue. And it often affects their memory of events. Very handy."

"It doesn't make it right," replied John.

"I know, but it's the best option we have."

John had to accept the situation. "Okay, but what about the cameras outside. Have you guys considered those? What if security has…?"

"We already have that one covered," explained Jenny. "I have a friend who has hacked into its feed, and she's got a loop running in most of hallways where the general public is not allowed. They won't even know we're here. Apparently it's not that hard. She was going to fire it up once everyone had been seated. In theory, it's working now. In any case, no one's noticed."

"…yet!" added John.

"Hey guys!! Keep quiet," said Karen. "We might have got in fine, but someone could still hear us outside. No talking unless necessary, and not until we have secured everything. If you feel the need to talk, whisper!!"

Jenny nodded in agreement. She signed for people to take their positions around the room.

There was a big roar from the auditorium, followed by a big cheer. Jenny looked at her watch and signalled with her hands that there was ten minutes left, which John assumed to be the end of The Dictate. Jenny walked over to John.

"John, if you don't mind, I need you to put on the *Delugional Guard*'s uniform," she whispered. "If Clive's guards think that you are one of them, it might just delay them a bit and give us the upper hand."

"If you think so?"

"Thanks!"

John went over to Ahmed who was attending to both of the sleeping guards. Ahmed was reinjecting the leg of each of them which John assumed was to top up their anaesthetic. He quickly whispered to Ahmed what Jenny wanted. Ahmed nodded. He agreed it made sense.

Ahmed cut the ties off the *Delugional Guard's* hands and started to strip his clothes off. John gave a hand, helping roll the guard sideways, so they could take his jacket more easily off. As he rolled the guard to one side to free his arm from the sleeve, John noticed a small minute ear piece in the guard's ear. He quickly checked the guard's lapel and found a small mic. *Oh Shit!! There's got to be a button,* he thought. *There's got to be one.* It was a very similar device to the ones used by the security detail in Australia. He quickly felt the guard's pockets and sleeves. He eventually found a small on-off button on the guards right sleeve edge. John was somewhat relieved to see that it was off.

"Hey guys," said John.

"Shoosh!!" said Karen.

"No. This is important. The guard's got an ear piece and mic."

"Is it on?" asked Karen.

"No. I don't think he's used it, but what would happen if someone tried to call him?"

Jenny and Karen shot concerned glances at each other.

"They could think it's broken," said John trying to ease their fears.

"Just in case!" said Karen. Karen threw Jenny and Ahmed a gun each, and quickly tucked one into her belt. She threw one at John which he missed as it fell to the ground. John winced worried it would go off, then remembered that it had a safety.

And besides, he thought. *If it went off like that, imagine how many people would accidentally kill themselves, not to mention the transport issues.*

The door suddenly burst open and two *Delugional Guards* came rushing through. Karen leapt into action from beside the door disarming one by twisting his arm back, which she then followed through by rapidly kicking the other directly in the head. Karen's gun slipped out of her belt. Her gun fell with a clunk to the floor. Karen had managed to catch them by surprise.

The second guard fell back, momentarily stunned. The first guard swung his free arm around with a knife launching at her chest. Karen released his arm, collected the other hand and twisted it back. The knife was immediately released, and fell to the ground. She then kneed him in the groin and sent an elbow into his head which was resting against the stone wall. The guard collapsed to the ground.

Karen then quickly came upon the second guard who was still lying on the ground but starting to regain consciousness. She quickly twisted him over whilst holding his head and arm in a powerful lock. He struggled against her hold. She pulled on his arm harder and he yelled in pain.

Ahmed raced over and zip tied both of their arms and legs. The guard under Karen's arms started to yell out more. Karen squeezed his neck harder whilst pushing down onto his chest until he eventually passed out. Ahmed quickly gave both the guards some of the anaesthetic drug from the syringe.

John was impressed with Karen's speed and skilled moves. "All I can say is thank God Karen that you left the IDF and joined our side!!"

"Absolutely!" agreed Ahmed as he recapped the syringe.

"Who said I left the IDF?!" said Karen, as she picked up her gun from the floor.

Clive, unaware of the party waiting for him, came stumbling into the room. "Why did you guys rush in so f.........Oh!!" he said.

Karen lifted her gun in Clive's direction. He put up his hands. Besides Karen, no one's attention was on Clive. They were all looking at Karen.

Obviously this is something new, thought John.

Chapter 30

"What do you mean, '*Who said I left the IDF*?'" demanded Jenny.

Karen had her gun still pointed at Clive. "It doesn't matter. Clive is here now. It's him who we want."

"No, No, No!! You cannot take that back! You cannot make that comment and not explain yourself!! What the fuck do you mean!?!?"

Clive wandered unperturbed through the room and took a seat by the large lit mirror on the side wall. He looked surprisingly pleased with himself. He wasn't scared. He wasn't perturbed. He was going to enjoy this as much as he could. He sat back and stroked his rough brown beard.

"I'll tell you later!" said Karen trying to sway the conversation away.

"No!! Now!!!" yelled Jenny.

Karen paused for a moment weighing up the situation. She realised she had made a reckless mistake. She lowered her gun. "Alright!! It's as I said," she replied. "Yes! I am still part of the Israeli Defence Force."

Ahmed took up the position of aiming at Clive.

"So what are you saying?" said Jenny. "That you've been playing us all along, all this time? That you never loved James? That you just used him as a conduit to get here? That you've played us all for a fool?"

"No!" replied Karen somewhat offended. "It's not like that."

"Well what is it like, Karen? I would really like to know! Why don't you tell us exactly what it's like?"

Karen looked nervous. "Come on. We've got Clive here, what we all want!!"

"No, no, no!! You have no right to fucking dictate what we're doing! Not now!"

"Okay, okay!!!" said Karen slightly nervous. "Look. Just to get two things straight, I am still on your side and I did love James. I still do, and it's because of pricks like that, that he's dead."

She was pointing at Clive. He didn't appear affronted.

"When I said that I left the IDF," she said, "it wasn't technically completely true."

"Ooh!! This is interesting!" said Clive. He leaned back in his chair, enjoying the ensuing drama.

"Shut it!" said Ahmed.

"I did leave the IDF," said Karen, "not voluntarily, but on orders, and it was nothing nasty."

She took a deep breath and continued, "The Israeli Government saw the sudden rise of *Delugion* with the great global floods as their biggest threat and quite rightly so. They saw it not only destroy their own country's culture and religion, but they saw it also destroy the culture and religions of their friends, even their long-time enemies in the neighbouring countries. Even though *Delugion* brought about peace to the region, it did so at the sacrifice of so much.

"The Israelis never wanted this. The Israeli Government of the late 2010's was already making major headways towards peace, having halted settlements, lifting sanctions and agreeing to land sharing deals. They felt that they could move towards a situation where all religions would come together and maybe help stop the scourge of ISIS by supporting the Muslims. Admittedly there were extremists in all sectors, including the Jews themselves, but it was hoped that, through cooperation, each religion could help control their own.

"But what happened with *Delugion* was something different. It was the worst threat of any kind and it destroyed all that was integral to the country, to the region. The heads of the IDF had their suspicions. They knew that something wasn't right. They knew of some background chatter, but they never knew exactly what it was. What they did know was that there was something happening, something in the back rooms, even further behind the governments."

Jenny looked horrified, as if she never actually knew who Karen was. Ahmed didn't seem any more at ease.

"They felt that someone, or some group was manipulating it all, and that Clive... no offence..."

"None taken," he said.

"... was just the patsy."

"Actually!! Offence taken," interrupted Clive.

Ahmed waved the gun at Clive in frustration to shut him up. Clive pretended to zip his lips.

"They wanted to find out," said Karen as she glanced at Clive in some annoyance. "They had tried to get people to infiltrate many of the mining organisations to get into their upper echelons, but that drew nothing.

"So someone came up with a different idea. They thought they should try the other way, create a target to draw those involved in. The others apparently thought it wouldn't work, but one person managed to convince those in charge to at least give it a try.

"The idea was to try and get someone on the opposite side of *Them* and *Delugion* to make so much attention, and to be such a threat that they bring the subversives out, get them to show their hand. So the operation was approved, and the search for suitable candidates ensued.

"They knew about my early academic studies in climate science and there was more. I was one of their more skilled members in combat and one-to-one activities. They decided that I was perfect, and felt that I should try and infiltrate my way. They sent me to the UK to East Anglia on a so-called scholarship to do my PhD. They felt that East Anglia was the perfect target, especially with climate-gate and all. The rest you basically know."

"Just one question?" asked Clive to everyone's surprise. "We all know… Sorry, I assume that we all know given that you all are now here… that *Them* would have easily found out about this through their computer hacking systems. But how did you escape their digital net? How come they never knew the truth about you?"

Karen was reluctant to respond to Clive, but no one had objected to his question. She reluctantly ceded. "It's because they never put it into any computer system. They never had it on any server or any database. They put their ultra-covert ops on paper files only as they want it to be completely hidden. It's therefore impossible to hack unless you actually go in and steal or photograph them."

"That explains a lot," said Francois quietly.

"What about James?" asked Jenny. "This is a betrayal of his love."

"I never betrayed him. Yes, he was the perfect person to align myself with, but I did fall deeply in love with him. You don't know how many times I saved his life during the whole Angel-gate affair. They kept on coming after him. I could've let him get killed by *Them*, and then come to your group on my own, but I didn't. I couldn't. I wouldn't. I protected him. I wanted us to have a peaceful life together after all of this finished, to let him continue with his passion in research. I never put him in danger. Sadly, his work did all of that."

"So why didn't you tell us all this?"

"Because they would've found out and come after us harder."

"And what is to happen with this and the IDF?" asked Ahmed somewhat still angry. "Is the IDF going to take it all over?"

"The IDF will help us get the messages out and help us take appropriate actions. They were worried you would fail."

"But how can we trust them?"

"You're right," ceded Karen. "You can't necessarily trust them. But then again, they haven't interfered with us all these years for fear of reprisals. The last thing they want is to actively be seen to help us. It would massively backfire. But, they are here to help us in any way through other means. How else do you think I got us all that equipment? Secret friends? Come on!! Jenny, even you turned a blind eye to where it all came from. You must have had your suspicions."

John looked over at Jenny. She appeared somewhat sheepish, refusing to face what had been really happening.

"The IDF won't do anything public unless we have a smoking gun. It's backfired on them too many times in the past not having the concrete evidence. With Clive, hopefully we now will. In combination with John's government, we can work together to get the message out. It is so important. I'm sorry I've lied to you all these years."

"Clive!" Karen looked at him with pleading eyes. "We need you to tell the world the truth, to end all the lies and deception. We need you to bring the world back to what it once was and hold those truly accountable."

"Actually, I don't think you want me to," he replied.

CHAPTER 31

"**D**ON'T GET ME wrong," said Clive. "I'm happy to do so, but I don't think you want me to."

"Why is that?" demanded Jenny, at the same time somewhat surprised at his willingness to cooperate.

"Was it so bad what we did?" asked Clive.

"Yes!!" they all said emphatically.

"I challenge that. We did a lot of good. We ended conflict. We settled disputes. We ended religious rivalries. We brought cultures together. We prevented what everyone knew would be a world war. I think what we did was a great thing, and I know and you know, there was no other way around it."

Karen and Ahmed looked wary at what he was saying. Jenny appeared completely betrayed by his comments. Francois however looked more or less bored. He obviously had discussed this with Clive many a time, and as such this was nothing new to him.

John folded his arms. He was somewhat challenged by Clive's beliefs, but at the same time curious. He was curious how an atheist and apparently learned man decided to take this path, one to control people. What Clive was about to tell them was his own truth, his own real beliefs and not some feigned story of discovery of one's religion or God. This was real. This was his vitality.

But to listen to it and understand it, for Clive to honestly say what he had done was right was truly confronting. No matter how infuriating and how hurtful it was going to be, John needed to know. He needed to know why these ideas were worth fighting for, for someone who had no seeming personal agendas, for someone like Clive. Karen, Jenny and Ahmed, he understood. Clive, he didn't. John needed to know why someone like this would allow his wife, Frank, Phillip and others to be killed, and ultimately in his own name.

"We were facing one of the greatest catastrophes to hit modern mankind with the rising waters," said Clive, "and we needed to bring everyone together to get through the difficult times and challenges. And to bring everyone together is hard, but if you don't, you have chaos and disorder, and potentially you have world order collapse. So to bring everyone together, you have two options. You either need a common enemy, and that will not happen in the near future, withstanding aliens, or you need to have world rule. And to have world rule you need to remove religion, because religions will always interfere.

"But the biggest problem with religion is faith. Whilst there is faith, you cannot actually remove religion. So you then need to remove faith, and the only way of doing this is proof of a new religion. So our solution actually was simple... Create a new religion.

"You see people want to be guided. They need to be guided. For example, after the September 11 American terrorist attack... and no, that had nothing to do with us. It was as it was. After the September 11 attack, what happened?"

Everyone remained silent.

"Nothing? Come on you people!" Clive grasped the air plucking an imaginary piece of fruit. It irked John. "People turned to religion. Why? Because it gave them black and white answers. God is good, and anything else is evil. That's what people wanted. That's what people always want. Simple stories, simple solutions. And that is what happened back then on all sides of religion worldwide – the Christians, the Muslims... but especially in places like the US and where the post terror conflicts occurred. Why do you think ISIS rose so quickly? People turned to religion because it gave them answers, simple easy answers. Rise up and fight. It's hard to argue with that as they think the result is quick and permanent, but it never is. It never actually resolves the problem."

Clive leaned forward in his chair. He looked at every single one in the room, staring them in the eye.

"Nothing is ever black and white. The world is full of shades of grey and people don't like that. It's too hard. They prefer for someone to tell them what is right and what is wrong. It makes them feel better. They don't want to think for themselves. Let's face it, that's why people join the military, or for that matter join the church.

"Actually, is there any difference?!? You get told that someone is the enemy whether it be foreign forces or supposed blasphemers. Only one tells you to go and kill, and the other... actually some may say the other tells you to do it even more, but I digress.

"Ultimately people want to be controlled. They need it. They crave it. With global warming with the worldwide disasters, they are desperate for it. And instead of having crazy people guide them— bigots, zealots, despots, it is better for someone with no agenda, no hidden past, and no hatred to lead them, like myself."

"So you're saying you sacrificed yourself to make the world a better place?" asked John.

"Well… Yes!!!"

"And you're the better one to lead them?" asked Karen.

"What? Would you prefer some Hitler figure blaming a minority group or an Ayatollah sanctioning a global fatwa or jihad? Look what happened with the supposed caliphate! There are a lot of crazy people in the world with crazy ideas, and you're not going to get rid of them. What you need is someone to nurture them in a way that they don't cause harm or damage. By having a leader that these people believe in, that will speak to them and for that matter for them, then we can create a better world."

"Surely people aren't all going to listen and follow you?"

"Of course not. I would be extremely naïve if I thought that I could get everyone's attention and guide them. But we have now ten billion following us and that is no small number. Anyone who would stand against this following would be cut down in seconds. So I am not worried about us having some figure trying to wrest control from me. No! I am actually more worried about those who try."

"Clive," said John. "You said there were only two options – a common enemy or world rule. You know there is a third option?"

Everyone looked at John.

"A common goal!"

"And John, what goal would that have been?"

John remained silent.

"Ahhh! Climate change perhaps?" Clive briefly chuckled. "The problem with the world is everyone has disparate views, personal agendas and even if there is a common goal, everyone has their own ideas on what needs to be done to achieve it. So what happens?

Nothing gets done. That's why we never succeeded in the early efforts in combatting global warming."

"But what about the Kyoto..?"

Clive laughed again. "The Kyoto protocol was about what minimalistic attempts everyone could agree on. If Kyoto was supposed to work, then we wouldn't be here now, and I wouldn't be the current religious prophet."

Clive leaned forward.

"You see, people hear what they want to hear. They choose to ignore whatever evidence they want to ignore. We now live in a time where people can create their own news list, listen to who they want to, find the story or person that reinforces their own belief. There's a good term for this, and it's called confirmation bias. Search engines and social media even help this. We live in a time where there is so much information out there, some reputable, but mostly not and whether you like it or not, people listen to the latter.

"People think that all sides should be heard regardless of the source, no matter how dubious that source is. So when we had oil companies funding climate research, pumping out information that people wanted to hear… Of course people didn't want to know what was really happening. That's why there was such a difference in what should've occurred compared to what actually did.

"And ultimately when things go wrong, people wanted to hear that everything's right, everything has a reason, and has a purpose. And that's where *Delugion* came in. Why do you think religions exist in all corners of the globe, because they explain the way the world is without question, and they don't require reason."

Jenny was getting frustrated. "This is bullshit!!"

"No. Hear him out," said Ahmed.

"What!?!!" said Jenny.

"I'm with her!!" said Karen.

"He's got a point," replied Ahmed. "We were never going to be able to stop global warming, and ultimately Clive is right. What would've happened is far worse. This is the better of two evils. It would've been chaos otherwise."

"I'm glad you understand," said Clive.

"Fuck off!!" said John. "It's a nice convenient story you have told us. It's what despots tell their followers, that they have helped save the world."

"Can you deny it?" replied Clive.

"Can you prove it?" said John. John caught a brief collapse in Clive's serene demeanour. Clive quickly rearranged himself in his seat.

"So what other options were there?" Ahmed asked John.

John struggled for an answer.

"Reality," replied Karen. "Let the world learn that what they did was wrong. Let science prove that what happened was not supernatural, but real. Then and only then, would the world realise that they had done wrong and try to act. Sure there would be victims, but the damage would stop. The world would act together. Clive was not there to cover up global warming. You were there to help continue oil production."

"You are truly naïve if you believe that," replied Clive. "People have dedicated their lives to their faith. People continue to believe in things such as Creation, Adam and Eve and the original biblical flood, not because it has been proven scientifically, because it hasn't; not because it is infallible, because it isn't; but because they have invested in it. They've put their time and effort into their beliefs, and after a while it is very hard to turn back. It's called investment justification, the more you invest in something, the more you have to justify it by believing in it.

"If we did nothing, if we sat on our hands, we would have had the radicalisation of those beliefs. The only logical step was to act before that occurred, to create a different trouser leg of time for people to follow down."

"I'm sorry, but Clive actually makes sense," said Ahmed.

"For fuck's sake," said Jenny. "You're surely not buying into this crap."

"Ahmed, how dare you!!!" said Karen. "Are you going to let this bastard tell us what he and *Them* have done is right? Are you going to let the memory of James be just that? A memory!?! Ahmed, surely you're not being swayed by this dickhead."

"Look," said Ahmed, "I know what he says is hard to take, but what he says seems true. Imagine all the extremists around the world suddenly fighting for their cause. Europe and England would be a war zone. Asia would collapse. Africa would be a slaughterhouse. None of us would have been safe."

"And what about your religion?" asked Karen. She had tears of frustration in her eyes. "And all the others that are becoming extinct?"

"Well maybe there is a time when things should end," said Ahmed.

"You know? It wasn't easy seeing that happen," said Clive. "Religions are my passion, my hobby, my being and for me to quash all that I loved – the culture, the stories, the spirit… let's just say was not easy. Every person who came across abandoned hundreds, no… thousands of years of culture. It was like destroying the relics of the past, to never be regained."

"It's not right," said Karen shaking her head. "It's not right!"

"It needed to be done," said Francois who was now sitting in the back corner of the room.

"No. I cannot accept it," said Karen. "Israel and the IDF are not interested in this false scenario. Chaos has always been and always will be. Maybe for short times, you can manufacture peace, but it won't last. It is not your right to destroy beliefs. People have always survived desperate times. We would've survived this. That is why I'm here. That's why you need me." She looked at Jenny and Ahmed. "You guys wouldn't have put this out there. That's why we needed the IDF!!"

Ahmed stood in front of Karen. She looked at him as if to dare him to stop her. For a brief moment the room was quiet, only interrupted by the heavy breathing of the anaesthetised guards.

Jenny looked dumbfounded at both Clive and Karen's arguments. She was obviously trying to work out the consequences of exposing it all. Certain things began to irk John. He felt uneasy.

"Just one question," said John. "Why the renditions? Why now? Why kidnap me?"

"Haven't you worked that one out yet?" replied Clive with a slight smile.

"Well it can't be about the email. That ultimately said nothing, but it did lead us to Phillip, Francois and eventually to you. Regardless, *Them* could have got rid of everyone on the email chain, which they have done, instead of my rendition. That would have destroyed the evidence trail and let you continue your work."

"Then why are you here?"

"I was flown to England…" John thought about it. Suddenly it dawned. "Oh fuck! Oh fuck!!"

"What!?!" said Jenny somewhat nervously.

"It's a trap. It's always been a trap. It's been too easy. Oh fuck!! How could I have fallen for it?"

"What do you mean?"

"Why are we here? Because they want us here. This is what it's been about all along. They brought me to the UK to lead you guys to him. Clive's been stalling us."

Clive smiled. "Well done," he said. "I'm surprised you didn't come up with that sooner. A religious figure will only become immortal and infallible once he dies. And I am willing to sacrifice myself for that. My final gift to you was some truth. I have done my work, and now I will live on forever."

Suddenly the doors burst in and several shots fired off. Something struck John's side and he abruptly felt the breath leave his chest. John saw Clive's body slump as a bullet hit his head. John collapsed to the ground as three figures in dark suits entered the room. One of them put his sleeve up to his mouth. He spoke with a strong Scottish accent, "Stage three complete. We've now entered Stage Four."

The room went cloudy and then John saw no more.

CHAPTER 32

JOHN FELT HEAVY. His mouth was dry. John's guts were aching and churning as if he had a bad meal the night before. His head throbbed with a relentless pounding. John felt his limbs slowly return to his body and realised his hand was cold. Something was in it. He flicked his wrist and the clunk of metal faltered from his hand. John tried to move his arms. They were sluggish in response, but eventually he managed to get them under his chest.

John felt strange, as if everything that happened couldn't be real. He tried to push himself up, but couldn't. He tried again and managed to get up a little, but then flopped back down. He heard sobbing, female sobbing. He needed to get up. He forced his hands under his body and rolled himself over. Everything was still slightly blurry, but was starting to get clearer. He pushed himself up further to try and sit up, but just barely got himself to be resting on his elbows. He looked around him. A gun lay next to him.

John looked further afield. He wished he was still asleep.

The scene was truly terrifying. Across the room lay Clive, his eyes staring up at the ceiling, frozen in the moment of Clive's final expiration. His shirt was soaked in blood. On either side lay two of the *Delugional* guards. John couldn't tell if they were alive or dead, but they were motionless making him assume the worst.

John pushed himself up more and looked around further. The two guards that were against the wall appeared to be shot in their heads as if to be executed, but what scared John, what he truly dreaded even more, was directly behind him. The sobbing. He turned around and his heart dropped.

Jenny had crawled over to the bodies of Ahmed and Karen. They had several gun shots in their chests and they lay where they fell with their hands held together in what John assumed was their last moments of comfort. Jenny lay over Ahmed in tears sobbing. It appeared as if there had been a fierce gun battle and they had been shot in the crossfire. Francois was nowhere to be seen.

John got whatever strength he could and crawled over to Jenny and his two friends.

"It's over," sobbed Jenny. "It's all over, and it's all my fault."

"Jenny," said John. "They all came on their own will. It's not your fault."

Jenny continued crying releasing all her emotions. She stopped momentarily with only a sniffle to barely escape. "My poor Ahmed, my friend, you had a beautiful soul. I never believed this would happen. And Karen, dear Karen, you were always there to look after us. I forgive you for your lies, but they ultimately meant nothing as your heart was in the right place." She looked up at John. "John, it's time we go to the police. We're over our heads. Use your ASIO friends…"

"They're not really friends."

"It doesn't matter. Just use them and let's expose them all. The police will help us here. They'll be able to tell that we didn't do it. They can use forensic evidence. They can tell we were drugged. It shouldn't be too hard."

"Jenny, I don't think you realise."

"Realise what?"

"Don't you understand?"

Jenny looked at John confused, struggling to cope.

"They've won, Jenny. They've won."

"What do you mean?"

"Clive is dead!" said John.

"So? We didn't shoot him!"

"But it looks like we did. And as far as the world is concerned at the moment, we killed the latest biblical prophet, their messiah. How long do you think we will last before we go to trial?"

Jenny's eyes widened.

"There are enough *Delugionists* in the police force alone to make sure that we don't even make it to the station. They're more likely to get off than we are. They've won Jenny. They've won."

"That's why they needed us to live!!" said Jenny in absolute shock. "It's what they wanted all along."

"Yes," replied John.

"Oh fuck!!!!" sobbed Jenny.

"We've got to go, Jenny. There's absolutely nothing we can do here. We've got to go and survive. We've got to be the memory of all of this. We can and will eventually expose *Them* and *Delugion*, but it's going to be harder than we ever imagined. We're not safe here, or that matter almost anywhere. We've got to run, Jenny, before the police get here. We've got to run, and somehow we need to survive."

Jenny nodded. They both stood realising that most of the drugs they had been doped with had close to worn off. They quickly picked up their gear off the floor.

John looked at his plant, the gun that had been left in his hand. It lay on the floor. He picked it up.

If this is the weapon I have been framed on, he thought, *it may as well be of use.*

He shoved the gun in one of the backpacks. After they had one final scan of the rooms for anything useful, they quickly left. They ran across the corridor and used the card Ahmed had obtained to get out.

It was dark outside and there was no one about. The crowds had left long ago. They ran across the parklands past the landlocked waves and manicured grasslands. They ran past various statues of religious figures including Clive. John looked about to make sure that no one was following and then saw a lone figure standing by one of the bridges far from where they were running. The figure stood alone under a light as if to make sure he could be seen. The figure waved at John and Jenny and smiled with a sardonic grin. John realised who it was. It was the Scotsman.

He wasn't after them. Far from it. It was as if he was saying his farewell. The Scotsman turned and slowly walked over the bridge sending a message from his phone. He disappeared off into the night.

Soon sirens sounded in the distance signalling their approach. The police were on \\their way. John and Jenny continued to run as they mounted one of the wooden bridges. The bridge bounced under their desperation. They continued to run. Flashing lights appeared on the other side of the island. The night's events would soon be news.

John and Jenny ran. It wasn't going to be easy, but John knew they had one last lead, one last option and it was going to be near impossible for them to achieve it. *Them* was no longer after them. John and Jenny were now too public a figure. They would be lucky to last a week or even a day, for soon the world would be after them and nowhere would be safe.

But John knew. He still had hope. He knew that one person would now be calling the shots. One person would soon control the intense masses of people that followed the false religion of *Delugion*, and the masses would listen. One person would have her own agenda. She wasn't as innocent as people had suspected, but this would soon change. The world would soon see. Maria Rodriguez would soon be the head of *Delugion*, and that was a far scarier prospect than Clive ever was. And yet, she was their only hope of surviving.

EPILOGUE

THE PAST THREE days were a complete blur. John was still trying to comprehend all that had happened and how he had escaped. The stories of what had spuriously happened were worldwide. The media gave continual coverage of the events of New London. People were baying for blood. The British forces were in crisis mode as people searched for John and Jenny's whereabouts. The UK government promised retribution. Nations mourned.

All John knew was that he was now relatively safe, far away from the dramas in the UK. Jenny was holed up in their room, staring out, barely communicating. John couldn't stay contained. He needed some air and went downstairs to the local coffee shop. His new appearance worked, and didn't arouse suspicion which had very much relieved him. He sat down with his coffee and stared at the white brown froth on top. It slowly dissolved away in the still air.

A seat pulled out in front of him, and a middle aged woman sat down.

"Sorry, I am expecting…"

"…someone? Really John? Are you really expecting Jenny to come down?"

John started to stress. His hand trembled as he moved the cup to his mouth. He placed the cup down on the desk. He now recognised the person in front of him.

"Why have you come? Surely they could have sent someone lower, less important?" said John.

"Because we cannot have too many people knowing about our knowledge of what has really happened. And to be honest, we feel somewhat responsible that you are now in this situation."

"And what situation is that?" replied John.

"That you are the new Judas, or Herod, whichever you prefer, and are now part of the modern mythology of Clive. You have cemented Clive as the modern religious martyred prophet, and they have cemented you as the villain."

"But you know we didn't do it. We didn't kill him."

"Yes we know. But I'm sorry, we aren't going to tell the truth. Too dangerous. Nobody is going to believe us. The story they have weaved you in is too powerful a narrative to break. You are on your own from now on."

"But you were never there to start off with!" said John with exasperation.

"We were. We contacted you, but you refused to speak to us. We could have helped you, but now it's too late. Besides, you should be grateful. We helped you get across the Channel."

"No you didn't. We managed to hide in the hold of a…"

"…lorry? Which miraculously didn't get searched? Come on John! After the assassination of the biggest religious leader of modern times, do you think that you would have got across the channel so easily? You really made our job somewhat difficult."

"So you knew all along!?!"

"No… we had our suspicions, and when we started to follow your trail, we came up with stronger evidence of *Them*'s involvement, but that information is now of no use."

"But what about Karen and the IDF?"

"Where do you think we got our suspicions from? The IDF were very careful in keeping their information secret, but we heard chatterings. They had a lot more to lose than us, hence their secrecy and lack of cooperation. I might add the word is now "had". You've put *us* in far more peril, not that it was entirely your fault. That is the reason why we are now being so careful. Most of our organisation has no idea of what really happened. There are some *Delugionists* who work for us, and they may not be so friendly to their employers if they found out what we know, let alone their mother-country for that situation.

"And as for the IDF, they're concerned enough that Karen will be linked by the public from you back to them. And that would possibly result in another holocaust. They won't risk that. You better watch out for them. I would keep quiet about her and the IDF. We have managed to just convince the IDF that even you are too strong a public figure at this moment to be assassinated by them. For now they are listening. Do not give them an excuse."

John felt sick to his stomach. He thought about back to home.

"And my sister and her family?" asked John.

"They're safe, for now."

"And Scarlet?"

"We've lost contact with her. We're not sure where she is."

John took a sip of the cooling coffee. The lukewarm liquid gave him no comfort. He placed the cup down on the saucer. People sat down at an adjacent table.

"One question," said John, "what happened to Francois? When I woke up, he was gone. The media says he is still missing, presumably murdered."

"Didn't you work that one out?"

"What?"

"He is one of the key players. He is the one who has been pulling the strings all along."

"No, but he helped…"

"…you get there? Really John? Are you still that gullible? He's the one who brought everyone who's involved into the fold. He most likely started it."

"So you can go after him?"

"No we cannot."

"You're really letting me suffer for all of this. I can't go back. I can't see my family again. You cannot… No… will not clear my name. I have no future."

"What do you expect from us John?"

"I don't know…" John tapped his fingers on the table. "So what do I do now?"

"John, that I'm sorry is up to you."

"Will I see you again? How can I contact you if I need help?"

"I'm sorry, but we cannot be seen together again, that is until you change the narrative once again. And I think you know where you might have to go for that."

The woman stood up and pushed her chair back in.

"You know, those dreadlocks do strangely suit you. I would have never have guessed it. God speed John! You just might need some divine intervention," ASIO director Jan Cover said with a smirk. She quickly left, leaving John to stare at his ever evaporating coffee. He was now truly scared.

www.ingramcontent.com/pod-product-compliance
Lightning Source LLC
Chambersburg PA
CBHW050515110726
47899CB00005B/1461